Meta Orred

Honour's Worth or the Cost of a Vow

Vol. I

Meta Orred

Honour's Worth or the Cost of a Vow
Vol. I

ISBN/EAN: 9783337047894

Printed in Europe, USA, Canada, Australia, Japan

Cover: Foto ©Andreas Hilbeck / pixelio.de

More available books at **www.hansebooks.com**

HONOUR'S WORTH

OR

THE COST OF A VOW.

A Novel.

By META ORRED,

AUTHOR OF "POEMS," "A LONG TIME AGO."

"I could not love Thee, dear, so much
Loved I not Honour more."—RICHARD LOVELACE.

"Der seltne Mann will
Seltenes vertrauen."—WALLENSTEIN.

Prospero. "Foolish wench!
To the most of men this is a Caliban,
And they to him are angels.

Miranda. My affections
Are then most humble; I have no ambition
To see a goodlier man."—*Tempest.*

IN TWO VOLUMES.
VOL. I.

LONDON:

CHAPMAN AND HALL, 193, PICCADILLY.

1878.

To

LADY WALLACE.

" God sees completion where we only plan."

The Painter's Ideal.

HONOUR'S WORTH;

OR,

THE COST OF A VOW.

CHAPTER I.

"Ernst liegt das Leben vor der ernsten Seele."

WALLENSTEIN.

"Why, Gladys! what an armful! Where are you going?"

"They are for Hermione's room," answered Gladys, holding up to Colonel Myddleton the exquisite bouquet of eucharis and gloire-de-Dijon roses which she had gathered, in one hand, whilst the other arm was laden with trails of ivy, sprays of myrtle, laurestinus, wild briar, bramble, and a wealth of wild treasures.

"What! *the* Hermione? Oh, she is fond of flowers, then?"

"Yes, she loves them. You should see her rooms at home; even in winter they are quite full of wonderful treasures: scraps of things, that you would never

B.

think were worth looking at till you see them in the vases—' weeds,' as Philip calls them."

"Do you know, Gladys, I am really curious to see Miss St. John; you all seem so very devoted to her."

"Ah! there's nobody like her in all the world," said Gladys, slowly. "She is beautiful in every way you can imagine. I know you will like her."

"I?—why, I don't think I shall. I never like people everybody likes."

"You will like her, because you like nobody," said Gladys, looking gravely at him. "You like such odd things that most people don't care about, so I know you will like her."

He laughed. "Well, Miss Sixteen, that is the reason I like you, I suppose. Odd things, indeed! It's complimentary to your friend, anyhow."

"Oh! she is not my friend," said Gladys, quickly. "She couldn't be my friend; she is Dorothy's, just like you are Philip's."

"And why couldn't she be your friend, too, as well as Lady Clinton's?"

"Because she is much older, and so clever, and so good, and so different; she couldn't be my friend."

"Oh! So you think friends ought to be of equal age? Well, I call that very unkind of you; for I am ever so much older than you are, and probably than Miss St. John is, and yet I always consider you as my friend."

"Yes!" with a glad, puzzled smile; "but then

you have known me from a tiny baby, and that's different."

" Yes, that is different, Gladys," he said, kindly. " You are right. Well, to please you, I mean to try and like Miss St. John."

It was a most beautiful evening, still and dusking fast; one of those soft evenings we sometimes have vouchsafed to us in late September. The hall door stood widely open, and Colonel Myddleton sauntered out and stood under the lofty portico, looking far away into the dreamy quiet of the sky. As he stood there, close to one of the great pillars, his tall, powerful figure came out in strong relief. He had a fine head, his hair was fast turning grey; his eyes were large and grave, and his mouth firm and yet gentle in expression. There was an indescribable look of repose, strength, and sadness about him; his very attitude expressed readiness, without hurry—a waiting, without expectancy.

The house stood on high ground, which sloped from it in every direction. Immediately in front of the portico it swept away, under groups of magnificent Scotch firs, to the mere, beyond which were belts and belts of trees—oaks, elms, and beeches —fading away into the blue and grey of the distant hills. Here and there the smoke from the village pierced the dusky masses, and went straight up to Heaven like a soul released. It was wonderfully still; the rooks called lazily to each other as they swung homewards. There was hardly any colour in anything; it was a light in which only the greys and yellows predominated.

The other gentlemen of the party staying in the house had not yet come in from shooting. Colonel Myddleton had returned early, on account of a slight threatening of ague to which he was liable since his fever in India.

Suddenly a water-wagtail flew close past his face, and, with a curious clashing of ideas, he thought, "Hermione! How strange that she should have that name, and I not know her! Well, it does not matter."

A carriage came up the distant drive. He caught sight of it in one of the windings, and, guessing it was Lady Clinton bringing Miss St. John from the station, he beat a hasty retreat.

Gladys was busily wreathing ivy and myrtle round the looking-glass, and filling the vases with flowers in Hermione's room. She was tall and slight, with a sweet, young, bright face, and she arranged the flowers with the most loving care and cleverness. Sir Philip and Lady Clinton had no children, and this little sister of his was their darling, and had always lived with them since the death of her mother, and his marriage.

"There!" she said, as she finished, and heard the carriage drive up; "that's beautiful. Oh! here's a dear little bud; that will just do for him. It's very odd that he doesn't know her. I know she said she knew him—but I suppose she meant by sight; she said it was long ago."

In the midst of her soliloquy she heard the bell, and darted from the room.

Hermione was first down, in spite of having had to unpack. She stood in the long drawing-room, by the great, open fireplace. She was leaning her head on one hand, the other, which was ungloved, she held towards the flame, showing the exquisite modelling of wrist and arm, bare to the elbow, where it was shrouded in filmy lace. She was in deep mourning, and wore no ornaments excepting one jewel, which glittered at her throat, yet shone hardly less than the extreme whiteness of her skin, which showed clearly against the square-cut dress. She was excessively tall, and so slight in limb and stature as to resemble more than anything a swaying, plumy reed. Her figure was perfect, and you felt that all lines of dress must necessarily fall in graceful folds against it. Her head, like her hands and feet, was very small and beautifully shaped and put on; her hair was fair, with a bright gold in it which shaded off almost into light as it lay against her brow; her eyes were dark violet, and the lashes were much darker than her hair, though not so dark as the eyes. Her mouth was intensely grave, with a strange, quiet, unspeaking look about the lips, that gave one a curious feeling of quietude and self-control.

She was apparently absorbed in thought, for she did not move when the door opened and Colonel Myddleton came in. He at first did not see her, but came hurriedly forwards in the dimly lighted room towards the fireplace, and saw her suddenly. He started violently, but with a great effort he put out his hand, and said, with only a slight trembling of the upper lip, "Lady Carruthers, I didn't know I was to meet you here!"

She, too, had put out her hand, but at his words it fell again; a shadow of crimson, a dusky flush, flew over her face and stained her very brow scarlet for a second, a wild look contracted her eyebrows, and then she said very slowly, with a grave dignity, "There is some mistake. My name is St. John."

"My God!"

He did not see that she was trembling violently, because she had turned away and was steadying herself by holding a chair. A grey shadow, which made him look as one dying, came over his face. He tried to speak—no sound would come; he held out his hand still, mechanically.

The door opened and Sir Philip Clinton came in; he only saw Colonel Myddleton.

"Halloa! old fellow; what on earth's the matter with you? It's all these confounded fogs after that fever."

"Yes, it's the fever," said Colonel Myddleton, in a husky, broken voice. "Let me go, Clinton, and take some of that stuff, you know."

He groped along to the door like one half-blind, and went out and shut it after him, just as Sir

Philip caught sight of Hermione, sitting in a great chair, half hidden by a screen.

"Poor fellow! I don't think he will ever get over that fever," he said, coming up to her. "He is such a good fellow, do you know, Miss St. John. It was all after the Mutiny—exhaustion and all that sort of thing. Of course, because he is worth his weight in gold, he'll go and die," he ended, discontentedly.

"Yes!" said Hermione. She, too, had caught sight of that death-like face as he left the room, and her heart was beating wildly. What did it all mean? What did he think? How dared he insult her so?

Just as the gong sounded, he came in again. At dinner he sat on Lady Clinton's left, and she said, "You can, hardly see her from here; but don't you think Miss St. John very handsome?"

It was one of those foolish questions that so rarely gets a true answer.

"I knew her formerly," he said; "but I thought she had married Lord Carruthers. I was told so as a positive fact, just as I was starting for India."

"That man!" said Lady Clinton, vehemently, as though any further expression of reprobation would fail to convey her feeling about him. "How could you believe it?"

"He told me himself," said Colonel Myddleton, quietly.

Lady Clinton was speechless. Then she burst out again, "How could you believe it?"

"How did she come to change her name, though?" he asked, absently.

" Ah! Of course, being in India and all that, you did not hear. Well, poor Mark, her cousin, was killed out hunting—at least he died from the fall. She came into the property and everything, and he asked her to take the name. You know he was always madly in love with her. It was like a kind of marriage of names, poor boy! She did it at once, and now she lives at the place. It is so lovely."

" I saw her mother died last year."

" Yes. Well, really, she was no loss to Hermione, she was so worldly and hard."

Colonel Myddleton was silent. He was not even looking at Hermione; he was gazing stedfastly into the flowers in front of him, going over in thought the last six years of his life and hers. What had hers been? what did she think of him? what could she think of him? and now he had insulted her by addressing her as the wife of a man he despised, and one whom all men despised. Would she forgive him, that proud, quiet, pale girl, whom he had so deeply loved, whom he did so deeply love, and whom, he saw now, he had so deeply wronged? "She will forgive me," he thought, " because I have wronged her. I shall never forgive myself. How could I believe that lie, of that pure, high-hearted woman? how could I believe she could marry that brute, that cur? And yet, yes, just because she is what she is, too good to know the

evil, she could have, she might have, married him, as
the best and noblest of women have done."

"I suppose she is a great heiress now?" he said,
suddenly; but Lady Clinton understood him, for she,
too, had been thinking about Hermione, and the error
of Colonel Myddleton had suddenly opened wide a gate
of conjecture to her.

"Yes; eight thousand a year, and that splendid
deer forest in Aberdeenshire, beside the English
property."

"Ah! I am very glad of that."

"Why? I don't think it a good thing for a woman
to have so much in her own power."

"Is it entirely in her own power?"

"Yes; stick and stock. Mark took care of that,
poor, generous fellow! I always think if he had tried
she might have married him, and then the title
wouldn't have dropped."

"Ah! yes, I forgot the title. How women love a
handle to their names!" he said, absently,

Lady Clinton laughed. "Now I call that unkind,
as if I cared whether Philip was Sir or Esquire, or
'Mister,' like a coal-heaver!"

"I beg your pardon," he said, hurriedly. "I wasn't
thinking of you, believe me. I only meant that men
would think of the money, though women would only
think of the title."

"In her favour, do you mean?" said Lady
Clinton, mischievously.

"No, against it," he said, rather sternly. "A man dare not owe all to his wife if he mean to keep his own self-respect."

"The wife is very glad to get rid of the responsibility, I should think," said she, earnestly. "I know Ione would be; she feels it a terrible burden."

"I dare say many would gladly share it."

"The question would be, would she?"

"That is indeed the question. I cannot imagine it, can you?"

"Hardly. She is so unlike other people, it is difficult to judge; but I have known one or two whom I think she might have liked."

"Might have!" he said, with emphasis on the last word. "Then there is no one now?"

"No; and let me say I never knew there was any one even. People talked about Mark, of course, but it was only talk; no one ever dared to say anything to her."

"I should think not. It is strange how she has always managed to keep so quiet and so cold," he added.

"Cold? Ah! you are like the rest of the world, after all, Colonel Myddleton, and take reserve for coldness; when, a thousand times to one, it is the consciousness of extreme power of feeling that forces self-control to act."

He turned and smiled his rare and very beautiful smile. "Lady Clinton judges by her own heart," he said.

"I do not judge. I know," she said, in an intense voice. "And I know because I love Miss St. John more than any woman I ever knew."

"You are a good friend," he said.

The long drawing-room at Charteriss was divided as it were in the centre by the fireplace; and at each end was a deep alcove. In one stood a fine organ between pillars of some rare marble; in the other an exquisite statue of Night. The room was hung with leather, richly embossed and gilt, of a pale buff, with here and there a boss of silver. It was very old Spanish, and exceedingly harmonious and quaint in design and colouring. Near the statue was a large settee, grouped round a tall stand of camellias and ferns, so arranged that they did not interfere in any degree with the view of the figure.

Hermione was crossing the room to look at the statue, which was cunningly lighted from behind, by some devise of Sir Philip's; when Colonel Myddleton came up to her and said, "I know everything now; it was a lie. Will you forgive me? I ought never to have believed it—but——" He stopped and caught his breath, then ended hurriedly, "It was so horrible I believed it." He held out his hand.

Again her eyebrows contracted, rising. Then, she said with a faint, shadowy smile, "I dare say you couldn't help it." She took his hand and shook it slightly.

"Then now we will start as though I had never

said anything, and you will forget?" he said, allowing her hand to drop the instant she attempted to withdraw it.

" Yes."

" You forgive me quite ? "

" Yes. It shall be just as it was before you went to India, if you like."

" Hush ! " he said, turning abruptly round with a ghastly pallor in his face. Then he said very slowly and wistfully, and in a low, faint voice, " That was six years ago ! I have died since then ! " He walked away, leaving her with a thrill of terror at her heart. Decidedly the fever still clung to him.

For the rest of the evening he did not come near her, or speak to her. Gladys came and talked to her, and all the others, too. Lady Clinton sang, and so did one or two others, especially a Mr. Freeman, an odd sort of grey-haired, wandering-Jew-looking person, a great friend of Sir Philip's, a man who always said the most bitter and unkind things and did the most unselfish and kind ones. He was a strange sort of friend and a still stranger enemy.

" I say, Miss Clinton, did you ever know any one who had seen a ghost? I don't mean a 'thought-I-saw-you-know,' but a real ' I-saw-it-with-my-eyes ' ? "

" No; did you ? " said Gladys, laughing. She was about the only person not afraid of him, " Quarl," as he was called, in allusion to his friendship with her brother (the monkey did exist but was kept locked up in the stable).

" Well, then, you may see one now—the saturnine, hatchet-faced colonel you are all so devoted to."

" No ! How do you know ? "

" I know he saw one this evening; you go and ask him."

Gladys went across at once to Colonel Myddleton. He was listening to the music, with an absent, grey look on his face.

" Mr. Freeman says you saw a ghost this evening. Was it the little man in brown, or the lady who stands weeping at the hall window ? "

" A ghost ? " he answered with a slight start—" a lady weeping ? "

"Yes; oh ! did you see her ? They say she means a marriage, which is odd, as she weeps ; she stands with her head bent down, all in white, and long dark hair, and her hands are all scarred, because, you know, she broke the window to get out. But the marriage that comes off after she is seen is always unlucky. Did you see her ?"

He stared a little wildly at her, frowned sternly, then burst into a low, mocking laugh. " Gladys ! how can you be so silly ? No, of course not. Who told you I had ? "

" Quarl," she said, disappointed.

" What made him say I had ? "

" He said suddenly you had seen a ghost."

Colonel Myddleton started, then looked coldly round at Mr. Freeman, who was balancing himself on the back of a chair. "I couldn't see anything more like a ghost than he is sometimes," he said. "But tell me, Gladys, what is the story, and where is the window?"

"The great window on the oak stairs. She was very unhappy; her husband beat her, he used to drink and gamble and everything," said Gladys, vaguely. "And then somebody was kind to her, and she liked him—Sir Sydney Clinton, the old black knight, who hangs up in the gallery. And one night her husband staked *her*, and Sir Sydney won, and she was glad; and he went away and said he would come the following evening to fetch her. And she waited. She had put on all her white satin, and no ornaments, because her husband had lost them all at play, but Sir Sydney had often said he did not care for them; and she went down and stood on the great staircase waiting. Her husband didn't care; he was drinking, and said she might go to the devil for aught he cared. And she waited and waited; the night went on, the dawn came, the day came, but—Sir Sydney never came. And then her husband came out on her and taunted her and beat her—beat her till she nearly died; but next night she went back and stood there, and night after night, and day after day, and week after week, and month after month, and year after year,—he never came. But they beat her and locked her up; she broke the window and got out, and came and stood where she had said she would stand. And then at last she heard he had married some one else, and gone away from that part, and would never come again, and the next day they found her dead, lying all in white, at the top of the stairs; her heart was broken."

Gladys, who had slid into telling a real story, a story she had heard over and over again from childhood, was telling it now with pale cheeks and quivering lips and eyes full of tears, to this man, who sat listening with his soul in his eyes; with working hands and stone-cold heart. She stopped short at last.

" Show me the window, Gladys," he said in an unnatural voice, which made her look round.

" Yes, come! " she said, greatly pleased by his rapt attention.

They went out, crossed the great hall in the moonlight, through the dining-room, lighted only by the dying embers in the grate, through a long stone corridor, along the cloisters, and came suddenly into a beautiful oriel chamber, the windows of which were filled with stained glass, and from the centre of which sprang a great branch oak staircase.

" There! " she said; then added, " Poor, poor thing! "

" It was a lie! " he said, in a deep, husky voice. " He never broke his word to her—his word of honour, don't you see, Gladys—some one *killed* him."

" The story does not say so," said Gladys, sadly. " I wish it had."

" Because you never heard his side, don't you see."

When all was still, and only now and then a quiet
owl's hoot echoed from the distant hanging woods, a
tall figure stood, with folded arms, at the end of the
lime-tree avenue, looking back on the Manor-house
glooming out against the dusky sky. It was a clear
night, and the colour of everything animate or inanimate was of a deep and sombre hue, indescribably
solemn.

"It is like looking at another's life," thought Marmaduke Myddleton. "And after all, that is the only
way to look at any goal ; to think how others would
act to win with honour. What matter if one falls,
even breaks a limb, or—one's heart ? Life is not all,
thank God ! Have I not seen that over and over
again in those nights in India ; in those scenes
through which women and children passed as through
fire, and came out with the very smell of blood and
death on them, and yet averred they would rather
have died ? I know it is not all, but—it is hard to
live sometimes because of others ; for oneself—re-
nounce and you win."

The cold night wind blew up his hair, and struck
sharply round the thin, worn cheek. He shuddered
slightly, for he was still weak from the fever. "Well,"
he thought, "I have given up most things ; I *can* give
up this. And after all, it's my own doing, like all one's
worst miseries. Of course I should not care half so
much if she knew why, and yet——." He turned
and walked slowly towards the house, losing words

even in his thoughts, and with a melancholy smile hovering round his mouth. A bat flew past with a little, soft "cheep," and he stopped again irresolutely half-way towards the house. "Must I go to-morrow?" he thought. "Go away and leave her, my darling, the only woman I have ever loved, to marry some one else, perhaps? and yet, except a miracle—almost—intervenes, I shall never, never dare to tell her I love her——." He stopped again in his walk, folding his arms more tightly across his breast with a wring. A star fell, shooting wildly down the zenith, and the flash caught his eye. "Why, of all stories, should Gladys tell me that? and why, of all nights, to-night? and how well she told it! Alas! my God, alas!" Again a pause; the lime trees had come to an end, tall hornbeams stood as hedges, and through the rifts and chasms in their foliage, made by the dying year, the wind swept with a dreamy and mournful undertone. "How strange it is that what one tries to do as one's best and noblest so often seems to be the undoing of every sort of happiness! Yet, after all, this will not touch her. Thank God for that; one can suffer in silence—alone. Yes, I will go."

Leaning back in the window-seat of her room, with the lights out, and the cold, passionless starlight gleaming on her wealth of hair which fell nearly to her feet, and glittered against the deep blue black of her dressing-gown, Hermione remained lost in thought, too. She was thinking of him. She had seen him standing in the avenue when he first came out into the light, and by a strange fascination she seemed unable to withdraw her eyes from him. Her head leaned back against the sloping panel of the window-seat, her hands were clasped round her knees, her face was extremely pale, and her dark eyes never moved from his figure. She had been sitting there, thinking of him, when he suddenly came before her bodily vision, and now she could not withdraw her gaze.

"How strange life is!" she mused, for her thoughts, by some magnetic current, perhaps, ran in nearly the same groove as his. "Why should I meet him here, of all places? and yet why not here, where he often told me he used to come? How changed he is—how aged—how altered! and yet, he has that same clear way of going straight to the point; that same way, unlike any one else I ever knew, of looking honestly and truly in your face when he is going to say anything that is painful to himself. Yes, he is unlike any one I ever knew; and what he must have gone through—from what Sir Philip and Dorothy say, it must have been awful. He looks like that—he looks as though he would never think lightly of things again or speak lightly of things either. Is it actually six years since I saw him last? It seems a lifetime, and yet as yesterday." Here his figure moved, and she paused in her thought and shrank a little. "Shall I ever forget his going to India so suddenly? And yet I knew he would go, I knew it directly I heard of it

somehow, but I thought he would come and say Good-
bye. Why didn't he? That is what I want to know."
A faint flush of colour swept over her face, it was like
carrying a light quickly past a casement. "And then
how could he think *that!*" She undid her hands
and wrung them hard; a half-stifled sob shook her.
"I didn't think he would; I didn't think *he* could go
and tell him that lie—for I know he told him, otherwise he would never have believed it; he said he
would, but I thought he had more manhood. Well,
at least, it spoilt our lives. I see it spoilt his; only
now, now he knows he did me wrong in believing it,
will he be happier? He looked so strange to-night.
What did he mean by saying he had died since then?
and he looked as though he actually had; and he
never spoke to me again, not even Good-night—and I
can do nothing; but I did say I forgave him. Did he
believe me, I wonder? And I am so horribly rich.
Oh! Mark, dear boy, if you only knew how miserable
it makes me! it is horrible to be so rich—horrible!"

The quiet figure was coming slowly down the
avenue now, and she noticed for the first time that he
had no hat on.

"What madness, just after that fever, too!" She
nearly held her breath, for she could hear his foot-
steps now faintly, and he was looking up, though not
at any window in particular, besides, her room was
dark and still as a grave. He passed on and turned
the angle of the house; but she sat for long, long

after, gazing out towards the place where he had
stood, longing with impotent longing to bring some
gladness on that grave brow, a smile on the stedfast
face.   And neither knew the other had thought alike.
If they had—— ?

CHAPTER II.

But Colonel Myddleton did not leave. Next morning at breakfast the butler came in and spoke to Sir Philip, who looked uneasily across at his wife, hemmed and hawed, and finally got up and went out of the room. He did not come back for some time, and when he did he looked rather anxious. This time he went straight up to Lady Clinton and said—

"I say, Dorothy, it's nonsense, you know. Here's Myddleton, wanting to be off home, and looking like death; do come and stop him."

"He only wants to be begged to stay," said Mr. Freeman, lifting up a saucer and covering up Lady Clinton's tea as she hurried from the room.

"How can you know what he wants?" said Mrs. Lane, with an angry flirt of a crumb at him. "You always say such cross things."

"Now do you suppose, my dear Mrs. Lane, that I ever say anything of which I am not as fully convinced as that you are always punctual for breakfast?" he said, lazily turning round, and allowing boiling water to run into a cup and putting in an egg.

"I know you always say very rude things," answered she, laughing. "I am never in time for breakfast, you know."

"But that is just the point," he said.

"A very pointless remark indeed!" growled old Sir Vere Temple.

"Not to those who feel the stab," murmured Quarl, getting up and going across to fetch a screen for Mrs. Lane's chair. "You shan't be roasted all round," he said with a smile.

Hermione was just coming downstairs, and met them in the hall—Sir Philip and Lady Clinton trying to persuade Colonel Myddleton to stay. He stood, looking very pale and ill, half steadying himself against the hall door. "Thank you very much, you are most kind, but indeed, Lady Clinton, I think I must go."

"Now, why? It's very unkind," pleaded his hostess. "Has anybody offended you? Is your room not comfortable? I know you'll go away and say, 'Clinton has got such a careless wife,' I couldn't stay; the eggs were bad in the fish sauce,' or something," and she laughed and tried to pull the wrap off his arm.

"You goose!" said Sir Philip. "But now, look here, Myddleton. Upon my word, you know, it's not fair on a fellow. You're only just back from India, after goodness knows how many years—— " ("And horrible adventures." "Which you haven't told us!" from Lady Clinton and Gladys, who had come running in from the conservatory.) "Hush!" said Sir Philip; "let me talk reason to him. Now, Myddleton, do be sensible. Where was I, Dorothy? Oh! yes, after years——" ("And adventures," *sotto voce* from his wife.) "And I want you to get to know Dorothy." ("I'll be, *oh*, so good!") "And she wants to know you, and Gladys wants to know about India. What on earth are you going off for again in a twinkle? Why, you've only been here five days, and we are going to have those theatricals, and a ball, and everything! Nonsense! you must stay."

Hermione had remained on the landing of the gallery. At this moment wheels were heard coming up.

" A dog-cart!" said the chorus.

" Yes, I ordered it, as I must go! Good-bye, dear Lady Clinton. The fact is, I—I—I don't feel very well; this fever has caught me again, and I had better go."

" Perhaps if they go down on their knees you will stay?" said the sharp, thin tones of Quarl, who had come suddenly on the scene. "Oh! try it; do, all of you, and there is Miss St. John only waiting an opportunity to throw herself downstairs, too."

" Freeman, really your jokes are unbearable," said Sir Philip, angrily, as Colonel Myddleton turned suddenly to speak, and half fell over the chair. "I do declare—why, hold up, Duke! Heavens!"

There was a slight scream from Gladys, a scuffle,
and Mr. Freeman and Sir Philip caught him together,
as he fell back in a dead faint.

With one rapid swing, noiseless and swift as a
bird, Hermione was in the hall and by their side. He
looked very awful, quite grey. Lady Clinton held on
to the trembling Gladys.

"Open the door—give him air—lay him flat,
quite," said Hermione and Quarl together. The butler
and footmen came in now as the dog-cart drove up.

"I say, Clinton, this isn't an ordinary faint; better
send for the doctor, and look sharp," said Mr. Freeman in a low voice; but Hermione heard, and the
next instant had gone to the door and given the
order. The dog-cart drove off full speed.

"Let's get him into the library," said Sir Philip,
not noticing who had given the order, but being aware
it was given. "Dorothy, you'd better go to breakfast;
he'll be all right directly."

"We've got him safe, Lady Clinton, he shan't fly
away now, I'll promise you. This all comes of his
nonsense; however, you may thank me for saving
your velvet gown on the hall floor, down on it you
must have gone otherwise. Look at Miss St. John,
she did stop his going, after all. Ha, ha!"

Hermione was ghastly, and she felt that she hated
Mr. Freeman.

"I never saw a man faint before," said Lady
Clinton, in an awe-struck voice.

"Oh! it's nothing," said Hermione, lightly; but she was shivering from head to foot. She linked her arm in her friend's and drew her towards the dining-room. "Come, Gladys!"

"Well! did Quarl stop his going?" said Mrs. Lane, as they came in.

"He fainted," said Gladys, in a low voice. "He can't go."

"No!"

"He is so stupid about going out late at night; so like all young fellows," grumbled Sir Vere, feeling that fate was unkind in having taken away his hostess before his second cup of tea had been poured out. "A man after a fever like that goes on for years with one foot in the grave."

"Oh, Sir Vere, really you do say such dreadful things," pleaded Lady Clinton, looking across at Hermione for comfort, who sat with a stony face, pretending to cut a very tough piece of toast, but whose fingers shook to such a degree as to be quite powerless.

"Don't believe him!" said Mrs. Lane. "Men often faint. I've——"

"Oh, oh!" from Sir Vere and her husband, who had just come in.

"Well, you know, Charlie, you did once."

"Why, who has covered up my tea, and kept an egg hot for me?" said Lady Clinton, laughing. "It must be that odd Quarl, for he was sitting next to me;

and, do see, he has run off in the middle of his particular pet dish, and left all the kidneys to get cold."

"But they shan't!" said Gladys, pouncing on the dish and running off to the fire with it. "He is a dear, good man, and I'll take some sugar to Disko."

"No, I'll have some more done for him. Ring the bell, Gladys."

In about half an hour the doctor arrived, and very shortly afterwards in came Sir Philip and Mr. Freeman. "He's all right now, come to, and gone to bed. The fever has come on again slightly, nothing to signify."

"He's caught some chill or other, or shock or something," added Mr. Freeman, passing close to Hermione's chair. "Men are such a plague when they're ill, falling about in that way, and spoiling all one's meals. Those Mutiny men think they can do anything and may be up to any pranks, and everybody is only too proud to be put out for them. Why, where *are* the kidneys?"

"Here, and don't be cross," said Gladys, putting a fresh dish before him, hot and delicious-looking. "And I have got six lumps of sugar for Disko; there!"

"It's no joke, though; it's a most ugly faint, I can tell you," began Sir Philip, with a cup of hot tea in one hand and a newspaper in the other. "It's all very well, Freeman, talking like that, but the fact is that—— "

"Pish!" said Mr. Freeman. "How can you go on like that, Clinton? You've said quite enough to make us all think we're going to have the fever, too, and as to what that fool of a doctor says, who would believe in him—a village saw-bones? He'll be all right in a day or two, only he always did like to make a fuss and be petted, and all that sort of tomfoolery."

"I'll tell you what, Freeman, you're wrong there; he's the last man on earth to stand, much less like, tomfoolery, and if he were to hear you——"

"Oh! I dare say," laughed the other. "Pas si bête! my friend. He'd eat me, I dare say, but I prefer eating, so let's be silent about him, do; it spoils one's appetite."

Here he got up, stretched across for an egg and gripped Sir Philip's shoulder hard, who shook his shoulder free, and said shortly, "Really, Freeman, you're impossible to manage; you're as peremptory as a king."

"Well, we all know the proverb about the one-eye'd man; don't go on," said Quarl.

"Let's go and see Disko get his sugar," said Mrs. Lane, suddenly, and away went the others.

Directly they had left the room, Mr. Freeman burst out. "I say, Clinton, how could you? Didn't you see that girl was nearly fainting herself? and when you began about the wound, I thought she would go off quite."

"What girl?" said Sir Philip, angrily.

"Why, Miss St. John."

"What on earth should she care for? why, she hardly knows him."

"Oh! doesn't she? Well, I dare say she was thinking of her cousin's death, you know; she saw him brought in, all mangled and crushed; and really Myddleton did look bad. Anyhow, I wouldn't say much before her about the wound."

"Why, I never said the word 'wound,'" said Sir Philip, bewildered.

"Well, then, don't," retorted Freeman, getting up and strolling out of the room. "Great ass!" he soliloquized, wandering off to the stables. "Blind indeed! twenty eyes wouldn't make some people see. It's a pity she has so much money, for she has a noble face, and what control! Well, he is a lucky devil."

CHAPTER III.

DISKO was a tiny monkey, with a most sad face, creased and puckered till all expression was merged in one deep line running just above the brow. He sat contentedly now on the back of Gladys' pony, stuffing sugar. She and Hermione stood stroking the pony; the others were wandering through the stable containing Sir Philip's hunters, fifteen splendid animals, all chestnuts. The stables at Charteriss were a sight indeed, even without the quadrupeds, so well built, so wonderfully lighted, and so thoroughly well managed. A border of flowers ran round the inner quadrangle, and flower-pots stood gaily in every window. Broom, the head man, loved flowers, and swore that his horses did too, and why not, he should like to know?

"What is everybody going to do to-day?" said Hermione, as she held a lump of sugar for Disko.

"Going out shooting, I think," said Gladys, kissing Prince just over his eye. "You little darling, I shall ride you, I think. Old Lady Dunstable and Miss

Thorold are coming to-day, and of course Robert
Watt and his father, the general, will come up in
consequence; and I want to go down and see Mr.
Fairfax and Miss Barbara and Josline. Won't you
come too, Hermione? you might ride Ruby."

"But what is Dorothy going to do?"

At this moment a servant brought Lady Clinton
a telegram, and, after reading it, she called to them
to join her.

"Gladys, will you tell Marton that Lady Dunstable
and Miss Thorold will come, dine, and sleep; and that
General Watt and Robert will also dine? I haven't
asked them yet, but I know they will," she added,
laughing. "Poor Robert! and really, Miss Thorold is
very handsome."

"'Handsome is as handsome does,'" said Mrs.
Lane, shaking Disko's paw rather irrelevantly. "And
all I can say is, if I were a man I should hate an
heiress being poked down my throat; they're bad
enough anyhow——"

Here she came to a sudden pause, overwhelmed
with confusion on seeing her husband turn away in
fits of laughter, Gladys become scarlet, Lady Clinton
draw herself up in haughty anger, and Hermione
plunge into a sudden discussion with Broom. She
hung her head and disappeared as Mr. Freeman came
sauntering through the quadrangle. Happy, indeed,
for her that he had not been present!

"Feeding that little brute of mine? How can

you?" he said to Gladys. "Nasty beast!" Here Disko, with a plaintive cry, leapt suddenly into his arms and nestled one black paw confidingly into his waistcoat. "Ha! thou familiar ape, thy manners are evil, and I misdoubt thy heart is as black as thy pate."

"You know you love him," said Gladys; "and he is a dear, wee thing. See how he gives me his little paw!"

"Yes; because he believes there's sugar in it. Ha! ha!" laughed Freeman, sardonically, as Disko withdrew an empty fist with a grimace of disgust, and shook it at Gladys. "He has not mental calibre enough to know that the way to get more is to appear to be satisfied with what you have already."

Just before luncheon Lady Clinton and Miss St. John were walking up and down the lime avenue, when the former said abruptly—

"Hermione, don't you think you would like to know something about the people who are coming here, and those who live round us?"

"Yes, I think I should," was the answer, rather absently given.

"Ione, how quaint you are!" said her friend, laughing. "You are really unlike any one I ever knew. I don't believe you have any natural curiosity."

"No, I don't think I am curious; but never mind me. Tell me about these people. Who is Lady Dunstable?"

"Well, she is a most enchanting old lady; and Miss Thorold is her great-niece, brought up abroad, very pretty, very silly, and will have a lot of money. They are all rather oddly mixed up together. Lady Dunstable was French, but married Sir George at sixteen, and is quite English now. Then General Watt is an old nonentity. He came here about three months ago with Robert, his only son. They are as poor as church-mice, and live in the old Red House, about three miles off. Well, it's rather romantic. Lady Dunstable was Robert's mother's greatest friend, and wants him to marry Mina. He is rather in love with Gladys, I think; but he is an odd young fellow, and Gladys thinks of no one. Then the Fairfaxes have lived here—at least, two miles off under the Ridge—from time immemorial. Old Mr. Fairfax is a dear old man, so refined, so courteous, charming. Miss Barbara is—— No, I can't describe her; you must know her for yourself. She is worth knowing, really."

"And who is Josline, that Gladys spoke of ? "

"Ah ! she is their niece; his only brother's only child, an orphan. There was a very sad story about her mother being so miserable with her father, who was a terrible scamp, that she died of a broken heart. Now, Hermione, I know one thing, you will *love* Josline."

"Yes ? "

"Yes, you will. She has the most exquisite,

pathetic contralto voice I ever heard in my life. She sings with her very soul in her voice."

" You seem to have a rather nice neighbourhood."

" Yes," doubtfully. " I don't know about Robert Watt; he is a rather dangerous young man; he has travelled a good deal, and he is *very* handsome, and he pets Gladys and—— "

" *Pets* Gladys ! " said Hermione, rather aghast.

" Yes. Don't look so shocked," said Lady Clinton, laughing. " They have known each other, more or less, all their lives; his mother and Philip's were cousins. I told you they were all rather mixed up, you know. Old Lady Clinton was devoted to his mother. Do you know, Hermione, I am sure that young Mrs. Fairfax must have been just like Josline; everybody loved her so greatly, and she died of decline quite young," ended Dorothy, with a pathetic sequence.

" How very sad for the girl ! " said Hermione, dreamily.

" Yes; but the Fairfaxes adore her; even Miss Barbara does, though she pretends not to. I couldn't answer for Colonel Myddleton even if he saw much of her."

" Do you think him so hard to move, then ? " said Hermione, looking back, and noticing involuntarily that they were standing on the very spot she had watched him occupy so long the preceding evening.

" I think most hard; but once moved—then I pity

him——" Here Lady Clinton took Hermione gently
by the arm, just above the elbow, and added, with a
wicked smile, "Just like you, Ione; and now you
both have met—well! we know, 'when Greek meets
Greek——'"

"I can imagine the tug to be terrific," ended
Hermione, with a cold smile, because her heart
began beating wildly. "But tell me a little more
about young Mr. Watt."

"Ah! you always care to know about *poor* young
men," said Lady Clinton, laughing. "Well, he is
interesting, and not easily led—for a young man. I
should like you to hear Gladys giving him good advice;
it's very comical."

"But what does he do? Has he no profession?"

"No, none. Of course it's a great pity; but the
old general would never let him leave him. He did
not like it at all, and wanted very much to go into the
army. As it is, there he lives, doing nothing whatever,
though his father pretends to farm a little."

"It does seem a pity. What a wasted life!"

That evening, when General Watt and Mr. Robert
Watt were announced, Hermione looked inquiringly
round. The general was exactly what Lady Clinton
had said—a nonentity: not very tall, ordinary figure,
shiny, silvery hair, no eyebrows, and weak eyes, with
a feeble mouth that seemed in a perpetual state of
gasp. But his son was very different: very tall, with
long limbs, which hung easily; the whole pose of his

body denoted strength, health, and manhood in its prime; his eyes were beautiful, very large and dark; his hair, that warm brown with almost blue shadows and gold lights; and the expression on the clear, open countenance was full of frankness, gentleness of heart, strength, and yet tenderness of will.

"No wonder Gladys likes him," thought Hermione. "He is the handsomest young man I ever saw; and what a fine, straightforward face! I am sure he is nice."

Lady Dunstable also took her fancy very much. She was a noble-looking old lady of about seventy-nine, slender and upright as a dart, in spite of her age. Her snowy hair was drawn tightly back and gathered under a black lace *fichu*, fastened under her chin by a single diamond. She was dressed in black satin and wore high-heeled shoes, and walked, slightly lame, with the aid of an ebony stick inlaid with silver. On coming into the room she made a stately reverence, including in the sweep all those she did not know; and Hermione, rising and returning the salute, felt as though she had suddenly returned to the days of history, and saw before her the unhappy Marie Antoinette.

There was a general introduction of everybody to everybody, and then they went in to dinner.

After dinner Hermione was standing by the organ, looking over some music, when Miss Thorold, who was lying back in a low chair, said in a drawling, half-awake voice—

"I wonder how people contrive to look so different from what they are?"

"What do you mean?" said Gladys, rather crossly, for she didn't like Miss Thorold.

"I was thinking of Miss St. John," said her guest, in a languid tone. "Who would think she was a great heiress? She hasn't put on her gloves after dinner; it can't be to save them, and I don't think her hands are pretty;" and she glanced down at her own very small and beautifully formed hands and feet.

"She hates wearing gloves," answered Gladys. "And besides, she is a person who never thinks how she looks; she has other things to think of."

Miss Thorold opened her eyes rather wider. "What's the good of thinking?" she murmured; "it only makes you thin and your hair grey. But "— with more energy—"you ought to think how you look; it's more ladylike."

"How could Hermione look more ladylike than she does?"

"I don't know, I am sure. Wear gloves."

Gladys, in hot youthful indignation, got up with a flounce, that made her friend turn round and smile and say—

"Gladys, I can't find this symphony of Beethoven. Do come and look."

She was so irate that she tossed about the pieces wildly.

"Why, Gladys! what is the matter?"

"She wants you to wear gloves," said Gladys, in a smothered voice of rage.

"She? Who?" said Hermione, laughing. "You silly child, to mind."

"I don't care. She has no business, vulgar little thing!" muttered Gladys, incoherently.

"I suppose you mean Miss Thorold. I should think she always wore gloves, Gladys; even came down to breakfast in them. She looks like it, somehow," said Hermione, calmly. "It's odd, for old Lady Dunstable only wears those mittens, and what beautiful hands she has! they are so perfectly formed, so white, so slender."

"I don't care for those sort of useless-looking hands," said Gladys, still on the quiver. "I like strong, noble-looking hands, like a face, don't you know."

"Yes; but you know, Gladys, Dresden china is very pretty too, even in hands," said Miss St. John, smiling. "And even you must say that Lady Dunstable's don't look useless."

"No, but she never would say such things."

"Well, never mind; I am just going to carry this to Dorothy, and ask her to play it to-night."

She lifted the symphony and was crossing the room when she was arrested by the incoming of all the gentlemen. She stopped short and sat down close to Miss Thorold, who, half-lifting her oval, full lids, said, "What a handsome boy that is!"

"Boy! said Hermione, rather surprised. "I don't see any boy."

"Oh! Robert Watt; he is only five and twenty."

"How pleased he would be to hear you say so!" answered Hermione, looking at the "boy," who was talking to Lady Dunstable.

"I hate boys! I don't hate him, much." Then, as Hermione was silent she went on, "It's a great nuisance being an heiress; don't you think so, Miss St. John? Everybody wants to marry one," she ended plaintively, holding up one hand and looking at each slender, rosy finger with the light shining through it.

"I have not found it so," answered Hermione, gravely, hardly knowing whether to laugh or be disgusted.

"Oh, but then you are so fearfully rich! I only have two thousand a year."

"Quite enough to make you miserable, it seems," said Hermione, lightly.

Miss Thorold looked up for an instant with keen inquiry in those blue, limpid eyes. She longed to say, "How much have you?" but she did not quite dare so to question that queenly figure by her side. "Don't you hate men?" she said at last with a sigh, relapsing into her chair as Robert Watt slowly approached them.

"Why should I?"

"Oh, I don't know. I thought you would; you look like it."

"Because I wear no gloves!" said Hermione,

maliciously. " I am sure you think me very strong-minded."

Miss Thorold coloured slightly and said, " You would never like to give in, not even to pretend."

It was Hermione's turn to be disconcerted. " Really, Miss Thorold, you seem to be studying your neighbours very closely."

" Oh, I never see anything," was the sleepy answer. " Aunt Dunstable says I am phlegmatic."

Here General Watt and his son came up together —the father very fussy, the son absent. He sat down, however, looking round the room till his eyes rested on Gladys; then he seemed more contented. Hermione saw this and made a sign to Gladys to come, which she did with alacrity; then, seeing her cousin she said—

" Ah, Robert, I just want to talk to you. Disko has burnt his paw."

" Why didn't he employ you as usual to get any-thing for him ? " said Robert, in playful allusion to her name of " White Cat," that he had given her as a boy.

Gladys shook her head at him and said, " I won't have you so impudent. Now do help me—I am in such a fright for fear Quarl should find it out, and—— "

" Miss Thorold, won't you sing ? " said Disko's master's voice behind her. Whereat Robert went off into such fits of laughter, silent and suppressed, that Gladys could hardly sit still.

" It's a great deal of trouble," answered Miss

Thorold ; "but I know Lady Clinton always expects people to sing."

"Yes, one generally pays for one's dinner in one way or another," said Mr. Freeman with a glance at Hermione. "If you can't sing or play, you have to talk to people who bore you. Miss St. John, are you bored ?"

"I think that is a very unkind speech to yourself, Mr. Freeman," said Hermione, beginning to dislike this odd man more and more.

"Ah ! ha ! ha ! very neat, I declare ; you mean that as it is I who am speaking to you, I imply you might be bored by me. Well, it's true, I am sure you are."

"No, I am not," answered Hermione, laughing in spite of herself.

He looked at her straight for a second or two, and then said, "No, I shouldn't think you were easily bored ; you would simply ignore people."

Gladys said, "That's just it."

"Miss Thorold, won't you sing, really?" said Hermione, disliking the personal turn of the conversation.

"My hands are cold," said that young lady, holding them out, as though to ask whether no one would warm them.

"Shall I bring you some coals?" said Mr. Freeman, gravely ; but just then, tap, tap, came a gentle sound over the thick carpet, and Miss Thorold rose with alacrity as Lady Dunstable appeared, saying—

"Mina, sing the 'Pré aux clercs,' va mon enfant, vite."

She had a sweet, clear, soprano voice, beautifully trained, and sang with more expression than Hermione could have believed possible. ·

"Have you heard Miss Fairfax sing yet, Robert?" said Gladys, in a pause.

"No."

"Have you seen her yet?"

"No."

"But why? I tell you you must. Why, you've been here three months."

"Well, it is funny, but I really have not seen her. However, old Crosbie says he will take me there directly he comes back. I say, Gladys, do you think *she* might be my Fairy Princess?" with a mysterious glance towards Hermione.

"Foolish fellow; *no*," answered Gladys, drawing a little closer to him. "She is too beautiful for anybody but—— " She stopped suddenly.

"Who?" and he bent forwards eagerly. "Tell me, there is a dear, good, little White Cat."

Hermione, who was speaking to Lady Dunstable, looked up at this moment, and her beautiful clear gaze rested on Gladys' face. The girl blushed to the very roots of her hair, as though she had deliberately insulted her, and she said hurriedly—

"Nobody; she's unlike any one I ever knew. I shouldn't dare to think of her marrying any one."

Her cousin laughed. "Silly pussy-cat!" he said. "Well, there! I won't tease you. She is very beautiful, and what a figure! and she has a sweet, kind, good face. It's a pity you can't be her page, Gladys; with your short hair, you'd look very nice as a page."

"Thank you for nothing," retorted Gladys, indignantly bending away from him, as he lifted a jewelled dagger from the table and ran it through one of the silken curls.

Gladys's hair was short, like a boy's, but it contrived to twine in delicate rings close to the open, pale brow, and round the slender curve of her throat. Her head had been shaved two years before, when she had nearly died from scarlet fever.

"Where is Colonel Myddleton? By-the-by, isn't he staying here?"

"Yes; he's got a return of fever; it's very unlucky," said Gladys.

"He is a thundering good shot, they'll miss him out shooting. Now he would just match that tall Miss St. John, don't——"

"Hush—sh—sh!" said Gladys. "I'll tell you what, Robert, you should never put people's names together; you know you don't like it when people talk of you and Miss Thorold."

"Well, one likes to have a choice," he said, absently; "but after all, Gladys, she isn't bad-looking at all, and she has lovely hands and feet."

"I dare say," said Gladys, quickly. "But she

meant you to find that out; she is always showing them, and they are absurd!"

"Well, I dare say they couldn't make a pudding. Now Miss St. John's are twice the size."

"I should hope so! Why, she is three times the height of that puny *thing!*" burst out Gladys.

"Why, my Cat! you really must put velvet gloves on your little paws, or we shall have a battle royal. What makes you so touchy to-night?"

"I am not touchy, but you are so silly, taken in by that girl."

"And what are you, miss, but a *girl?* and two years younger too! Never mind, Gladys, she's got a lot of money, and of course I am to marry her. Don't you see, my father and old Lady Dunstable have made up their minds? and there is that old fogey, Sir Vere, making the running; I'm off to cut him out."

He rose with a merry twinkle in his bright eyes, and Gladys angrily took up a book. In a minute he was back again. "I say, dear little Cat, don't look so cross; you know I never mean to marry, but rest a bachelor for thee!" he ended, with a tragic air, stooping so that no one saw his action and letting a kiss fall gently on her hand.

"You may marry Josline, but not that girl," said Gladys, very low.

"I thank you, my furry Highness!"

CHAPTER IV.

UNDER the shadow of a splendid walnut tree, in front of the smithy, stood Tubal Partridge, talking to Josline Fairfax; to put it more correctly, he had been speaking to her. At this moment he was silent, leaning on the huge hammer, with his rusty leather apron twisted upward round his immense frame. Tears were in his eyes, and one had gathered ominously near the edge of the lid, like dew on a crater. His face was grimy and strongly marked, but the tightly curling hair tossed round a fine brow, and though the mouth was large, there was nothing coarse or hard in the man's face. He stood regarding Josline with a strange and touching reverence, and presently, shaking his head till the great tear rolled over and hung on his cheek, he said—

"I do bless you, little madam, it is the first night she has slept at all."

"I will send her some more, then," said a clear, low voice. "And ask her when she would like to see me."

The girl moved slowly away, and the great hammer came down with a will.

It was a dewy, cloudy evening. A damp odour penetrated with flower scents met you softly, like an embodied voice, touching with tender chord the memories you loved the best; over the hedgerows, amongst the crimson buds of hawthorn, oak saplings, hazel, and beech, a cow's head looked now and then, and the great eyes pursued the girl's lonely figure as she went quietly on her homeward way. A little bird would start with a rustle and cry from the rank herbage at her feet by the ditch-side ; a great moth floated solemnly past ; a beetle stopped swinging on the dock leaf and lifted inquiring antennæ.

Suddenly the mist in the low-lying valley parted like the sweep of a grey robe, and the evening star shone palely in the dreamy sky.

Josline paused on the high ridge to which she had reached, and folding her arms against the bank, leant forward and looked down on her home in the hollow.

You could not see much of Old Court; a few twisted chimneys, a few gables curiously carved, a few points of ironwork, a stone ball gleaming here and there, a petrified moon against the old yews ; but, towering over all stood the grand old walnut trees, the pride of the country-side. Even in this dim light you could see the exquisite whiteness of the giant boles, the rich gem-like velvet of the moss and lichens.

In the hush of the eventide Josline felt as though she were passing into another life ; as though her spirit had slipped from its outward covering and was floating far away in indistinguishable essence over the home where she had spent most of her young life. She was not sad, yet the look of mingled yearning and unacknowledged pathos on her face gave you the impression of a grief subdued. She stood in her life alone in spirit ; and, unknown even to herself, the fact weighed heavily on her heart at times like these. In these quiet hours, when none were by to mark the droop in her limbs, the shade on her brow, she would give way to fits of depression that would have been hardly credited by those who only knew her in the ordinary run of life's progress.

Those whom the world concur in calling blessed— so joyous, so free from fret or stain, seem their lives— are, perchance, the very souls who live most completely a quiet existence of sorrow of their own. It is probably owing to this that we sometimes remark with inward wonder that sudden shade and gloom which fall on faces whose outward gaze is generally so calm to the world. The world is often baffled by a smile, though it forgives nothing to a tear.

A horseman came riding along the ridge, but the tramp was not heard as he rode on the turf at the side ; a great pollard oak stretched its branches protectingly between him and the girl. A few paces more and his eye caught her figure.

She was leaning against the bank, slightly sideways; her dark grey dress outlined her slender form,
and the white kerchief which covered her shoulders
was knotted carelessly just above her waist; her arms
were closely shrouded by the tight sleeves buttoned at
the wrist, and her large beaver hat swung behind her
head, throwing it out in exquisite relief. The prim-
rose light in the sky shone on her upturned brow and
gave an unearthly transparency to the colouring of
her temples and cheeks.

A subtle delicacy of expression was peculiar in
Josline's face; an expression penetrated with purity,
it appealed to the soul as well as to the human
tenderness of another, and inspired thoughts of and
desires for lofty ideals and noble aspirations. No
head I ever saw at all resembled hers, except, perhaps, the head of the Madonna in Raphael's picture
known as the " San Sisto."

Robert Watt was struck by its beauty at once and
for ever. In the light of those deep eyes he saw
reflected each noblest dream of his boyhood and
youth; in the delicate sea-shell tinted skin, in the
coils of shadowy hair round the small, perfectly poised
head, he saw his unacknowledged ideal of beauty
in woman. He had checked his horse unawares, and
whilst it snuffed delicately at the short growth on
the banks, he lifted his hat from his head and let it
swing at his knee, thus showing his fine brow and
the open frankness of his eyes.

The pause made Josline turn; as sound ceasing will always affect us, however undisturbed we may have been during its continuance. The grave sweetness of her face underwent a quick thrill as their eyes met, and the electric spasm ran through all her limbs. They both acted alike, though from different motives. He gathered his reins together and rode forward, still keeping his hat lowered. She turned, drew her hat on her head, and paced slowly on to the road again.

She held between her fingers a spray of myrtle, and as she went it slipped from her grasp and lay beneath her feet, unnoticed. She passed on. Robert was off his horse, had it in his hand, and had re-mounted before she turned, missing it, and looked up the road. He had a thousand minds in one minute of time. Should he? Should he not? He waited. Her eyes on the ground, she paced back by the way she had gone, looking quietly and earnestly along the track; once or twice she shook her head softly. He let her go up the ridge till her figure stood on the verge of the downward dip. Then his heart smote him; he went after her, sprang down, and held it towards her, saying—

"Did you drop this?"

"Thank you," she said. "Yes, it is mine," and she stretched her small, white hand for it; but he held it, and, drawing a little nearer, said—

"It was yours, but now may I keep it? it is very sweet," and he lifted the buds to his face.

"Ah ! no," she answered quickly, and with a grave tremor in her voice. "I could not give that spray to any one."

"Why not ? " and he held it more closely.

"Because it is from a grave."

A sudden pallor passed over the young man's face as he gave it back to her, bowing very low. She fastened it in her dress, bowed quietly in return, and went on again. He remained, leaning on his horse's neck, and watching her go from him with a strange, sorrowful feeling, as of one who has gone through a great grief, and with an intense yearning to have at least touched her hand once. Her fair, sweet form, dim and grey, half melting in the mist away, passed on down the ridge ; and then, when he began to think her appearance had been altogether a vision, a sudden glory burst from the setting sun, turned the mists into a golden lake of vapour, smote from the low-lying hills around, and fell at his feet in floods of glamoured light. She went into it : the light took her.

CHAPTER V.

THE cedar parlour at Old Court was a quaint old room ;
panelled to the ceiling with slabs of the sweet-scented
wood which gave it its name, and into which, at
intervals, were let old portraits of the Fairfaxes and
their ancestry. Two windows, with broad seats,
lighted it, and you gazed out on to a trim garden,
filled with sweet-smelling flowers. Within, the
curtains, the old damask furniture, the books, the
engravings, had all a perfume of rose-leaves and spice.
Before the fire, the "person of the house," yclept the
white cat, dozed the long days through, unless a robin
or a chaffinch sang too loudly at the casement and
roused too keen a longing for a dainty morsel, when
she would rise, and with a green light in her eyes, she
would stalk to the window, failing happily to find the
invitation, aught else save sound signifying nothing,
or just in time to see the flash of wings on the lowest
bough of the walnut tree. She had her revenges,
though—she would curl on the broad, warm sill in the

sun, stretch out her furry length, and straighten her
claws to the warmth with an ominous curl of her
whiskers, that held a world of repressed longing and
mischief.

A large banksia, whose pale globes of light shone
creamily in the dusk in their season, twined clinging
arms round the stone mullions—a sweet-scented
banksia, which bore wealth of buds to nod and toss
above the pussy's head, and whisper love secrets to
the butterflies and bees, in early summer. Then
came the stretch of velvet turf, with the old twisted
seat, on one of the arms of which was the carving
Josline so dearly and so curiously loved : two hands
clasped beneath a heart, from which sprang a daisy,
and this device beneath, " Fleur de ma vie et de mon
amour," and the initials "M. F." and " J. F." Were
they, she used to wonder, the initials of those two
Fairfax cousins who had loved one another so dearly,
in the troubles preceding the Commonwealth, but
whose families had taken different sides in the war,
and who had been parted to—die ; he killed at Naseby,
she to pine away slowly for love and life ?

Leaning her head backwards against the old gnarled
seat, held together as it was by a kind of rude
masonry, part of a levelled terrace, she would dream
over those clasped hands. Or, standing in the cedar
parlour, gazing on the sweet face of Margaret Fairfax,
dead for love in her youth, Josline would sigh a
piteous sigh of sympathy and ruth ; though, indeed,

the sweet anguish of love was as yet unknown to her. It was but the dim forecasting which all the purest and noblest hearts feel the earliest—that generous exodus of the soul towards all those who suffer, which is so divine in the tenderest natures, and almost the strongest and most lasting possession of such lives.

Beyond the seat came the group of walnut trees, old as the hills, or the Fairfax family; the largest bole might well have been their very genealogical stem, with its bark of pure silver gloss and coats of moss of such hue, depth, and softness as are only to be found on walnuts. They stood grandly and calmly erect in the wildest storms; not proudly, with flinging arms, but restfully secure in their own tenure. They were one of Miss Barbara's "prides." When we say that the "person of the house" was another, we shall have given a broad gauge of her sympathies.

Near them stood a bed of tiger lilies; such a bed as is never seen, save in very old gardens; a kind of blazon of armorial coats. They were splendid plants, and towered in their scarlet bravery like sentinels of an enchanted ground. On the border of their bed, sunk in periwinkle leaves, stood various earthen pans, kept always filled with water for Josline's doves, who would come tumbling, on windy days, adown the garden wall, like pearly clouds, cooing, bending their painted throats, and casting soft shadows on the turf, like fairy-boats with their sails filling.

Miss Barbara thought them "just like Josline! so

foolish to care for such things, that made a rumbling in their throats;" but the doves were not afraid of Miss Fairfax, nor had they reason to be. Little winding paths, under dense masses of clematis, may, ivy, and laurestinus, took you round to the back door, or out to the front door, by the great wild sweetbriar hedge, where the laburnums drooped golden water over the wallflowers and violets.

It was a sweet old garden. When you stood on the low, broad step of the old square porch, you saw a peep of wind-rocked elms, blue valley, low-lying hills ; and the ridge, with its sturdy pollard oaks and sombre yews, at intervals. You turned, and your eye fell over the low wall, with its stone balls, into the thick-set blossoms of the garden, or caught the spire that tipped the tower of the small grey church.

Shadowed by the trees, the cedar parlour caught none of the glamour that had bathed the ridge, but Miss Barbara recked little of that. She sat stiffly erect in her high-backed chair, her face as grim and nearly as dark as the lion heads that terminated the short arms of her seat, overlooking a curious scene.

On the polished surface of an ebony table stood three candlesticks ; by their side, in snowy whiteness, lay three wax candles. In front of each sconce stood a damsel, with face of different hue ; one was pale, one was red, the third was nearly purple.

" Now, have I sufficiently impressed on you not to be so rough, Mary?" said Miss Barbara's wrathful, high-pitched voice, as she pointed with straight finger like a dagger towards one wax taper, lying on the table, snapped across. "Do you think you can be a fit domestic for my brother's service, if you even lift a candle with such force as to break it?"

The pale maiden of sixteen summers gave an inarticulate sob, made a forward grasp at the candle, and then as hastily retreated beneath that lowering gaze.

"Now, begin all of you, and put those candles in."

Dead silence in the room. The great white puss stretched itself, yawned, and rose majestically to watch.

Mary seized her candle between finger and thumb, and lifted it to its place. It fitted, but hung a little waveringly on one side. She broadened her palm and pressed; it snapped, and rolled a white stem on the floor, not paler in hue than the destroyer's face. Puss advanced, and tapped daintily at it, with soft paw. Miss Barbara's face darkened.

Zilpah seized hers, and forced it down in the candlestick. A fringe of wax spluttered round the edge, and stood appealing against such treatment.

Phœbe scratched at the ends of hers, till fragments lay scattered round the candlestick, which she pressed off the shining table, till long seamy lines told a dire tale of mischief. Then it went neatly into the socket, and she held it up triumphantly, with a crimson face of exultation.

The ordeal was over.

Miss Barbara rose with severity. " You are all of you very careless, hard-handed, rough girls, unfit for service. But it is my duty to help in some way in the village, and as Eliza will go and marry John, I must take on another servant." (Long pause.) " Mary, you may go ! " (Retreat of Mary, sobbing.) " Zilpah, *you* may go ! " (Retreat of Zilpah, glad to get away, on any grounds, whatever.) " Phœbe, you are very little better than the other two ; show me your hands ! "

Phœbe, more rosy than before, came forward, and held out a pair of strong, bony hands, the nails of which were thickly lined with wax.

" Dirty girl ! " said Miss Barbara, " go to Mrs. Turgoose, and beg her to give you soap and water ; wash your hands, and then bring me back a damp duster, a knife, and a piece of wash-leather."

Phœbe retreated, and Miss Barbara returned to her chair, and waited for her in dignified disgust.

In about ten minutes, the little maid returned, still glowing. Miss Barbara then wiped the table carefully with the damp duster, rubbed it still more carefully with the leather, till the surface was as bright and unclouded as before, and finally, taking out the wax candle, so cruelly maltreated by Zilpah, from its tight socket, she pared it with the knife to the required roundness, and showed Phœbe how to set it firmly, then to sweep up the scrapings of wax on a sheet of paper, and finally to range all the candlesticks on the buffet, at the end of the room, in readiness for the evening.

"Has Miss Josline come in yet?" she asked, when all was done, and Phœbe was about to retire.

"I believe so, madam."

"Let her know I wish to speak to her, then."

Phœbe understood by this command that she was henceforth enrolled on the much-thought-of list of the Old Court servants. She had passed triumphantly through the dreaded ordeal by candle. It was one of Miss Barbara's whims that a servant could not be a fit servant unless they could set in a wax candle properly or approximately so, by instinct or otherwise. She never deviated from this trial, and would aver with extreme force and some asperity that the test had never failed her.

Dimmer and more dim grew the light in the cedar parlour. Miss Barbara had closed the open windows and paced the floor, on the red pattern only—for she had days for each colour in the carpet, and to-day the blue and olive had a rest—till she was tired; but Josline did not come; and ever grew Miss Barbara's wrath at such braving of her displeasure, such wasting of her time.

Miss Barbara had very severe ideas, which she carried into practice, too, as to the subserviency of youth. Josline, as young, should have no opinions, no thoughts save such as flowed naturally from contact with her aunt's strength and redundancy of

mind. Perfect submission of body and intellect was
the very essence of Miss Barbara's teaching, and in
some respects she had worked her will on her niece's
gentle nature—indeed, she had acknowledged this
even to others till quite lately; but an uneasy sense
of laxity in Josline's mood had befallen her of late,
and began to steal with insidious power over Miss
Barbara's mind—she hardly knew how or why.

In this gloaming, so grave, so colourless, so calm,
there came to her a sudden conviction that a veil had
been lowered between her power over Josline and her
niece's will to obey. Such things come to us now
and again with a force that we cannot explain or
define; an embodied sense takes us by storm, and
shows us what we cannot deny and yet cannot realize
fully till some further action has set in motion the
current of thought, and our minds have begun to
work in the new groove.

As the full conviction of this change in Josline
struck with ever-widening force on Miss Barbara's
mind, she stopped short in her march, looked up
without seeing, till the grim look on her brow cut like
a black knife between her eyes, and said severely to
herself, "Humph! this is folly! it will be the ruin
of her! I will never give in." Yet stronger than her
will was her love for Josline, and stronger still,
though unknown and unacknowledged, her jealousy
of that love. "The idea of keeping me waiting! the
little chit."

With care to tread only on the red, she went to the door, opened it, and crossed the low, wide, and nearly dark hall. A strain—it seemed from Heaven, so far away, so sweet, so low it came—of violin music, met her like a love look on a face. She stopped, unknitted her brow, undid her hands behind her back, brought them to a more womanly position into the little pockets of her small black apron; and trod less heavily towards the opposite door, nearly lost in the gloom below the oak staircase. She opened it gently enough, in spite of her bony hand, and stood on the threshold for a second, looking in.

In the large bay window stood Josline; her head had fallen slightly on one side, her slender fingers were laced in front of her, one small foot beat unconscious time. The last dying rays of light smote at her feet, striking a tender halo upwards from some heads of the white lily, which reared their silvern splendour from out a great vase of dark blue porcelain near her. Her eyes held and burnt with a dreamy peace, the "Light that never was on sea or shore." The iridescence of the flowers seemed reflected on her pale, sweet brow, and round her floated, like a spirit raiment, the music Miss Barbara had heard without.

Seated on a low stool in the shadow was an old man, a fine and stately figure, in spite of age; he it was who was drawing the soul of sound out of his violin. His head was bent now over the instrument, anon thrown gently back as some long, throbbing note made his every nerve thrill. He was playing very softly, utterly enwrapped in sound, and in the joy and the peace of perfect harmony. The room was low, wainscotted high, filled to profusion with gems of art, exquisite cabinet pictures, here and there a bust, books everywhere; a cabinet of intaglios, cameos, antique seals, and rings. A tall myrtle stood by the window, barring half the light, its pearly buds showing like eyes of silver on the sombre curtain of the evening shade.

" Dux ! "

The violin stopped; the small foot ceased beating the measure ; the spell was broken. But so also was Miss Barbara's exordium, for Phœbe announced at the door ajar—" Supper, and please, madam, Mr. Crosbie."

CHAPTER VI.

" Ah, Crosbie! I am glad to see you back at last
from your long holiday; when did you come ? "

" Last night; and here's a friend of mine, come
to live near us all. Robert Watt, a fine specimen
of inches, eh ? "

" Well-favoured and welcome," said kindly Mr.
Fairfax, holding out his thin, white hand, which
Robert grasped in some confusion on catching sight
of Josline in the shadow.

" Miss Fairfax, Mr. Watt. Josline, I've brought
you some one of your own standing at last, and not
only an old fogey like myself, to grumble and squeak
on wood and catgut," said Mr. Crosbie.

Josline smiled, and, clasping her hands round her
uncle's arm, said, in answer to the small, bright man,
" I don't think anything can surpass the grumble
and squeak, though ! "

" Except, perhaps, the rumbling of doves, eh ?
my dear," he said, laughing.

Here the "person of the house," who had seated herself in expectancy on a crimson leather chair close to the table in the dining-room, and whose delicate susceptibilities could no longer withstand the aroma of a lobster, uttered an appeal ending in a high note, which caused Mr. Crosbie to laugh still more and say, "An appeal from the cat in another form; well, pussy must be listened to."

Later, they went into the study, Mr. Crosbie brought out his violin, and some exquisite music was made.

Miss Barbara and Robert made friends, wonderful to relate. She found it impossible to resist the courtesy of his manner, the charm of his ready conversation, and, above all, the bright beauty of his face. Miss Barbara, though stern in her code regarding young men as well as maidens, was, nevertheless, prone to be propitiated by the former, more especially when, as was now the case, much was said and done to win her favour and forbearance. Robert was by nature inclined to yield deference to elder men and women, and this evening he was bent on being peculiarly devoted to the grim-looking, rather harsh-voiced guardian of the vision he had thus again so strangely, and, he could not help thinking, so fatefully met.

His whole being was pervaded by a sense of holiness and peace whenever his eyes rested on Josline. Each word that fell from her in that soft, low-pitched voice thrilled him with a curious sensation of having at last met with something long indefinably yearned after. When she sang, as she did before the evening was over, in that exquisite contralto that Gladys had spoken of, as he watched the languor of her pose, the droop at the corners of the sensitive mouth, the absorbed look in the eyes which seemed filled with dewy light; he grew more and more possessed with her image, more and more held by the longing to know her well.

When the music ceased, it being a warm, soft evening, they strolled into the garden.

"Where had you been to-day when I met you?" he asked, as they fell behind in the narrow walk.

"I had been to see Tubal Partridge's wife; he is the blacksmith."

"Do you go often amongst those people?" he asked, thinking how like a spirit of light this young girl must seem to them when sick or sorrowful.

"I know a few of them very well. Poor Nan has just lost her baby; I went to tell her I had planted a myrtle on its grave, and give her a spray."

"Was that the spray you would not give me? Why did you not give it to her?"

"She was asleep, and so I brought it home. I have it here for her," she answered, pressing it against her breast, where it lay nestling in the folds of her kerchief.

"I wish you would not wear it," he said, earnestly.

"Why?" she asked, looking up at him in the moonlight.

"Oh, because——" He paused, then said again, "Oh! I *wish* you would not."

She smiled faintly.

"You would not give it to me," he urged.

"Ah! but that was different," she answered, "and I am different." She ended in so low a voice that he hardly caught her words.

Had there ever been any one like her before? he wondered, as they walked on in silence; any one who could so move, win, possess a man in so short a time as to become his ideal of everything beautiful and divine?

"Do you like going to see poor people?" he asked at last.

She stood still, looking quietly downwards, then moved on more slowly, drawing each foot after her as it were in a kind of glide. "I am not sure about the liking, and at one time it used to make me very sad, but I see now it is one of the best things I can do for myself, so I suppose you will say that after all I do like it?"

"Do you analyse your motives so much?" he asked, rather surprised.

She looked up hastily at him with an intense earnestness in her eyes, then said—

"I try not. I should so often be afraid of acting if I went too deeply into motives."

"Do you think, then, that actions are right or the reverse according to the motives that prompt them?"

"I think that actions are so far coloured by intention, as for it to be possible to mar the noblest, or crystallize the lowest."

"How mar the noblest? Do you think a good action can be quite spoilt by a bad motive?"

"Yes; evil touching good is, to me at least, more powerful for debasement than good touching evil powerful for purification."

"How sad a creed!" he said with a sigh. "And how young you are to have thought it!"

She smiled. "I was a very merry little girl," she said.

Something of intense pathos in those few words smote on the young man's heart. "You *were*? and yet you are so young."

"I feel younger, indeed, since I began to think," she answered smiling, but more gravely, and leaning sideways till her lips touched a great white gloire-de-Dijon rose. "I love more things, and with knowledge comes a strength for loving I would not part with, though it may sadden me a little at times."

"It is very strange I should never have known you before," he said, abruptly. "I have often stayed at Charteriss."

"My uncle and aunt never go anywhere hardly, and never by any chance when there are visitors staying at a place."

"But you know Gladys Clinton and Lady Clinton?"

"Yes, a little. They have been here a few times. But I don't mind not knowing people," she said brightly and yet absently; "I am very happy as I am."

"Gladys wanted me very much to know you, anyhow. But I have been away for a little, and besides, I did not like to come until Mr. Crosbie said he would introduce me. I only came back last night; Gladys will be glad to think I know you now."

Josline was silent.

"You will not mind knowing me, will you?" he said desperately.

"No, I know so few people. Are you going to live near here?"

"Yes, my father has taken the old Red House; it's about five miles off."

"Oh!"

A sudden bend in the dusky walk brought them on Mr. Fairfax and Mr. Crosbie. The tall, stately old man was walking along with his hands clasped behind his back, his head bent, and in his steps much of the glide his niece possessed. The little, bright Mr. Crosbie went along with short, crisp steps, like an excited robin. They were discussing some subject with extreme quietude on the part of the host and exceeding volubility on the side of the guest. As the two young people met them face to face, Mr. Crosbie cried out—

"Ah! Bob; come here and tell Fairfax about Gabriel Vannier; that man would be a painter after his own heart."

"He must, indeed, be a rare genius if he is all Crosbie tells me," said Mr. Fairfax, looking up gravely, almost anxiously in the dim light.

"He is, I am sure, all Mr. Crosbie can tell you, and more almost than any one can imagine," said young Watt. "He is a rare fellow in every way; I fear not long for this world, either. His is a sad story; I hardly know the rights of it myself. I found him out quite by chance; the only artist I have ever met whose ideal seems to me to be as high as must have been that of the Old Masters; who paints because he cannot help trying to render his vision of beauty and perfection, and thus beautify other lives than his own merely, and not only as a means of income, though he is awfully poor. I am sure you, sir, would thoroughly appreciate his nature, his longings, his ardent worship of all things good and beautiful."

"Where does he live? far away?"

"In London; he is coming down to stay with me soon," said Mr. Crosbie.

"That is, you have kindly asked him," said Robert with a grave smile, whose full significance was perhaps only grasped by Mr. Fairfax and Josline.

"If he is all you say, perhaps he might like to come and see my antiques, and one or two of the pictures," said Mr. Fairfax, thoughtfully.

"I am sure he would, and thoroughly appreciate them, sir," said the young man, eagerly. "You don't know what a rest and joy it would be to him. He is very quiet and silent, too ; you would not be annoyed by him in any way. Somehow his work impresses my mind with the two attributes, repose and silence, more than any others."

"Therein would lie a great strength," said Mr. Fairfax. "Art in these days is too complex. We are not content, as were the Greeks, and till the age of the *renaissance* the Romans likewise, to render one idea or feeling in our pictures or sculpture. Our souls and intellects are so restless in thought, so manifold in action, that we involuntarily imbue our ideals with the many-sidedness of our modern experiences, and thus must lack for ever the noble simplicity, the grand repose of the ancients. Repose is not in this frantic rush of our lives, it is a feeling we have none of us actually experienced—we are too breathless to obey reverently and in silence, and thus our work is never stamped with that severe self-control which, in the art creations of old, still exercises so exquisite and profound an influence over us."

"Obedience appears to me the primary element in art," said Mr. Crosbie; "but not servitude, or we become weak imitators only, not creators."

"How many of us are fit to do aught else than serve ? " said Mr. Fairfax. " That, at least, we might possibly do well, whereas, in striving beyond, we fail

every way, and hinder those who, deterred by the con-
sequences of our incompetency, stand idle and allow
precious gifts to lie fallow."

Robert was looking at Josline. He saw her lips
move faintly and caught the words: "'Those also
serve who only stand and wait.'"

Here Miss Barbara, in a large, black hood, came
upon the scene, with such warning of storm in her
eye, that Mr. Crosbie bid a hasty farewell and carried
off Robert.

CHAPTER VII.

"WHERE is that lazy, good-for-nothing Robert Watt, I wonder?" said Lady Clinton. "Why, he has not been here for I don't know how long."

The odd fact was that everybody always abused Robert for doing nothing; but the instant he was employed otherwise than talking to them they missed him.

"He was going away for some days, he said, the last time I saw him," answered Gladys, who was holding Disko by a slender chain, and watching his incessant endeavours to climb and perch on the top of a dahlia stick.

They were out in the Terrace garden. Miss Thorold had gone out riding with Sir Philip. Mr. Freeman had gone in to fetch out Colonel Myddleton for the first time. Lady Clinton and Hermione were walking slowly up and down, waiting.

At this moment, bounding down the slopes, came the young fellow in question, with a triumphant air of a "very good boy."

"Eureka!" he called as he ran. "Found! found! I told you I would, Lady Clinton; the very thing, or rather——"

Here he stopped, breathless, as they all said: "What? what?"

He dropped on to a stone seat at the end of one of the terraces, under some large, deciduous firs. "Well, you know, Philip wants an artist? Well, I've found one, such a fellow, and he shall come and paint Gladys!"

"What! a real artist?—paint me? But perhaps he won't want to," said Gladys, with a droop of eyelid and lip.

"Oh, yes, he will, for love's sake, too," said Robert. "He's devoted to me, and would paint even a cat!"

Gladys laughed, and jumped Disko at the end of his chain. "But where have you been to find him?" she said.

"Ah! in an enchanted land—in the Castle of the Sleeping Beauty," he answered, with a merry twinkle of his eyes. "But don't you want to know any more about my painter?"

"Oh, yes; do tell us all about him," said Lady Clinton, drawing Hermione down by her side.

"Well, the truth is, all is very little. However——" he began; but Gladys interrupted—

"Now begin at the beginning. Where did you first see him?"

"In an old shop, staring wistfully at a piece of tapestry. He took out a pencil and outlined the foliage carefully on the back of a bit of wall-paper. The man saw him at last, and was so angry and wouldn't let him take it away, and he yielded at once and begged his pardon, and went quietly out with such a hungry look on his face. Well, I bought the bit of tapestry," said Robert, rather shyly, "and went after him and said I saw he was an artist, and I wanted very much to have the foliage copied in colours, and would he do it for me as a great favour, though I didn't know him, and all that sort of thing." Here he blundered and got very red. "Well, of course, then we began to talk, and he took me back to where he lived, not far off, and he sketched rapidly in chalk a sort of ideal of the Virgin and Child, and showed me how the foliage would come in as a kind of arabesque for her robe. It was beautiful, and then I thought I would like to have it, and so—well, Gladys, your eyes will certainly fall out if you make them so big. Well, oh! well, you always say I get all I want; so there, I ordered the picture."

Lady Clinton burst into a peal of merry laughter. "*You* ordered a picture, Robert! Why, I never thought you cared a bit about those sort of things; besides—— " She stopped short, and bit her lip hard, turning scarlet.

"I know what you mean ; you mean where am I to get the money ? " said the young man, with a burn-

ing flush. "It's all right, though; I've paid for it,"
he went on lightly. "I've taken it on trust; I'm so
harum-scarum, I thought it better to make sure whilst
I happened to have the money; and besides, I know
he will do it beautifully."

"It is really very good of you," said Lady Clinton,
with an earnestness that thrilled all over her face.

"The great thing will be to get Philip to let him
paint Gladys," said Robert, quickly. "An order like
that would do him no end of good. I'll tell you how
you would look well: in a great, black hood, and a
tall sunflower nid-nodding at you—so!" and he made
a comical face at her and shook his head.

Gladys laughed. "But perhaps he wouldn't like
it so."

"Yes, he would, it would be like light in a shady
place, your fair face under a black hood, and then we
could paint a long scroll waving elegantly out of your
mouth, with 'As flowers to light, so I to my love.'"

Gladys threw a dahlia at him, and he immediately
gave chase, and she fled over the garden, Disko tucked
under one arm and emitting little shrieks of excitement and joy.

"How could I say such a thing?" said Lady
Clinton, laughing and remorseful. "I am sure it
hurt him, and he is so good and kind and so unselfish.
I wonder how on earth he got that money; he never
has a farthing."

"Do look at them!" said Hermione. "They are

most absurd; but he is a nice fellow. Really, Dorothy, I think it's very dangerous."

"Oh, no; they've known each other all their lives, two children together. I wish I had not said that."

"I don't think he really minded; he didn't seem to."

"No, because he saw I was vexed. He is so good, he made light of it, for my sake. I'll make Philip give him a cheque for Christmas, and I'll double it."

"Pax!" said Gladys, at last, breathless. "Now, Robert, do be good, and come and tell me more about your artist."

"Vain atom!" said her cousin, squeezing up the monkey's face between his two hands. "You know you are dying to be painted, eh! my monkey?"

"Now, don't be silly; what's his name?"

"Gabriel Vannier."

"What a beautiful name! Well, tell me all about him, do."

"I'll tell you what, Gladys, it's an awfully sad story, that's all," he said, suddenly grave, and dropping Disko's face he drove his two hands into his pockets and went on slowly.

This was the subject of his report :—

Gabriel Vannier was the son of a French father and an English mother. His paternal grandmother was Italian, and he had thus inherited all the passions and some of the gifts of the South.

His father, an artist, had married his mother, an

English lady, "for love." They had run away together; both little more than children. His father
died suddenly whilst Gabriel was still a baby, leaving
his wife almost destitute; but she was a noble and
all-enduring woman. She worked early and late,
and by selling slowly some of the poor artist's pictures and early studies, she contrived to rear and
educate the child. He grew and throve on scanty
fare and much love, to be a noble-looking boy of
nineteen, when she died, went quietly home to her
first and only love, having "done what she could."

Gabriel had inherited all his father's love of art,
and was endowed with tenfold his power of creation.
On his mother's death he began studying in deep
earnest, and worked early and late till his fame was
becoming rapidly assured.

Suddenly the gifted and promising young artist
disappeared. A few weeks later and the Roman
world knew why. He had married, after a few days
of wild and passionate courtship, a girl of sixteen,
beautiful as the morning.

She drank. . . . . This was his history now.
Every effort he made to rise, she dragged him down.
Often and often, in fits of drunken fury, she had marred
or destroyed his pictures. He could not endure his
shame. He left Rome, where he was beginning to be
well known, and where a promising future was opening before him, and was lost to sight. Yet Gabriel
still loved Viola, because without love he could not

live, and because his was a nature that having once loved, loves for ever. Never once, even in her wildest moods, had he spoken roughly to her, though she was surely breaking his heart.

She was still beautiful, exceedingly, with a strange, unearthly wildness that was inexpressibly saddening to see. Viola loved her husband passionately with a blind, adoring, animal affection, that wrought her occasionally into fits of agonized remorse, which exhausted her bodily without bringing any increase of strength to resist the temptation. She did struggle against her sin, too. Yet if after days, nay weeks, of overcoming she seemed to be growing into a faint reflection of her former self, suddenly the fiend within would break forth and rage with redoubled force for the temporary holding.

At such times her fits of fury were appalling. Her passionate and unavailing remorse was as fearful. She would creep to Gabriel's feet and kiss his hands and dress, weeping wretched, bitter tears, and vowing she would never yield again ; or she would threaten to kill herself and so rid him for ever of her degrading presence. Had she loved him less, she would have done so long ago, but she could not tear herself from his loved presence. She worshipped the ground he trod on, the air he breathed, the inanimate things he touched ; the very love he had for their child was a grief to her jealous, craving nature. But stamina of mind she had none ; she was like a soulless being, and

her only goodness and truth consisted in her belief
in her husband.   Hers was a love without bounds,
indeed, and without restraint.

"There, it's awful! I don't know why I told
you," he ended at last.

"It's all very sad," said Gladys, looking up with
wet eyes and pale cheeks. "What a noble man that
Gabriel Vannier is! and oh! Viola——"

"But she loves him, too ; you should see her watch
him."

"Do you call that love ? " said Gladys, slowly, with
a curious tightening at her heart.

"Why, what do you know of love, White Cat ? "
he said, looking up with a roguish smile.

"I know this (Hermione said it once), love is the
most noble feeling on earth ; it makes life like God's,"
answered Gladys, very low. "She was talking about
being kind to people and all that, only she put it
strongly."

Robert was silent. There was something in the tone
of Gladys' voice which struck a new yet aching chord
in the young man's heart. Involuntarily the pure,
passionless face of Josline rose before him, and he
wondered what she would have said in Gladys' place.
He thought he would tell her Gabriel's life and
hear.

"I say, Gladys," he began presently, "you are
growing awfully old in your ideas."

"I am obliged to keep pace with your grey hairs,"

retorted Gladys, holding Disko out at him to hide the blush on her face. "One never can be in earnest with you without your thinking one is so old; that's just like a man. I suppose one may think, sir? Not that I do much; just short, happy thoughts; they don't go on like a book, like Hermione's do."

"Bother Hermione! Why can't you have your own?"

"I thought I wasn't to have any," meekly.

"Gladys," he said suddenly, "I have found the Princess."

She stopped short. "Some horrid creature, I daresay," she burst out.

"Child," he said with preternatural gravity, "you yourself said I was to marry her."

Gladys turned very white. "Well?" she said shortly.

"Now, don't show your claws," he said, laughing, "or I'll put on the gloves. Just fancy, if she saw how fierce you look, how amused she would be." He made a pounce at her, but with one quick bound sideways, she avoided him.

"I don't think she would be amused," she said, with a curious beating in her voice, that startled her. "Who is she?"

"I will be good," he said, grave again. "Come and walk by me, little Cat, it is stupid of me to tease you. It's Josline Fairfax."

Lady Dunstable stood on the verge of the upper

terrace. She had heard all the last part of the
conversation, and gave a start at the name pronounced. Then she looked curiously down on them,
and said softly, " Robert, will you help me down the
steps ? "

Gladys, who had not had time to speak, looked
up in the grand, gentle, serene old face, and then
with a kind of quivering smile she turned away to
run after Disko, who had by a sudden leap escaped
from her grasp.

Lady Dunstable came down the sweeping steps,
and Robert hastened to lend her his arm. She looked
very grave, and he did not speak. He knew not why,
but he felt as though a sudden bar had fallen between
himself and his unspoken, indeed hardly defined,
thoughts of Josline.

" And so you have been to see the Fairfaxes ? "
she said, at last.

" Yes."

There was the slightest, almost imperceptible
pause. Lady Dunstable's head settled itself like
that of a bird when it lifts its steady eyes, so keen,
so deep, so beautiful, to fix the gaze of some intruder
on its nest.

" Ah ! and the family ? "

" Mr. Fairfax is not married." Pause the second,
then a hasty rush of words. " But his sister, Miss
Barbara, lives with him, and (more slowly) his niece,
Miss Jos——, Miss Fairfax."

"What a strange name for a young girl—Jos!" said the old lady, with a stateliness which covered the absurdity of the thought.

"Her name is Josline," said Robert, hastily.

"Ah!" Then turning to look at him more fully, she said, "I have heard of Miss Josline Fairfax; is she not very pretty?"

"No, I should not call her pretty," answered he, quietly, for he was beginning to steady his heart by this time.

"Beautiful, perhaps?"

"Yes, the most beautiful face I ever saw in my life," he said, looking round at his questioner now, and speaking in a full, earnest, reverential voice.

Lady Dunstable turned a little pale. He saw it and said, "I fear you are suffering to-day, madam. Will you not sit down?"

"I am much fatigued to-day," she answered, with a saddened cadence in her voice.

They had reached the old stone seat under the firs; two or three dahlia buds, picked by Disko, and thrown at him by Gladys, lay glittering in scarlet and gold. Robert tossed them on one side to make room for Lady Dunstable, took out his pocket handkerchief and dusted the stone, and then she sat down.

"Do you know anything else about the Fairfax family?"

"Mr. Fairfax plays the violin most beautifully. He was very kind to me, and is going to ask a friend of mine, Gabriel Vannier, a painter, down to stay there."

" And Miss Barbara ? "

Robert felt the chord tightening. " She is rather like a dragon," he began, smiling ; " but seems very much attached to her brother, and—I suppose—her niece."

" And Miss Josline ? "

" What of her ? " he said, smiling uneasily.

" Does she seem happy ? are they kind to her ? "

" Kind to her ! " he said gravely and surprised. " Oh, yes, her uncle is devoted to her and she to him ; they could not help, she is so good," he ended incoherently.

" Ah ! "

" Why, Lady Dunstable ! " he said in turn, startled by her manner.

" They could not bear the brother's marriage ; he married a Roman Catholic, a Vavasour. There was some great quarrel about the child."

" Is she too a Catholic ? " asked Robert, a flash of light, sinister and lurid, illuminating his idea of sorrow being in some way connected with Josline.

" Ah ! that is what I was wondering," said Lady Dunstable, musingly. Then she added half to herself, " Quite in his power ; he need leave her nothing or everything. I remember the talk about it now ; but if he loves her so, I suppose she will have Old Court, and then—how curious ! the property will go back to the Catholics and the curse will come true. Robert" (aloud), "have you seen much of Josline Fairfax?"

"No; oh, no; but I feel as though I had known her all my life," said the young man, with a sudden outburst of feeling. "I don't care if she is a thousand times——" Then recollecting himself he stopped, overwhelmed with confusion.

Lady Dunstable laid her white hands gently one over the other on the ebony handle of her stick. She was pale as alabaster to the very lips, the blue veins stood in lines of colour on her brow; and she said slowly, without looking at him, with her eyes fixed far away on the distant hills, "Josline's mother was my only child's greatest friend. She was the most perfectly lovely being I ever knew, in body and soul, yet she died of a broken heart because she married out of her faith——"

A dense mist seemed to fall on Robert's heart, icy cold, and heavy as a shroud. Once more the figure of the young girl appeared to move from him over the ridge down into the light, and the light took her—he remained in the darkness.

The old lady rose and moved slowly back to the house, on his arm. "My only child's greatest friend," she murmured, "and they are both dead; and hopes die like friendships." Then looking up in his face, she said with grave sweetness, "I shall like to know Josline Fairfax—she must be very lovable."

CHAPTER VIII.

THEY met Colonel Myddleton and Mr. Freeman on the steps. Colonel Myddleton looked very pale and thin, but his eyes were bright, and there was a general air of relief on his face at being at last allowed out again. Lady Dunstable greeted him warmly, and Robert shook hands for the first time since his arrival.

"We are going on to the terraces," said Mr. Freeman. "Are you just going in, Lady Dunstable?"

"Yes; but Robert will gladly go back, I am sure."

"I shall have to go directly, so I may as well go and say good-bye to Lady Clinton," he answered, and they strolled slowly down the bank.

Lady Dunstable went quietly into the great conservatory, and sat down in a kind of hall running at right-angles to it, with one or two statues in niches, and goldfish in a fountain that sang on quietly to itself the long days through. She drew from her pocket a filmy handkerchief and shed a few quiet tears. "After all," she thought, "if she is not a Roman Catholic, why should he not marry her instead of Mina ? Though his mother was my great friend, her mother was Lucille's ; only I had so set my heart on it. Mina is a dear child, and then we could have lived much together, and I still think marriages are better arranged—but then I am only a silly old woman after all."

At this moment some one came hurriedly into the conservatory and passed rapidly across the front of the recess. It was Hermione. She started violently on seeing Lady Dunstable, and then passed on.

"I never saw any one so pale as that girl," murmured the old lady. "I am sure there is something wrong with her heart. I dare say she never got over the shock of her cousin's death."

Lady Clinton, Gladys, and Disko received Colonel Myddleton rapturously. He looked round for Hermione. She was just disappearing into the conservatory. "She can't go away to-night at dinner," he thought with a throb of joy.

"Good-bye, Lady Clinton," said Robert. "I must run all the way home, or I shall be awfully late."

"Why ! where's Redskin ? "

"Oh, I've—I mean—he's gone," said the young man, hurriedly shaking hands and looking flurried.

"Gone ! what *do* you mean ? Surely, Robert, you haven't sold him ? "

"Oh, well; a fellow wanted him, and—one never knows, if I had refused he'd have got kicked or something horrid ; so there it is."

Lady Clinton was silent; Gladys buried her face between Disko's paws.

"I hope you don't mind," he added. "I forgot you were all so fond of him. He was an awfully nice beast, but," with a short laugh, "horses are no good, and I was getting too fat, so now I mean to run."

"Well, you'll never get anything like him again, Watt," said Mr. Freeman. "I hope you got a good round price?"

"All right; I got what I wanted. I know what I am at," said he, rather savagely; and then with a "Good-bye, Gladys," he was off up the bank and out of sight in a few seconds, doing justice to his legs.

"Extravagant dog! Debts, I suppose," said Quarl, with a growl.

Gladys looked up mournfully. "Such a dear beast!" she said. "I used to ride him."

Lady Clinton made no remark for a few seconds, and then she lifted her head rather high, and said slowly, "He is the most noble, unselfish boy I know."

"To pay debts of honour?"

"Don't joke!" she said. "I will tell you. I *know* he sold Redskin to pay Gabriel Vannier."

"Now, Gladys, my dear, don't weep," said Quarl, with a pathetic blow of the nose.

Gladys's eyes were full of tears. She got up and walked away, saying, "No one knows how he loved it; he sat up with it two nights running when it was ill last winter, got staked or something in a wonderful run they had."

"I shall tell Philip," said Lady Clinton decidedly; "and Hermione; that is just the sort of thing to make her fall in love."

"Let us all sell our horses," said Mr. Freeman, grandly. "Myddleton, you shall have mine."

"You've nothing but a hobby," said the colonel, grimly. "Lady Clinton, are you going in? It seems to me rather damp here."

"Yes, it is. Won't you take a turn with me on the upper terrace? I dare say Hermione will come out soon."

Quarl and his monkey departed to the stables, and Dorothy and Colonel Myddleton went up on the high terrace.

For some time they were silent; and then Lady Clinton said, "I wonder Hermione does not come out."

"Does she always come out about this time?" asked Colonel Myddleton.

"Yes, generally. I'll go and call her, and then we will go down to the 'head.'"

In about ten minutes they came back together, and then all three started for the "head"; it was not very far from the house. On the right of the portico you struck suddenly into a deep-cut road, overhung by fine trees, which dipped rapidly towards the mere. It was curiously wild and unkept-looking, but it was one of Sir Philip's pet walks, and he never allowed it

to be much meddled with. Now their feet rustled
through the dying leaves, and the long ribbonlike
grasses swept over the edge of the bank, and showed
where the wild geraniums and strawberry leaves were
turning scarlet, with here and there a strawberry
plant coming into bloom again; and here and there
three and four violets turning up pale faces, with their
snowy beards and bright pointed eye of scarlet. A
thrush was singing exquisitely not very far off, and
the dank, subtle scent of autumn seemed to follow and
cling to them.

"What force!" said Colonel Myddleton, as they
stood just by the 'head,' and saw the water coming
down, all foam and wildness.

"Oh! this is nothing," said Lady Clinton. "I
saw it once, three years ago, when it was within two
inches of the bridge; everything seemed to shiver, the
air was full of foam and spray. As to hearing yourself speak, it was impossible. Philip stood by me and
roared in my ear, but it was just a kind of whisper,
meaning nothing. I am quite sure some day the
bridge will go."

"I like it," said Hermione, walking on to the frail,
rocking, little wooden bridge. "It seems to be
carrying one away with it, in the rush and whirl. I
should like to stand here in a great storm, when the
waters are out."

"Yes, you always like such odd things," said
Lady Clinton; "but I hope you never will, for I am

sure, if you came here, you would try to cross, and then—"

"I wouldn't if I knew it was not safe," said Hermione, "because that would be foolish. I only meant I should like to feel the triumphant rush of the water."

"I should think you liked everything with a dash of conquering and danger in it?" said Colonel Myddleton.

"Not for the mere reason of conquering, I think," she answered, not looking at him, but watching the swirl of the foam bells. "But when everything is smooth in one's life, one does sometimes wonder whether one would have strength if it were necessary. And then I like to see things escape; there is something so glad, and yet so lasting and so unconquerable, in the rush of water. It seems as though it must go on for ever."

"Yes, most things are so short-lived," he said. "When you see people happy, when you are happy, you know it is for so short a time, and besides, you wouldn't be happy, if you could know all."

"Ah! there I don't agree. I think you would be happy if you knew all; it is because we only know in part, that we grasp so hardly at our joys as to kill them. The fact is, the minute you *say*, 'I am happy,' the bubble bursts."

At this minute, a view halloa made them start. Sir Philip and Miss Thorold were riding slowly across the road and saw them, and Lady Clinton set off running up to them. The other two stood still watching, then slowly began to stroll back also.

Suddenly Colonel Myddleton said, " Do you really think that it would be better for us to know everything in its entirety ?"

"I am not quite sure about everything," answered Hermione, slowly. "Perhaps I was generalizing too largely—yet no, I think I would rather know a subject in all its bearings."

"Stop, please," he said, hurriedly, almost stepping in front of her. "I wish—do you really mean what you say? Think before you answer me."

She stood still, outwardly as calm as marble, though her heart began beating thickly. He was breathing hard, and looked white; and the keen anxiety of his expression alarmed and startled her.

"There are some things we never can know in this life," she said in a low and not very steady voice. "I suppose it is intended we should not do so."

"But you would wish—you would like—you would care to know? For God's sake, answer me truly." His hands, which were clasped on his stick, whitened with the pressure of his grasp.

Hermione paused. The thrush was still singing, a rabbit skurried across the road. She looked up, was going to speak, but caught sight of his face; something in the dilation of his eyes, in the ghastly pallor of his cheek, shocked her, and she said hurriedly, not knowing what she had said even till she had spoken, and never afterwards being able to assign any reason to herself why she had so spoken—

"There are some things it is better never to know."

"You mean that?"

"Yes, I mean it," she answered, looking him full and clearly in the face.

He was silent, then he bowed, and went slowly on again. In front of them the thrush ceased singing, the rabbit's tail spun through the tall, yellowing fern, and the riders rode quietly forwards with Lady Clinton holding on to her husband's saddle.

Hermione was wondering at herself. Hers was a mind which often apparently leaned the most strongly on the side actually opposed to her real convictions; more from a kind of unacknowledged wish to balance the very force of her feeling than from any definite desire to contradict others. At this moment, she was wondering at the whole tone of the conversation ; for hers was not a nature to render up her ideas easily. Back to her mind came days long gone, when she had sometimes talked in the same kind of strain to Colonel Myddleton, and then—well, he had gone to India.

Colonel Myddleton was thinking over and over again so intensely, on one subject, that at last he said it out loud. "Would to God I had never gone to India!"

The thought expressed, startled Hermione so much, that she said "Oh!" and then, in utter confusion, was going to hurry on, when he said—

"It's no good thinking so. I did not mean to speak."

"Nor did I," said Hermione, with a slight tremble on her face.

Their eyes met, and they both smiled a little sadly.

"I wish you would tell me something, Miss St. John. When you spoke just now, were you thinking of yourself, or—— ?" He stopped.

"You, you mean," she ended. "Neither; I meant it. I don't even know why I meant it—I mean it," she added distinctly. "I will tell you something. We think a great deal too much about ourselves. There can be no justice, if you are judge, till you put yourself out of court. The only way to get on at all is to think of others."

"Hermione! A strawberry! Do get it for me," said Miss Thorold.

Hermione was so taken aback by hearing Miss Thorold address her by her Christian name, that she simply stared at her, and that young lady, suddenly becoming aware of the circumstance, felt herself coerced by the pale severity of the gaze to say, "I beg your pardon; but could you get it, root and all? I will wear it in my hair to-night."

Hermione obediently was going to fetch it, when Colonel Myddleton hooked it out with his stick, and then the conversation became general.

They were met on the steps by old Lady Dunstable, who carried off her great-niece to change her habit at once, much to that young lady's discomfiture. The rest went in to tea, which was round a blazing fire in the morning-room, very snug, with plenty of plain leather and deeply stuffed chairs, for the gentlemen, and delicate silken seats for the ladies. Sir Philip, with a large cup and some hot muffins, suddenly became aware in the plentitude of his comfort of the absence of Gladys. It had begun to rain, and he said—

"Halloa! that little puss will get wet. Where is she, Dorothy?"

"Oh! she came in ever so long ago. The fact is, she is very low, for fancy, Phil, Robert has sold Redskin."

"Nonsense!" said her husband, throwing half a muffin to Jerks, the skye, in his horror at such news. "What has he been up to? Some stupid bet, I suppose; or, just as likely, some fool in distress has got round him."

Then, of course, the whole story came out, and Hermione heard it. Colonel Myddleton watched her keenly. He was standing in the window, half hidden by the curtain, and saw her face flush as she listened.

"Well, it's a stupid thing to do," grumbled Sir Philip. "Why, he can't hunt at all now; it's all very well, Dor, but you know he'll be an awful bore hanging about with nothing to do. I wish to goodness men wouldn't have such inconvenient generosity fits.

Well, where is Gladys? Just ring and send for her; it's pouring, and she'll catch cold again."

Just then came her voice singing along the gallery overhead, and in a few seconds she opened the door, with a basket of hothouse flowers in her hands. "Come, all of you, and choose your flowers," she said, in a kind of refrain; and they went up to her—at least several of them. "Here's one for you, Philip," she said, bringing it to him, and holding it down over his forehead, so that he could not see it properly.

He stretched up and caught her wrist and drew her down beside him. "Are you sorry Redskin is gone?" he asked.

"Yes, very," she said, readily; "but it was wonderfully good of Bob; he is just always such a good old fellow."

"Well, I think he's rather an ass in this case," said her brother, angrily. "Why, Redskin would have carried you to perfection. I don't know where I could get another like him, so high-couraged and thoroughly broken. Why couldn't he let me have the refusal of him? I would have given him his own price."

"Oh, but Phil, he couldn't have let you, you know. Why, you mightn't have wanted him, and it would have been like a present."

"Mightn't have wanted him! Just listen. In a stable like this, at the beginning of the hunting season, too. There, go along with you, silly child.

I tell you you may never get such a chance again, Why, Mab to-day carried Miss Thorold horribly. He is the very horse I wanted. I declare I'll give Master Bob a good pitching into."

"You are just as cross as you can be," said Gladys. smoothing his hair. "It is a pity, but we can't help it, and it would have been a great trial for Bob to have seen him going out day after day, and——"

"And you riding him!" said her brother, laughing.

"No, I didn't mean that," said Gladys, laughing too.

"Well, I hope the old general will give it him well."

"He's sure to tease him, whether he deserves it or not," said Lady Clinton. "Poor old thing! he must worry somebody."

"What do you think of it all?" said Colonel Myddleton to Hermione.

"Poor fellow! he must have minded very much. I think it was very good of him."

"That is just a thing a woman would admire, and a man cavil at," he answered.

"Yes, but you see a man did it," she said. "I have the greatest faith in men doing noble, unselfish things in a large way, though I think they are more selfish than women in small ways."

"That is the foolish way women spoil us," he said, with a restless sigh. "They let us be cross and unreasonable, and say we are tired of this, that, and the other; but I don't think they understand a great worry that makes a man silent and moody."

"No, perhaps not; but I think the fault lies in both. Men so rarely trust women fully; they think they can't and won't help them to bear anything, when often and often a woman is only thinking painfully how she can best aid and comfort a man, but is afraid to speak for fear of making things worse to bear, or seeming to be prying."

"I don't think there are many women like that, Miss St. John, or I hope we should be better than we are," he said, drawing a little closer to her chair.

"That is what I believe, though," she answered, knowing without seeing that he was looking earnestly at her, and feeling irresistibly inclined to look up; but she would not, but drew her brows tightly together instead, and looked out of the dim window into the drifting rain.

He was silent for a little. They were nearly alone; the others had all gone into the hall through the folding doors, and were examining the raised dais at one end, with a view to the tableaux which were to come off soon.

"Do you think it a good thing to trust people, then?" he said abruptly.

"Yes, if you want to—I mean if you must; it is safer to trust nobody."

"But if you want to—if you have to?" His voice sank lower, and again that expression of tension came on his face; but she was fitting Jerk's ears over his eyes to hide a certain trembling in her mouth.

" I think it is a noble thing to trust people," she said, suddenly sitting up straight. "I have always thought so; only, trust them fully, tell them everything. I don't think a real trust has ever been betrayed."

The firelight caught and held her small beautifully poised head in a kind of glory, and lit into rare softness the usually grave mouth, and her eyes looked up clear as "shining after rain." There was something wonderful, strong, womanly, divine about Hermione at that moment. The man was struck by it— a shiver of emotion flew over his face, he took two steps forwards, he held out his hands, and said in a voice which was clear from extreme lowness—

" Oh! do you remember before I went to India— the last evening in Curzon Street——?" He stopped suddenly.

" Yes," said Hermione, with a breathless gasp, thinking in an agony that they would all, or some of them, come back.

" I did not trust you then," he went on, hurriedly. "And now—now——" His voice began to quiver and break. He pointed to a magnificent half-hoop of brilliants on her left hand. There was a pause. Hermione looked at her ring too. It was an heirloom that Mark had begged her to wear. It seemed alive—every separate facet sparkled like a point of fire. She felt

as though she were being pierced all over with them.
"You are so—rich!" He turned and walked quickly
out of the room.

She was perfectly stunned. She had risen on his
hasty exit; she had tried to speak, to call to him by
name; not a sound would come. Then with a hasty,
violent movement, she tore the ring from her finger,
and held it as though about to fling it into the fire.
Jerks, expecting a game, sat up and begged.

"Ah, no!" she said, slowly, and the small dog
sat down again. But she was not speaking to him.
She gently put the ring back on her finger, and kissed
it. "Ah, no! poor Mark! I do owe you this, in spite
of all."

Then she wrung her clasped hands till her slender
fingers nearly snapped with the strain, and went
quickly into the hall to the others. Everybody was
in a great state of excitement. Mr. Freeman, high
up on two chairs, was measuring with a fishing-rod,
whilst Sir Philip was pacing out the distance from
pillar to pillar. Miss Thorold was leaning over the
balustrade, looking very pretty, and Gladys was helping Sir Vere Temple to rummage in an old chest.
They were all talking and laughing merrily, and,
coming out of the dim morning-room into this hubbub
and glare, Hermione put her hand to her eyes.

"What a pity the Lanes had to go," said Miss
Thorold. "She was so merry, and so good-natured."

"And he was an uncommon bad shot. Seventeen,

eighteen," said Sir Philip. "There, I've finished;
this will do capitally. Do come down, Miss Thorold,
and sing us a song. I am worn out."

"And still in your wet things!" remonstrated Lady
Clinton.

"Never mind. Do sing, Miss Thorold. I shall be
eternally grateful."

"Till you forget all about it," she laughed, coming
rapidly down, and going into the drawing-room.

Hermione went slowly upstairs after a little. As
she came out on to the long gallery, she saw a girl's
figure standing at the head of the haunted stairs; it
was Gladys looking out at the rain. She went up to
her and touched her gently. Gladys turned round
with a start, and her eyes full of tears. Hermione
appeared to notice nothing, and said—

"What a wet evening! I am going to read in
my room. Why don't you go down and listen to the
music? That girl sings well."

"I don't want to go down," said Gladys, drearily.

"Would you like to come and sit in my room?"
said Hermione.

"Oh! might I, really? Wouldn't you mind?"

Hermione smiled, and carried her off. They
installed themselves, Hermione in a large arm-chair,
and Gladys on the rug, leaning her head against
Hermione's knee. Hermione laid a gentle hand on
her head, and they sat silent a long time. Then she
said—

"Gladys, I wish you wouldn't cry, dear."

Gladys turned suddenly, laid her head against Hermione's breast, and sobbed.

"He was such a dear beast! I loved him so!" she said.

Hermione was silent. She felt convinced that something far deeper than the sale of the hunter had stirred the merry, light-hearted Gladys, to cause such grief. But she knew there are things that are better never put into words. Her conversation with Colonel Myddleton flashed back to her; so she only stroked the soft hair lovingly, and drew the head a little closer to her. Hermione was one of those rare people who have the gift of silence. A rather dreary sense of the whole world being out of joint came on her, though, in the silence.

Gradually Gladys calmed down, and then she expatiated on the merits of Redskin, till she seemed a little soothed; and Hermione quite agreed with her that it was very noble of Robert to have sold him, and that very few men would have done so.

Then they sat silent for a long time, and Hermione went incessantly over and over again those few words, "And now you are so rich!" Oh! how she longed to throw off the burden of these intolerable riches. If he were only rich, and she poor! It was counted nothing for a girl to marry a rich man. People only said, "What a capital match!" But if a man married a great heiress, men said, "It was, of

course, for her money." Why should it be so? Why
should there be this strange, horrible injustice towards
men only? Was it not a patent fact that girls married
every year solely for the sake of money, position, lands,
a title; and yet how many cried shame on them?
None. Whereas, how rarely men had the chance of
marrying for money, even if they wished! and how
intensely men dreaded its being thought they had or
would do so!—proud, noble, straightforward men like
Marmaduke Myddleton, above all. Of course, supposing she ever were married, the kindly world would
always say it was for her money. Then what did it
matter who it was, provided she cared for them, and
they for her? What would she care what the world
said, as long as she knew in her heart it was she who
was married, not the money only. Staring into the
fire, she thought over the time when she had first
known him, when she, too, had been poor—at least
not rich. How they had always been friends, for
years back now; and then that going to India, and the
long blank, and this sudden meeting. She had heard
of him all through the Mutiny, as being one of the
most determined, courageous, daring of officers. She
had heard of his wonderful exploits and noble stead-
fastness; and then of his being desperately wounded,
and the fever supervening; and after that a blank,
dead silence of over two years. What had happened
to him during that time? Lady Clinton said he had
gone a long tour in the hill country, then into Persia,

then back again into China and Tartary, shooting and hunting. He had had another attack of fever, she knew, and had then come home. He never alluded to the Mutiny himself; it was impossible to get him to talk about it; but Sir Philip and Dorothy had often and often told her about him.

Meanwhile, he was walking up and down the conservatory, smoking and thinking what was to become of him. If he stayed on here, he would be obliged to speak—he felt it; he felt he had gone too far already not to have said more. Should he tell her *all* and abide by her decision? Was she not sure to judge honourably and truly, and in the best and highest way for them both? And yet—and yet, as long as he said nothing, they could go on being friends, if nothing more; but if he spoke, he must go away for ever; and could he bear that? Perhaps not though; she might decide not—there was that chance. He would, of course, abide by her decision. And then there was another view of it. It was possible she did not care for him. Possible? It was horribly probable. Probable? It was almost certain; and then he needn't go at all. His brow darkened. Could he go on bearing this slow fire day by day? They were going to have tableaux and this fancy ball. Could he hold on through it all? Would it not burst forth in spite of him? Certainty, certainty—he craved for certainty at almost any price. What was she doing now? he wondered. Had she still that grave, sweet look in her eyes, that was enough to madden any man into desperate things? How could she speak such gentle, noble thoughts in such a clear, cold voice? But he knew she meant them and would act up to them, too. She was a soldier's daughter, and would make a noble wife. Ah! his darling! And yet what right had he to think of her as his darling? Oh! just for once to hold her clasped in his arms, to feel her heart beat against his, to hear her say, "I love you!" It seemed that it might have been once. She had not been rich then. He was far the richest of the two, and they were both free. But now, there was the barrier of great wealth, and—what he had himself placed there, willingly. "I suppose I shall get over it in time; I did once before," he muttered, with a half groan. "Of course, that was easier, for I thought it was done for for ever, when I believed her to be married. And isn't it now? Yes; God knows it is," he said, with fierce and savage energy. "Well, if I tell her anything, I'll tell her all. But why couldn't I forget her in all I have gone through? Why should I just hold to her and no one else—not one? I thought I had, to be sure; but, of course, there it all lay smouldering—— "

Here the great bell rang for dressing; and, throwing away his only half-smoked cigar, he went into the house. Miss Thorold was still singing, Sir Philip was dozing in his chair, Lady Clinton and Lady Dunstable were going upstairs, and Sir Vere and Mr. Freeman were standing in the hall. He went on through the morning-room; the chairs were still standing as they had got up and left them. Jerks was worrying something on the rug close to Hermione's chair; it was a glove. Colonel Myddleton lifted it quickly, with a gesture full of passion and joy, rolled it up, and put it in his pocket hurriedly, as the men came in to carry away tea.

In his own room he took it out, smoothed it, kissed the palm, and placed it in his pocket-book that never left him. It was currently believed that Jerks had eaten that glove. He danced round the ravisher all the way to his room, believing it had been rolled up for a better purpose, namely, to make a ball for him, than merely to be laid carefully in a pocket-book. Hermione thought she had lost it at the "head." One does lose gloves in droll places at times.

She noticed that evening that Colonel Myddleton held aloof rather from her, and seemed much engrossed by the music generally; or, was it only her fancy?

CHAPTER IX.

It was late on in the night, but Josline stood at her open window, leaning out into the quiet and soft gloom. It was like looking deep into the heart of a flower, so entirely were all things steeped in mystic, warm, glowing fragrance, coming no soul might tell whence, but pervading and tinging each thought as it rose winged, as thoughts can only be in the entire stillness of the night.

Scents of autumn, dying exhalations from the flowers passing away with the months, stole up confounded in essence, piercing heart and brain with subtle power.

Josline leant out still further, absorbed in thought. She was clothed entirely in white; her long, shadowy hair hung fine and soft as silk—a cloud to her knee; her small, white feet and hands shone in the faint starlight like mother-of-pearl in the purity of their tinting. On her right hand was a ring—a ruby heart with a coronet of diamonds, the one spark of colour about her.

Dreams were in the deep, grave eyes; dreams in

the every fold of her robe, gathered like a stole about her; dreams in the falls of cloudy hair; dreams in the linked hands. Dreams, but not a girl's dreams of love and a happy, intangible future.

She was praying—praying softly in words learnt years ago at the knee of a young, dying mother. When she had ended she drew from her bosom a crucifix of ivory; gazed earnestly in the exquisite sadness of the pale, agonized face, kissed it reverently, and murmured, "I remember, mother."

Then she leaned out once more, putting her hand tightly over her heart as a little wind stole like the sigh of some one near, through the creepers, stirring them faintly like a hand on a weary quest; but it was only the Spirit of the Night; and she closed the window, and lay down to rest with one hand clasped on the cross on her breast.

Early in the dewy freshness of the following morning, Josline was crossing the silvered lawn when she was arrested by Miss Barbara's voice, and, looking round, saw her aunt standing at the window of the cedar parlour.

"Josline! where are you going at this time of day?"

"I was going to see Nan Partridge, aunt."

"Nonsense! I can't think what you want to be always running in and out of the smithy for! it's not very seemly, I think. In my day girls were content to stay at home, and not be so forward."

"Oh, aunt, if you think—but I promised Tubal to go as soon as I could again."

"All sentimental folly! and you are sure to be late for breakfast again. I've no patience with these new-fangled notions."

Bang went the window, causing the "person of the house" to jump hurriedly down from the window-seat with a fluff and miau.

"Such silly things girls are!" soliloquized Miss Barbara, giving her gigantic morning cap a fierce shake, very detrimental to that erection, and nearly coming to grief over a footstool in her hurried effort to avoid treading on a red square; to-day being a "blue" day in more senses than one apparently. "There she goes, wasting all her strength on those sort of people," continued Miss Barbara, saving herself with more skill than dignity; "when any one can see she is not fit to do anything but drink new milk and eat fresh eggs; and how she can live as she does, on nothing at all but music and flowers, I'm sure I can't think! Such nonsense, and Dux is worse than she is."

Josline stood as she had been left, smitten by those words, "Sentimental folly!" Was it really that?

Just then came a few notes of the violin, and with a sudden impulse she turned and went round by the nut-walk, coming out by the study window.

"Dux!"

"Anima mia!" The violin stopped its throbbing and ended in a faint wail.

"I want to know what you think about my going to Nan Partridge?"

"How early you are out with your small feet in the dew!" said Mr. Fairfax, gathering his Belovèd under his arm and coming up to the window.

"It will not hurt me, Dux," said she, earnestly, laying her cheek against the beautifully shaped hand that was clasping her shoulder. "Nothing seems to hurt me."

"A little Una who witches the heart out of things evil," said her uncle, half-absently, stroking the hair that lay as smooth as the glossy wings of her doves.

If he had one feeling more strongly developed than another about Josline's personal appearance it was about her hair, which he always would declare was "düftend," like that of Schiller's Cassandra. "So nasty!" as Miss Barbara said, "smelling hair;" but then her brother would dryly add that he knew she had looked out the word in the dictionary, and did not give it its proper signification relatively to Josline.

"What do you think, my Dux?" she asked again.

"I think you will be sure to decide rightly though perhaps not wisely," he answered, still absently. "There, you are quivering to be gone—go!"

And she went.

She found Tubal, under the shadow of the great tree, fashioning some instrument of iron. He gladly

went with her to his young wife's room. They opened
the door gently.

Nan was sitting in a hard, wooden arm-chair.
She was dressed in a short stuff petticoat and a loose
bed-jacket. Her face was entirely colourless; her
eyes were closed and sunk, and dark purple shadows
round the sockets made her cheeks look still more
hollow and wan. The strong man's voice shook and
his eyes filled with tears as he began—

" Nan, my dear—— " There he stopped.

Josline made him a sign to go out. Then she
went and sat down by the young mother, very little
older than herself, took one limp hand in hers and
said, laying the spray of myrtle on the cold, lifeless
fingers—

" This is from baby for you, Nan."

A strong shudder went through the woman's frame,
and she tried to withdraw her hand, but Josline held
it firmly, though softly, and she desisted.

The window was open, and you could hear a hen
clucking triumphantly, and the resonant stroke of
the hammer. Neither of them moved for some little
time. Nan kept her eyes closed, though two large
tears had pierced the lids and swam in the hollows
round them. Josline was looking out of the window
over the little orchard, waiting for the broken-hearted
mother to take her time. The young girl was thinking long thoughts about death, which it seemed to her
stood alone in its completeness; for death has but one

country to which we must all go, and from whence
none can return till all have been there; so that
actually those who are dead are more within the scope
of our comprehension than those who, though still
remaining on earth, may have been compelled to
wander in another hemisphere to which we may never
attain.

At length a faint voice said, "I don't like to keep
you sitting here, young madam."

"I am quite content to stay a little longer, Nan,"
said Josline, gently; "but won't you try and look at
me once?"

"I fear me I shall weep if I do; your face is
so——"

She stopped, quivering all over as a child's cry
rang down the road. She made a violent effort to
regain self-control. Josline held her hand tighter.
After a few seconds she said with a convulsive
gasp—

"I'm that tired of weeping, and he never wept
at all."

"But you would rather have it so, Nan, wouldn't
you? You would rather grieve for him, than that he
should have cried for you?"

She shook her head faintly. "He couldn't have
grieved this like," she said.

"Ah, Nan! you don't know what it would have
been to have left him. I think so often and often of
my mother's agony when she had to leave me. I

believe it's worst of all. She used to lie and look at me, and you could see the sorrow killing her all the quicker, and yet she grieved and grieved the more. It's very lonely, Nan, to have no one to love you like a mother does. Sometimes when I am tired, I think if she could just be there once more and kiss me, all the pain and grief would go. Nan, you would not want baby to feel that, would you? you can't realize now that he would have grown up and wanted you; that he would have hurt himself and no one would have looked after him or cared. You didn't mean that, did you, Nan?"

The simple words of the young girl, so simply said, seemed to touch Nan deeply. She closed her fingers tightly round the clasping hand, and unclosing her eyes at last, she said, as the tears flowed gently—

"You are a very angel, dear young madam; and it's quite true as Tubal said, you'd know all about it; and I will try and think that my dear baby is spared my grief, and that his mother bears it for him. Perhaps," she added, timidly, "you will come and speak to me about him whiles?"

"Indeed, indeed I will, Nan," said Josline. "And won't you come and lie down a little now, and try and sleep? See, I will shake up the pillows for you."

So Nan lay down, and Josline covered her up, drew the white curtain across the window, and, laying the spray by her, stole quietly from the room. And, worn out and yet comforted, Nan fell asleep.

" Nan is going to sleep," she said, as she stepped
out into the blaze of light. " She is quieted now,
and I hope will wake more like herself."

She saw Robert at this moment. He was standing
just behind the smith.

" Good morning," she said, feeling the thrill she
had felt before as their hands met.

He watched the delicate colour fly over her face,
and knew she was moved.

Then she turned and walked quickly away up the
lane. When, at breakfast, she mentioned Robert's
name as having seen him at the forge, her uncle
said—

" Why did you not ask him in, Josline? I want
to inquire more about that Gabriel Vannier."

Josline was silent, but Miss Barbara said sharply—

" Dux ! What next ? Ask him in, indeed ! He
must have thought it odd enough to see her there ;
then he would have thought her mad ! "

" With method then," answered Mr. Fairfax, " for
I shall go and fetch him myself." And out he went.

Robert had gone on his way thoughtfully. Was
Josline a Roman Catholic ? How was he to find out ?
He could not ask any of her own people, since Lady
Dunstable had said it was a subject of disunion
amongst them. He wondered whether any one knew.
Did Mr. Crosbie ? Surely the clergyman of her village
would know. Did she go to church or not ? Was she,
perhaps, compelled to go ? Compelled ! but by whom ?

Not by Mr. Fairfax, he was far too much attached to
Josline evidently. By her aunt? Yes, she might be
severe enough to drive a gentle creature to any
expedient, and yet there was a quiet peace about
Josline's look, in spite of her subdued melancholy,
which forbade any supposition of compulsory life.
After all, was he frightening himself at shadows?
Was there any real question of her faith at all? Lady
Dunstable said there had been a great quarrel about
the *child;* doubtless it was all settled then. The
quarrel had been between the parents, or between the
father and uncle, or, maybe, between the mother and
aunt. He would not worry over it, and yet, if she
were a Roman Catholic, would she have anything
to say to him? any words of love for one of a different
creed? Was hers not just the nature that would
cling deeply to a faith misprized by others, but
held to and suffered for by her young, dead mother,
who, doubtless, she had dearly loved and reverenced?
If he could only know how she felt and thought on
the subject at all!

He had been brought up in the faith of his parents.
He had gone to church, as a rule, because all
English gentlemen went; it was the way and custom
of the land, and there was something nice and quiet
in it now he came to think of it. He said a prayer
night and morning, also as a rule—the simple prayer
he had learnt at his mother's knee as a child. He
read his Bible now and then, when he read any other

book which made reference to its teaching, or when he heard discussions about the East and its customs. He had often thought too, in so doing, how inconsistent seemed its deductions; how impossible its conclusions. He believed what he had been taught, and never troubled himself about the niceties of his creed. In fact, his belief was summed up very much thus: "Our Father which art in Heaven; *my* Father who created me, and whom I am to serve as an honourable, upright Englishman, speak the truth, and forgive my enemies, and not despise them more than I can help."

This sort of general belief had stood him in fair stead till now; but now he began to wonder what was his creed? how should he define it if asked? What would be her creed, supposing she were a Romanist? In what consisted the supreme difference of the two? His ideas of the Roman creed were even more vague than his conception of his own; a kind of vague jumble of Purgatory, Virgin worship, confession, penances, and doing pretty much as you liked, provided you paid for it! This could not be Josline's creed, though. What was it? What was the faith, the beauty of which could give that calm peace, purity, and strength to her expression? or had she been born with that look on her face, and had her religion nothing whatever to do with it? Oh! what would he give to talk to her about herself, her thoughts, her inner life. Should he ever dare? If,

as Lady Dunstable said, there had been disunion
about her religion, or rather her mother's, would she
ever be likely to approach the subject, and with a
comparative stranger too? Alas! it was most unlikely.
And yet how tenderly, how reverentially he would
handle it; all her thoughts should be sacred to him
as the most holy things; anything appertaining to
her soul should be as entirely her own as though
unknown of save to the Almighty. Had her father
been thus lenient to her mother? Ah! there, he felt
at once, lay the great question; the one bar, which
might utterly prevent any the very faintest possi-
bility of her caring for himself. The more he thought
over Josline, her life, her nature, the more imperative
became his longing for certitude.

The greatest longing of our souls, the yearning
towards God, receives the strongest reciprocal
guarantee, and this is why a great and unique love
must always partake more or less of the nature of
adoration. Nothing but the peace which follows
single-hearted, soul-absorbing worship can satisfy so
intense a feeling.

Striding over the fields, uplands, and fallows,
quickly towards home, he thought over these things
more deeply than he had ever thought over anything
in his life before, all becoming more confused in his
mind from the very efforts he made to disentangle
cause and effect. He strove hard to believe that all
his uneasiness was so much folly; but he became

more and more convinced, against his will, that there was only too much ground for anxiety.

"Father," he began at breakfast, "had you known Lady Dunstable long before I was born?"

"Well, let me see. Oh, yes, a few years. She was your mother's great friend, though she was twenty years older, I should think. I liked her very much; she was a wonderful old lady always.

"She seems very kind to me now. I can remember her giving me tips when I was quite small."

"Yes, she took to you tremendously when your poor mother died. She wanted to adopt you and all sorts of things. 'Elle avait des idées,' as she always said; but my ideas were rather different, you know!"

"Had she no children?"

"Yes, one daughter. Ah! that's an odd story. I don't think my lady had much religion personally, brought up in that heathen France, and at that time, too. She worshipped Marie Antoinette and the Prince d'Artois; but she had this girl brought up very strictly in a convent with a lot of English girls, amongst others that lovely Vavasour girl, who afterwards married wild Jack Fairfax.".

"What! Jos—— Miss Josline's mother?"

"Exactly so. She *was* beautiful; none of your piny, dreamy, bread-and-butter misses; but a tall, elegant woman, more like Miss St. John than any one I've ever seen. And deep! I am sure she'll play

them a trick or two still, in her grave. She hadn't
those eyes and that mouth for nothing, I can tell
you—a little twist at each corner of her lips ; that
girl has got it. I saw her the other day. It's just
as well Jack died before her. Shot in a duel he
was, good-for-nothing dog; for I don't think she would
have kept quiet much longer, though she adored
him. He drove her nearly mad, though. It's all
very fine bringing up that girl as a Protestant. Mark
my words, she'll turn as soon as she gets the bit in
her mouth. She is a quiet little devil."

" Father ! "

" Oh, yes! my boy, you'll find it out, I can tell
you. The quiet, gentle women are the ones who
never give in. Far better be content with Mina
Thorold."

Robert got up violently, shoved his plate into the
very centre of the table, and said—

" I hate the very name of the girl," and strode
out of the room.

" How can he speak so ? " he thought, beating his
hat on to his head, lighting a cigar furiously, and
striding out to the gate. " It's revolting ! a sweet,
gentle, loving creature like that ; I don't believe she's
double, or would live a double life ; and how can she
help it if she does ? " he urged to himself, with a
lover's kindly sophistry. " I dare say they'd be out-
rageously cruel to her, poor darling ! "

At this moment horses came cantering down the

lane, and Sir Philip and Gladys came up, followed by a groom with a led horse.

"Hurrah!" shouted Sir Philip; "this is luck. I say, Bob, there's going to be an awfully jolly day at Crumb's Corner, so I've brought over Rat-trap. Just go and get on your things in a twinkle, and come along with us."

Robert gave one gulp of delight, nearly swallowing his cigar, then flung his hat in the air with a "view halloa," and dashed into the house. When he came down again, which he did with wonderful rapidity, he found that Sir Philip had ridden on to join the rest, and Gladys was waiting for him.

"I say, this is good of Phil. What a stunner he is!" he said, red and happy, vaulting on to Rat-trap's back, and starting gently. "Quiet, old fellow! I could kiss you, you splendid brute!" and he stroked the neck of his horse, who was anything but quiet, but bucked and capered and curvetted in fine style. At last they all steadied down, and then they had a delightful ride through the keen, delicious air along the ridge. Soon Robert noticed how silent Gladys was. "Why, you look as melancholy as I felt just now," he said, with a slightly forced laugh. "We are a nice pair to be going out on a hunting morning! Yoicks!"

Gladys laughed too; she couldn't help it. "I am so glad you are happy," she said.

"Well, but look here," he went on; "I want to

know what did you mean by that mysterious threat to me the other day that I was not to get all I wanted?"

"I think you have got it now," she answered. "You get too much what you want, you'll never be really happy."

"Come now, Gladys, I can't have you going on philosophizing in this way. You won't be any more my little cat; and tabbies demure I can't endure."

Gladys smiled and was silent. He was silent too for a little, and then he said suddenly—

"Tell me, Gladys, what you mean, really, by my not being happy if I get all I want? I surely shan't be happy if I don't get what I want."

"Yes, you will," she said, earnestly. "Don't you see, Bob, if you had *all* you want, you would have Redskin, and yet have paid for the picture, too."

"Gladys, you witch! you blackest of white cats!" he said, colouring deeply.

"Well, you have now a sort of painful pleasure about it, and nothing to regret."

"Painful pleasure!"

"Yes, you know you were thinking about it when we rode up. I saw you did not want us," she said, vehemently.

"I was thinking, certainly," he answered, gravely; "but I don't know that it is good for me to think too much on that subject, and it did not make me happy."

"It wasn't about Redskin, then? Oh, Robert, I

am so sorry," said Gladys, with quick sympathy. " I
thought it was about him, and that Rat-trap had
made it better to bear."

" But," he went on, with a change of tone, " you
don't want me to be happy, you say it is bad for me."

" Because I *do* want you to be happy, don't you
see ? " urged Gladys, flushed and eager. " If you
get all you want at once, quick, you won't care really.
I know you won't; one never does—it's all jam and
no bread."

" Why do you think so, Gladys ? "

" Oh ! because I shouldn't—no one does."

He laughed out. " Ah, Cat, now you are generalizing ; judging everybody by one standard."

She was silent, switching at the bushes in the
bank. Then she said, " Robert, I *know* it is true, only
I can't say how ; you know it, too."

He made no answer. " Disko is just the same,"
she said again. " If I take away his ball and hide it,
he tares all over the place and wants me to play ; but
if I leave it by him all day he doesn't care a bit."

"I don't think I am quite like Disko," said Robert,
gravely.

" I think you are," said Gladys, with decision.

" You are very impertinent, miss ! "

" Well, you'll believe me some day," she said.
" You'll get all you want, and then you won't care ;
or else you won't get all you want, and then you will
care."

" But then, anyhow, I am to be wretched, bad
Cat ! "

She was silent; the hot tears burnt in her blue
eyes.

" Well, anyhow, I'll always have you, my puss;
and I can revenge myself by teasing you."

" No, you won't ! " she said hastily. " I shan't let
you have me just when you don't want anything
else ! " Then, with a little defiant shake of her head
and reins, she cantered on and joined the rest of the
Charteriss party, who were just coming into sight
across the common.

" Well," thought Robert, " I wonder what has
come to Gladys ! what thoughts she has, and very
clever ones, too ! What was that phrase my old
dominie used to be for ever quoting, not at me, but
about his own dusty old manuscripts, which never
were printed, poor dear old fellow ?—hard reading
they would have been, too ! What was it ? "

Here he lost the current of his thoughts, for he
joined the rest of the party. They were all there :
Lady Clinton and Lady Dunstable and Mr. Freeman
in the carriage, Sir Vere, Hermione, and Miss Thorold
mounted, and Colonel Myddleton, too. Hermione was
too slight to look really well on horseback, but she sat
beautifully, and where she had contrived to hide her
masses of hair so as to show only one thick coil under
her hat, remained a mystery. She was on Ruby, a
beautiful blood mare, that carried her to perfection;

and her great height did not show at all too much
even in the perfectly fitting habit, on the tall chestnut.
Hermione had a power of making people feel she liked
them in the very way she held out her hand. Robert
felt it now, and was quite inclined in consequence to
believe that Josline's mother might have resembled her.

"It is a very noble face," he thought. "Such
a fine brow—so frank! and how she holds that mare,
soft as silk and nervous as steel!"

Colonel Myddleton's horse was so troublesome that
he had to keep at some distance, and he was inwardly
fuming at not being able to stand alongside of the
rest. But his grave, quiet face showed no trace of dis-
composure, and as the animal wheeled and reared
and kicked, and finally tried to bolt, he sat with no
movement, keeping it well in hand.

"That grey is quite wild to-day," said Sir Vere.
"I don't believe many men could stick on."

"Oh! he likes to show off," said Mr. Freeman.

"At any rate, he is not *afraid*," said Hermione,
with a slight tremble of her eyelids, as the grey gave
a side jump that would have unseated many a good
rider.

"No, he doesn't sit in carriages, for fear of breaking his neck," whispered Robert, with a glance of
supreme contempt at Mr. Freeman.

"Nor ride other men's horses," said Quarl, who
had overheard the remark.

Happily at this moment the fox broke cover, and

in a few seconds every man and horse were doing their best. Hermione and Gladys were to follow for a little; and the grey had sobered down like magic to the sound of the hounds in full cry, and was going along like a gallant ship under full sail, neck and neck with the chestnut mare.

"This is glorious!" said Hermione, as they rose together at the first fence, went over it, and flew across the broad pasture-land like birds released. The wind whistled keenly in her small ears; her eyes glittered with excitement; her colour, generally so evanescent and faint, deepened into vivid carmine, as, with her hands close together and well down, sitting well into her saddle, steady as a young tree swayed gently in the growing, she smiled for the joy of the rapid pace.

Colonel Myddleton was close to her, his every nerve tingling with the excitement of the ride, and sympathy with the intense eagerness of the noble animal he was riding, who, hard held, was going along with his whole heart in his stride. He looked up as Hermione spoke, and their eyes met. She turned very pale, there was something so intensely mournful in his look.

"Once," he began, "I rode for my life. I never speak of it, but only—well, I didn't want to save my life then; I had a duty to do, though. I got through all right."

"I am glad," said Hermione, breathlessly, as he paused.

"I should not ride for it now," he said.

Check! and they were nearly into the hounds.
And then every one came gradually up; and then off
again faster than ever. But it was over for Gladys
and Hermione; the country was very severe, and Sir
Philip shouted to them to go home. It was easier
said than done so far, for both Ruby and Prince were
quivering with excitement, and their riders little less
so. However, it had to be, and by degrees riders and
horses calmed down and the day was over.

"I *wish* I were a man," said Gladys. "Look,
Hermione, there go the grey and Rat-trap!"

Hermione looked, and far away went the grey like
a meteor. "It is glorious!" she said. "Never mind;
we are only women!"

Hours later, riding home in the cool grey twilight,
suddenly back to Robert's memory came the phrase he
had forgotten, with a strange new meaning and force
—"I wish for myself, and for those for whom I care,
that sometimes we may succeed, sometimes fail, and
so pass through life, rather than succeed in all things.
For never did I hear of any one who succeeded in all
things, and did not at last end ill, utterly perishing."

He drew rein, and sat looking into the light of the
western sky; and as he murmured the words to himself, he thought of his boyhood, and his mother, and
his kind old tutor in his snuff-coloured clothes, with
his big books, and his spectacles.

CHAPTER X.

"Now when will you all settle about the tableaux?" said Mr. Freeman.

"*All* settle?" said Lady Clinton. "I think it would be much better if you would settle the whole thing. Give us our parts, and we'll do as we are bid!"

"Do you mean really?" said Quarl, with a gleam of joy on his harsh thin face. "Well, you couldn't do better; I'll suit you all, and you'll like your parts, I can safely say."

"As long as you don't give me a solo piece," said Sir Philip, laughing. "I couldn't stand up and be still, to be stared at."

"Now, don't begin at once to say what you couldn't do. If I am to manage them, everybody must *obey*."

Hermione looked up curiously, and he said at once, "Do you mean to obey me, Miss St. John?"

"I don't mind," she answered. "I dare say I shall do to come in, in the crowd?"

"Very usefully, you are so like the general mass," he said. "But now, once for all, will every one promise me to obey implicitly?"

There was a general chorus of "Yes," and then he said—

"Very well. Now, I shan't speak about it again for two days. I must think."

For the next two days he was very absent and odd, often coming suddenly on each individual in turn, and standing before them and contemplating them gravely, making them laugh at each other.

"What sort of thing will he choose, do you think?" asked Miss Thorold, who was most anxious to be dressed up. "I can't think; he is so odd about things—something that is not usual, I imagine."

A sphinx could not have been more impenetrable than the master-mind, though. He went with Sir Philip into the gallery, and chose out wonderful weapons; he went with Lady Clinton into the so-called bower-chamber, and chose out marvellous brocades; he ransacked her jewel-case; he then went down to the blacksmith, and much startled Tubal by some orders; then to the saddler, who was even more amazed. Every one, though pretending they did not much care, was excessively curious.

At last the decisive evening came; and, after dinner, they all collected in the hall to hear what was to be the fate of each. He made them all go on to the daïs, and he stood at the other end contemplating them. There was a little silence, and then he said—

"Ah!—well, I'll tell you all the one large tableau; but the others will only be known to the individuals who will act them."

"Oh!" General excitement and disappointment.

"It's no good; I won't say. One has only just this moment come into my head. I *see* it. Now, if only the saddler is worth his leather," he muttered, seizing his chin in one hand with a curious rounded snatch, peculiar to him.

"Well! but what's the general one?" from everybody.

"Catherine Douglas barring the door. Hush! don't all speak at once. Here is everybody down: Miss Thorold, Queen Joanna; Lady Clinton, Miss Clinton, Lady Dunstable, ladies in waiting; Sir Philip, Colonel Myddleton, young Watt, forcing the door—pikemen; Sir Vere Temple and myself, spectators."

"Catherine Douglas—Miss St. John," said Sir Vere, bowing to her.

"Exactly," said Quarl.

Hermione coloured. "Well, of course, as you order," she said, with a laugh; "but I hardly call that one of the crowd, and I am too tall for Catherine Douglas."

"Oh, you'll look perfect," said Gladys, much relieved to find she was only one of three, as it were.

" What are the others, and how many more ? "
said Lady Dunstable.

" Oh ! there will be three more only ; it's no good
having too many.   And now, will you all renew your
vows of obedience ? "

They did ; and he plunged into the library, and
summoned each in turn to consult over the dresses,
and generally lay a plan.   They mutually came to
the conclusion that it would take a fortnight at least
to get everything arranged.

The only two who did not seem at ease were
Hermione and Colonel Myddleton.   They were longer
with Mr. Freeman than anybody when · it came to
their respective turns, and both came out looking
vexed and puzzled.   Hermione went straight across
to Lady Clinton.

" Dorothy," she said, " do you really think Mr.
Freeman is to be depended on ?   He is so odd.   I
mean, don't let him turn us out as something
supremely ridiculous."

" Dear, I don't think he would do that, really ; he
has too true an appreciation of everything perfect and
beautiful.   And really, I must say it, you are one of
the only people I ever knew him sincerely admire and
like.   No, I am sure you at least are safe."

" But it is so odd ! " said Hermione, musingly.

" What ? has he told you of a tableau all to yourself ? " said Lady Clinton, curiously.

" He won't say whether I am alone or not.   I think

not, from his manner. But the dress is too extra-ordinary; I don't like it."

"What is it? Oh, do tell me."

"That's just it. I can't. I promised not, before he told me. It seems stupid to make a fuss, but——"

"Oh, Hermione! don't mind, please. I am sure it will be something beautiful."

But Hermione was anything but easy, and Mr. Freeman was evidently not very sure of her, for he was continually coming up to her that evening, and during the rest of the time, to remind her that she was "under orders," and on "honour," not to dis-appoint him. He was tremendously strict with every-body's dresses and the grouping, and used to be having constant rehearsals in the different ways he thought would look best. Indeed, he was so earnest, and took such pains, and was altogether so kindly and encourag-ing, that they all grew quite fond of him and deferred to his every wish.

"I've got it quite on my mind," he said to old Lady Dunstable. "I can see how it will all come. I tell you what, it will be the most perfect thing of its kind that ever was."

"And what are the other tableaux going to be?"

"Ah! that's my secret. Why, nobody knows, except Colonel Myddleton."

"Why did you tell him?"

"I only told him about one; he doesn't know what he's going to do in the other. By-the-by, I must be off after the saddler," and off he went, swinging arms and legs down the approach.

"Now, I wonder if he is going to be with Hermione in the one Dorothy says she is uneasy about," pondered Lady Dunstable. "Quarl is quite capable of doing something allegorical between those two; and they would make a wonderful match."

The funny thing was that, even in consulting together, the different "figures" did not know what they were going to be at relatively. It was a capital idea of Mr. Freeman not telling them, as it caused great excitement; and so particular was he about Hermione's dress, that it was ordered in London.

"What are you going to wear in your parts?" said Hermione to Colonel Myddleton, when he came in late one evening from the village.

"Principally leather," he said, "and then armour. Freeman is gone wild on the subject of fit, and my jerkin seems to be impossible. What are you going to wear?"

"As Catherine Douglas, a riding dress, and then——"

"Hush!" said Mr. Freeman. "Come away, Myddleton. Why, if you go on like that, you can't get up the expression for your part. You are to care for nothing, see nothing, hear nothing, look at nothing."

"Then he is to be dead, I know!" said Gladys, quick as lightning. Hermione gave a little shudder.

"Not quite," said Mr. Freeman, with a curious look at her. "You never can get up rigidity enough for that sort of thing. No, my tableaux are to be perfect; and whoever winks an eyelash shall have Disko set at them."

"I know I am to be very nearly dead, anyhow," whispered Robert to Gladys. "I wonder who is going to save my life? Are you?"

"No; I am only going to act in Catherine Douglas," said Gladys, a little sadly now, on hearing her cousin was going to have an extra part. "I do wish we could get Josline Fairfax up here for the whole thing. How she would enjoy it!"

"Do you think so?" said he, wishing quickly that he might act with her, though the idea of her in any character struck him at once as extraordinary and incongruous. "I am not sure, I think she would be too shy; and then Miss Barbara would never let her come."

"I wonder if Dorothy went and asked her?" mused Gladys.

"I'm afraid it's no go, Cat, and besides, they've asked down Gabriel Vannier. I say, here's an idea! he'd better come up here, and paint us all."

"And me, then! for I am going to wear *such* a dress!" said Miss Thorold, holding up her little hands, and spreading each finger wide. "You don't know how beautiful, and so becoming to me; and they are going to friz all my hair, and Lady Clinton has sent up for the emeralds and the rubies, both *parures*, and all the diamonds are coming out, too, to be worn down the front, white velvet and black satin."

"Oh! but I don't understand," said Gladys. " Queen Joanna would not wear those jewels in the Catherine Douglas scene."

"No, it's for another scene; and I'll tell you what," she added, a little pettishly; "it's all the fault of Miss St. John that we don't know our parts."

"Why?" simultaneously from Gladys and Robert.

"Oh! because Mr. Freeman thinks she wouldn't do it, if she knew, and so he does not dare to tell her till the last minute, and he does not like it to be particular, and therefore, he won't tell anybody. Heiresses are rather a plague!"

"I don't think it's that, really."

"Yes, it is; he almost said as much. I don't see why she should be so absurd. She told me she didn't hate men, so I suppose she can't mind who she acts with. And she is much too tall to look well with any one."

"She is the most perfect and beautiful height," said Gladys, hotly. "Isn't she, Robert?"

"Well, I think both you and Miss Thorold would look too tall, if you were her height; but somehow, she doesn't look too tall."

"She makes every man here look dwarfish," said the fair little Mina.

" Thank you ! " he said, laughing. " Perhaps you don't know I am six feet, and Colonel Myddleton is six feet two; and Phil is five feet eleven, and Sir Vere Temple—— "

But Miss Thorold tucked her small hands up to her ears, and shook herself angrily. " The fact is, I don't like her. Can't you see it ? and she is too tall for me," she said.

" Well, she is rather above you, I must confess," said Mr. Freeman, who had been quietly listening to everything, as usual. " You need not be afraid; you're not going to act with her."

" Of course not, I wouldn't."

" Yes, you'd have to, if I said so. Never mind, it would be a pity to eclipse you."

There was nothing for it but to laugh, as usual, at Quarl.

" I have a suspicion, Miss St. John," said Colonel Myddleton, coming up to her and sitting down by her, a thing he had not done deliberately since that evening, in the morning-room.

Hermione felt curiously glad. " Yes ? " she said, looking up, and laying her right hand over her left, to hide the flash of those tiresome diamonds.

" I wonder if it has struck you ? I think we are going to be in a tableau all to ourselves."

She was silent; but a crimson flush mounted to her forehead, and she dropped her eyes.

He looked at her keenly. " Shall you mind ? " he said.

"No, of course not; why should I?" she said, looking up, but as quickly letting her eyes fall again. "I must do what I am bid, you know."

"Not at all," he said, earnestly. "If you dislike the idea, I'll refuse point-blank, so you will have no trouble."

She hesitated a little, and then said, "I think that would be a pity, don't you? He has so set his heart on this tableau, evidently."

"This tableau! What? Which?"

"Well, I mean the only other I am going to act in besides Catherine Douglas."

"It shall be just as you like," he said. "Of course, I like it. I wish you would tell me what you are going to wear; it might give us a clue."

"I don't like the dress; it's too extraordinary," she said, looking up again. "It's all white from my head to my feet. I shall look like a ghost."

Colonel Myddleton started so violently that his elbow upset a cup of coffee standing near him, and in the confusion, consequent on wiping it up, made no further allusion to the subject; on the contrary, he got up and moved hurriedly away.

"What can I have said now?" thought Hermione. "I'm always saying stupid things;" and it was rather wistfully that she looked towards the end of the drawing-room, where Colonel Myddleton had drawn Mr. Freeman, and was talking to him, evidently most earnestly. Mr. Freeman looked round once or twice.

" I say, Freeman; you're not going to make me act any tomfoolery, now, about that ghost story here?"

" Why? "

" Because, simply, I won't do it. I hate that sort of thing, and frankly, my dear fellow, I won't do it."

" Ha! hum! Well—— " oracularly.

" Now, come, Freeman, out with it in time; get somebody else, but I won't do it."

Quarl was silent, holding his chin; then he said, " Well, would it make any difference as to who was the ghost?"

" Yes—I mean no; of course not, why? "

" Oh! j'ai mes idées voilà tout! " said he, looking across at Hermione. Then suddenly, " I'll tell you what, Myddleton, it'll be an awful shame if you cut out at the end. Now look here; stop a bit; listen! I've got such a scene in my head—it will be perfect— there are only two people here who can do it; you are the man. Now then, be quiet, do! Who do you think looks in the least like the woman? "

" I'll tell you what, Freeman, this is all very fine, but I won't act in that scene. I hate such rubbish; it's a shame to bring a woman in as a ghost. I couldn't stand it."

" Bah! are you afraid, absolutely? " Quarl said it curiously and slowly.

" Yes—well, I am—of that scene," answered Colonel Myddleton, in uncontrollable agitation.

"Well, then, Miss St. John is to act in it. Now do you mind?"

"Just the same," with a spasm at the corners of his mouth.

"Then you would rather somebody else was the old faithless Sir Sydney?"

"I won't act in it."

"Well, we must give it up, then," said Quarl, in a quiet way, "more especially as I had never thought of it at all till you put it in my head."

"Why, you said——"

"Nothing at all," said he, imperturbably. "Only you jumped to some extraordinary conclusion. Now then, look here, who in this room, has a truly noble, spiritual face?"

"They are all too young," said Colonel Myddleton, coldly, turning deliberately away from looking at Hermione.

"I don't agree with you. Miss St. John's face was never young, and it will never grow old. *She* will act the scene with you; and I can tell you this—I think she would be the one to object, if she knew, not you. She will only be your good angel." Then he walked off to make Gladys play.

Colonel Myddleton walked straight across to Hermione, as she had done to Dorothy, and said, "You are not going to be a ghost, only my good angel."

The excitement went on increasing. All the invitations were written and despatched; there was to be a dance afterwards, and a fancy ball the next night but one. The gardener was forcing flowers; the housekeeper was nearly beside herself with anxiety about the supper; the maids were working day and night. The men under Sir Philip and Mr. Freeman were arranging the hall and the daïs. Temporary pillars were raised in front of the dais, hung with tapestry, and between them was slung the curtain. A band was ordered down from London, and was to be placed in the gallery that ran round the hall, at half its height. Everybody worked for everybody else, and nobody did what they ought to do. Mr. Freeman had induced them to keep secret what they were all going to wear at the fancy ball.

"The general world will think Charteriss has suddenly gone mad," said Gladys, dancing with glee.

"I think the general world has gone mad itself," said Lady Clinton. "Do listen ; Mr. Fairfax has said Josline shall come with Mr. Crosbie, only not in fancy dress ! "

Robert Watt, who was polishing a partizan, coloured to the roots of his hair.

"I am sure Miss Barbara doesn't know, then," said Gladys, "for I saw her yesterday, and when I began about it, she sniffed and snuffed, and said she didn't see what young people wanted with all these pinkettings ! so I didn't dare say any more."

"Ah, but I went off to Mr. Crosbie, and he got round that dear Mr. Fairfax; but, of course, I shall have to go in person, and ask Miss Barbara. It will be rather fun, though. Hermione shall come, will you, Ione?"

Meanwhile, day by day, Colonel Myddleton and Hermione seemed to say less to each other. It was not so much on her part as on his. He kept away as much as he could, and when he could not refrain from sitting near her, he hardly spoke. But there was something so held down in his whole manner and bearing, that Hermione was bound by it too. All the old freedom of feeling that had had such charm for her, the feeling that whatever she said he would understand, was gone. She felt, instead, as though he weighed and watched for her words, her inflection of voice, with painful earnestness and often disappointment; he seemed to her to hear what she was saying through any buzz of talk—even if he were speaking to others, in some way her voice appeared to reach him; she knew it by some sudden turn of shoulder and head. It made her restless and feverish; but she had great self-control, and no one found it out, unless perhaps Quarl. She and Mr. Freeman seemed to have arrived at some strange unspoken alliance, offensive and defensive, and she began to like the strange man.

"Gabriel Vannier is coming to Old Court, and I am going to stay there whilst he is there," said Robert Watt to Gladys.

"You will like that, won't you?" said his cousin.

"Yes, awfully. I say, Gladys, it's so odd—I think I really have fallen in love at last."

"So it seems; I knew you would with Josline. What does it feel like?" she said, wistfully.

"Oh, very horrid, but rather jolly too. Of course it will all be no good."

"I don't see that!" indignantly. "Why?"

"Oh, I'm so poor. I say, I didn't mean to say all this."

CHAPTER XI.

A FLOOD of light through the branches of the tallest walnut tree made golden mist in the small chamber where, perched on a four-legged stool, Miss Barbara was giving out household linen to Mrs. Turgoose and Phœbe. The carefully wired lattice window stood wide open, letting in streams of warm air, thrills of birds, and boom and hum of insects. Sweet scents of rose and lavender and thyme came from each press as Miss Barbara opened them in turn, and handed carefully out the snowy and shining piles.

"These will go into the blue chamber, and these into the west," she said, giving down some fine sheets.

"Will Mr. Watt be in the blue chamber, madam?"

"Yes, that delicate artist must have the west, Mr. Fairfax says."

"My lady's own!" ejaculated Turgoose, letting Phœbe take the sheets from Miss Barbara.

"Yes, Turgoose, my lady's own," answered Miss Barbara, severely. "Have you any objection?"

The housekeeper turned round with an angry glare

at the sheets. " Take care, Phœbe," she said, sharply;
" you are crumpling those fine pillow-cases; you're
not fit to carry such linen."

Phœbe, with an alarmed air, stroked the tiniest
crease out of the pillow-case, as you might touch a
gem in the Royal Crown.

" Well, Turgoose, I think I have given you all you
require," said Miss Barbara, closing the presses with
an inward smile at the old woman's look of suppressed
anger. " You will see that the blue chamber and my
lady's own are prepared by this evening."

" Will you give me some more sheets, please
madam, before you close that press?" said Turgoose,
in a voice portending storm.

" I have given you all you want, I am sure,"
answered Miss Barbara, carefully bolting the half of
the old press, and avoiding her housekeeper's eye.
" Phœbe, carry away that armful."

" I beg your humble pardon, madam, but if Phœbe
may put them down here for a moment—girls are
that careless, and all that fine linen," she added, in a
voice of penetrating anxiety.

Miss Barbara closed the remaining door of the
press, and still Turgoose stood expectant.

" Come, now, you must both go," said her mistress,
turning to the window.

Phœbe caught her superior's eye and went.

Miss Barbara leaned out in silence. She hated a
struggle with the housekeeper, and foresaw one now.

At the same time her own temper was rising like a thermometer in the rays of Turgoose's heated feelings.

"I hear the gate swing, madam."

"I have told you to go, Turgoose; there is nothing more for you to do."

"If you please, madam," as she stooped, separated the pile of linen, and came towards her mistress with her arms full, "I am waiting for the sheets for my lady's room."

"Now, Turgoose," said Miss Barbara, turning round suddenly, sitting down on the four-legged stool, and clasping her black mittened arms behind her in her wonted manner, when she meant to be obeyed, "I have given you that linen and I mean you to take it away and use it."

"Certainly, madam, it shall be laid out in the blue chamber most neat, as you would wish."

"Then what are you waiting for?"

"Sheets for my lady's room."

"What sheets? Your arms are full."

"These are the fine sheets, madam, the best pearled linen."

"Well?"

"And for my lady's room?"

"You will put them on, and bring away the lace counterpane, when I will give you out the quilted Persian."

This was a fine stroke of malice on Miss Barbara's part. She thought by rousing more anger to break the force of the whole.

"The quilted Persian ? Very well, madam; and the lace for the blue room ? "

"No. Mr. Watt will not want a counterpane at all."

"There has always been a counterpane on the blue room bed."

"There has never been any but the finest linen sheets on the west room bed," answered Miss Barbara. "Now, Turgoose, don't be such a foolish woman—you know it's of not the slightest use struggling with me. My brother wishes that artist to have the west room, and having the west room he must have the appurtenances thereof."

"My lady's own ! " murmured Turgoose. " In my lady's time it never would have been."

"In my lady's time, Turgoose, you would no more have dared to stand bandying words with your mistress than I choose to allow it now."

Miss Barbara rose and walked past the housekeeper to the door. "Follow me ! " she said.

Turgoose deposited her armful, gathered the others, and followed.

Majestically her mistress passed the blue room door and went on to the west chamber. Phœbe and Mary were opening the windows, beating the rug, settling the furniture generally. They were chattering like two birds, but the step of Miss Barbara caused instant silence. She turned round to speak to Turgoose. No one was there.

" Turgoose ! " she called. A faint voice answered—
" Yes, madam."

" Where are you ? "

" Putting on the sheets in the blue room, madam."

" Phœbe, go and fetch the other pile of sheets
here," commanded Miss Barbara.

Phœbe went. Mary went on dusting and arranging. Down below came strains of the violin and
Josline's voice singing. Presently Phœbe came back.

" Put the sheets here, and tell Mrs. Turgoose I am
waiting."

The housekeeper came.

" Now, Turgoose, bring me the counterpane."

With careful hands, but rather shaking, the
housekeeper drew off the lace counterpane, folded it
carefully with Phœbe's help, and brought it to Miss
Barbara.

" That's right. Now I have a little word for you
all. Whilst I stand here, you Turgoose, and you
Phœbe and Mary, will put the sheets on that bed."

" I will go and fetch them, if you will give me
your keys, madam," said the housekeeper.

" They are at your elbow, Turgoose," said Miss
Barbara.

The housekeeper turned with a start. There in
snowy freshness lay the sheets. She gulped, then
said, " Madam, I *could* not put them sheets upon this
bed for the artist gentleman."

" You *could* not ? " said Miss Barbara.

" No, madam."

" Then, not a servant shall touch them," said Miss Barbara, with a sudden blaze of wrath. " Stand where you are, all three of you. Oh, but this is too much ! "

She stalked to the door and called in a voice whose shrill clearness made the oak hall ring.

" Dux ! Dux ! come here at once."

Mrs. Turgoose stood pale, silent, shaking in every limb. Phœbe and Mary, appalled and aghast, held on each to the opposite ends of the rug, mid air, as though they were about to toss some victim to Miss Barbara's wrath.

The violin sounds ceased, and Mr. Fairfax's voice answered, " Yes, Barbara, I am coming."

Miss Barbara, with a pant, stalked to the window, and called, " Josline ! "

A cloud of doves rose, wheeling, as Josline tossed them from her arms and shoulders and hastened in.

The astonished Mr. Fairfax and his niece found themselves in the west room on obeying the summons.

Miss Barbara, with purple stains of anger on her cheeks and forehead, and her cap tossed on one side, stood glaring near the bed, drawing off her long mittens.

" Dux ! " she began, " is this our mother's room ? "

" Yes, my dear."

" Did you wish the artist to be put here ? "

" Yes, my dear."

" Did you give me that order ? "

" Certainly, I asked you."

" Did you expect everything to be as nice, as thoroughly well-arranged, as though you yourself were coming here—you, a Fairfax ? "

" Certainly," answered her brother, raising his head a little loftily. " My guest is before myself.

" Good; then sit in that chair, please. Now, Josline, tuck away those hanging bobbins of yours, and help me to make the bed."

Josline, with a hardly repressed smile, lifted the sheets with her beautiful arms, and proceeded to make the bed with Miss Barbara, and assuredly never was couch more well-arranged.

Mr. Fairfax was asked to inspect it, and gravely pronounced it perfect, and then Miss Barbara turned on Turgoose.

" Now, Turgoose," she said, sardonically. " As you were quite unable to make a bed, your mistress has taught you in her own mother's room, who was the daughter of an earl."

The housekeeper's face twitched, and she suddenly covered it with her hands and sobbed—" It was because she was—— "

" Let me speak, Barbara," said Mr. Fairfax, quietly. " I don't think you quite understand each other." Miss Barbara heaved. " You both mean much the same thing, only you look at it differently. You, Barbara, give of your best to a guest, because you know your mother would have done so, as being the truest, noblest, only thing to do, no matter whether they stand high or low in the social scale. Turgoose, loving my dear mother's memory and reverencing her beyond all things and people, is grieved to think any one should approach or in any way be placed on the same footing—— "

" Yes, yes, Master Giles ! " from Turgoose, now quite softened and melted.

" Yes ; but you forget, Turgoose, that that is not what she would have wished. Who so kind, so thoughtful for others, so unselfish as my mother ? Did it make any difference to her whether they were rich or poor, high or low ? "

" No," murmured Turgoose.

" Did she ever speak more peremptorily or harshly to you because you were her servant ? "

"No."

" Did she ever tell you to do anything you would have dreamed of questioning ? "

" No," still more low.

" Well, then, it is settled in this way : my mother was by birth a lady, and by every feeling of her heart and mind tenfold so. Knowing that the higher God has chosen to place our rank, so much the more are we bound to consult the feelings of those around us with the true nobility of soul which comes from the sense of how high above us all is the God who yet took up His abode amongst the lowly."

A grave silence followed Mr. Fairfax's last words. Miss Barbara had lost her angry colour, and was looking gently at the housekeeper. Phœbe and Mary stood, with tearful eyes, nearly adoring their master for his goodness. Josline was holding his hand. Presently Miss Barbara drew on her mittens with a jerk, and going across to Turgoose, held out her hand, saying—

"If I was too severe with you, Turgoose, and you not sufficiently obedient to me, we must forgive each other. We were both working, as my brother says, from the same motive, wrongly."

The old housekeeper kissed her mistress's hand gratefully, and murmured, as Mr. Fairfax's footstep died away down the passage with Josline's and Miss Barbara's—"They are real, real gentlefolks."

Mrs. Turgoose, Phœbe, and Mary worked away with a will to make the west chamber look quite at its best. The Persian quilt made the bed look resplendent. The bay-shaped windows stood wide open, letting in warmth and flickering lights. A few delicate flowers, sent in by the gardener, were arranged in tall Venetian glasses, and a large chair, with side-wings, stood in the angle of the window and table, to rest weary limbs.

As she turned to leave the room, Mrs. Turgoose gave a small sigh of regret that it was only an artist who was to profit by such refinements and joys.

Gabriel Vannier's heart ached with longing for his

mother that night when sitting in the old chair, his throbbing temples pressed in his hollow hand. The refinement, the quiet, the serenity of sights and scents, brought vividly back to his memory the mother, who, through all her troubles and poverty, had yet contrived always to surround her child with something of the subtle distinction and beauty of her nature.

Could the housekeeper have known what perfect rest and refreshment this room brought to the sad-looking young man, whose slight, husky cough had startled her kind heart that evening as she passed his door late, she would have been repaid in full for her struggles.

CHAPTER XII.

THE church bells were ringing that melodious peal, full and sweet, rarely heard out of England, or, indeed, out of a village, which seems to say, with a silver beat, like a sob of joy, "Come to chur—urch! come to chur—urch!"

Robert was walking up and down the velvet lawn in a state of feverish anxiety. Gabriel Vannier was watching the doves. The "person of the house" was gravely parading, with dainty steps, down the nut-walks; her lifted, curling lips far from uttering prayer or praise, I fear; her soft coat gleaming as though she had donned a new dress in honour of the day she fully intended desecrating with a slaughter of inno-cents, might she but only entice some winged mes-sengers on to the bough whereon she was about to spring, curl up, and lie in wait.

One bell alone took up the strain now. Robert's head, which had been lifted, scanning each window of the house in turn, fell as the garden door opened, and

Miss Barbara and her brother came out. His heart
sank with a bitter feeling of disappointment, too great
for explanation, as, without further waiting, they
nodded to him to follow; and, passing along the
low wall, turned the corner by the stone balls, and
went down the narrow path to church.

"Then it is true," he thought to himself, standing
still and forcing his cane far into the turf at his feet.
"I don't see why I should go to church at all, either.
I'll stay here with Gabriel, and perhaps I'll see her
that way."

"Are you not coming, Mr. Watt?" said Gabriel,
suddenly.

"Are you going to church?" said Robert, amazed.

"Yes, I shall," answered he, with a slight hesita-
tion. "It will be so quiet."

"I should not have thought it much in your way,"
said Robert, laying a hand on his shoulder.

The artist smiled sadly. "It was my mother's,"
he said.

How small a thing will sway us? In five seconds
Robert and Gabriel were hurrying along the narrow
pathway, to be in time; and although Robert was
growling and murmuring to himself about the "bother
of it," and "missing Josline," still he felt irresistibly
impelled to accompany the artist, whose will, however,
exceeding his powers, they were forced to pause to get
breath, at the old lych gate.

Mr. Fairfax and Miss Barbara had disappeared.

One or two villagers were hastening in. The bell had stopped, and discordant screams of a trumpet, trombone, bassoon, fiddle, and the occasional thump of a drum, made the men look at each other, and Robert burst out laughing; his companion was too exhausted to speak or laugh. His extreme paleness made Robert stop and say, anxiously—

" I fear you are terribly weak, Vannier. Take my arm."

The colour ebbed slowly back to his face, as they sauntered into the porch, where they were met by a small, fussy man with a blue wand, tipped with gold, and led into a deep pew.

When Robert looked up, he saw they were sitting about the middle of the church, which was long and very low, with thick, short pillars. Immediately in front of them was a superb old tomb, surrounded by carved angels bearing coats emblazoned ; and, on their right, running at right-angles from the wall, and raised above the body of the church about three feet, was a small chapel, or rather what had been such. It was now used as a pew by the Fairfax family, and contained a large oak table, heavy oak chairs, and an open fireplace, filled at this season of the year with green boughs.

Robert's heart gave a violent bound, for there knelt Josline, her face buried in her hands. The revulsion of feeling was almost painful. Miss Barbara's stern glance met and reproved his ardent, wistful gaze of joy, as she leant forward and said, in a loud voice—

" You were very late, or you would have been here ! "

He bowed deprecatingly, and only just in time to stifle a smile, as the trombone gave a fearful moan in the closing harmony.

Perhaps Robert had never been so attentive in church before. The sense that he was near Josline, that she was praying with all her heart—she must be, or how could she look so perfectly divine ?—the joy and relief of knowing that thus she could not be a Romanist, completely overcame him for the time being, and filled heart and soul with gratitude and worship, whether for the Creator or the creature he did not care to define. Under Miss Barbara's watchful gaze, he did not dare to look too often to his right; but during Mr. Crosbie's sermon, which was delivered with short, sharp emphasis, he kept his eyes fixed on the beautiful east window, with the altarpiece below it—the Holy Dove hovering, surrounded by angels' heads, each small face between wings, bearing a different expression of joy and happiness. The warm light from outside played up and down it, and one face, with gleaming curls and deep eyes, reminded him so strongly of Gladys in a merry, half-serious mood, that involuntarily he caught himself smiling at it.

The service was over, and they all met at the lych gate.

"I was afraid you were not coming, Miss Fairfax,"
were the first words Robert spoke, looking down at
Josline.

"I think I might have thought that of you," she
said, smiling. "You were so late, I began to think
the painter had kept you."

"Oh, no!" he answered, with hurried eagerness.
"It was entirely his doing that I came at all."

"Don't you go to church, then, as a rule?"

"Yes, but I was waiting for you, and then I thought
you weren't going, and then I thought I wouldn't go
either." He stopped short, hitting at the brambles
hanging over the hedge.

Josline made no remark, a faint colour tinged
her cheek, and a new and vivid feeling shot through
her heart.

"Where were you?" he began again. "I was in
the garden near your doves, but I never saw you go."

"I went first of all to Mr. Crosbie's, with some
flowers, for him."

"Do you put flowers in the church here?"

"No, they were for his room. I always take him
some on Sunday morning."

"Who is that altarpiece by?"

"Hudson ; it is thought rather good. Do you like
it?"

"Yes, it's an uncommon subject, too ; some of the
children's heads are charming. I saw Gabriel
Vannier looking at them for ever so long."

"And some one else too," she said, smiling. "I saw you looking at them as though they were old acquaintances."

"One was like my cousin Gladys," he said, with a happy feeling to think she had noticed him. "She is such a dear little thing."

In the evening there was some most beautiful music; Mr. Fairfax drawing sounds from his violin that Orpheus might have sought in vain to rival, and Josline's exquisite voice, singing Mendelssohn's "Auf Wiedersehen," till even Miss Barbara's eyes filled.

Strangely enough, Robert, though perfectly enthralled and entranced, kept thinking more of Gladys and the seraph's head in the altarpiece, than even of the singer.

Gabriel Vannier leant out of the window, drinking in scents and sounds with the peculiar powers of his artist mind and soul.

After a short pause and silence, Josline began "Che farò senza di te Eurydice."

Mr. Crosbie, who was talking to the "person of the house," curled up on his knee, gave a start that precipitated puss between his legs, then got up and went over to the window to Gabriel.

"This is the very thing I wanted you most to hear," he said, in an almost inaudible voice, "though I did not think she would have sung it to-night, with me here, too, the little minx."

The artist did not move, his eyes were fixed on

Josline; he seemed drawing her with them on a mental canvas. Her head was bent slightly on one side, her eyes were half closed, her lips seemed to open only enough to breathe gently; so perfectly full of repose was her whole figure, she might have been singing in a picture, but that the full sorrowful anguish of sound filled the room with waves of melody.

She held them all spell-bound, as that song should always do, yet apparently by no volition of her own; it was as though her very life floated out in the cry, "Eurydice! Eurydice!"

When she ceased at length, each person heard the beating of their own heart; a profound silence reigned in the room, and then Mr. Crosbie noticed Gabriel's head had sunk on his breast. He touched him, shook him, the artist had fainted.

"It was the joy of that ineffable singing," he said, when at last recovered he found himself lying on a low settee by the open window.

"You had stood too long, I think," said Miss Barbara, anxiously. "I am sure you've looked ready to faint all day, and all these flowers in the room; such nonsense of Josline, who will go on about flowers and birds." And she gave a push to the great blue vase full of the silvern lilies.

"Oh! I *love* flowers," said Gabriel, earnestly; "they never hurt me."

"They made you faint, though, I'm sure," she answered.

He sat up hurriedly, very pale. "I am so sorry to have given you all so much trouble," he stammered. "I will go up now. Will you thank Miss Josline, oh! so much for her great kindness in having sung that song to me?—the last time—my mother——" He broke off, got up and walked quickly to the door.

"Go after him, Mr. Watt, he'll faint again, poor fellow."

But swiftly the artist had reached the landing, on the top stair he stood gasping slowly, and as Robert bounded up to him, he heard him murmur to himself, in a voice full of wistful misery, "Gran' Dio! morir' si giovine io che ho penato tanto!"

CHAPTER XIII.

The following day Gabriel Vannier came down early, but not so early as Mr. Fairfax, who was already playing softly in his den.

"Ah! up so early!" said the host, laying aside his bow, and holding out his hand to take and hold that of his guest. "I fear you do not rest enough, but I find as a rule that those who want most rest take least."

"I have no time to rest, yet," answered Gabriel, with a dim smile on his wan face. "Rest comes only to the weary, and I have so much to do, I am never weary."

"Ah!" said Mr. Fairfax, with dreamy terseness, and as his fingers fell on the strings, he pressed and drew out a long note, lifted his bow and fell back again absently to music.

The artist leant against a tall-backed chair, the colour flushing and fading; he saw again the singer at the quaint but sweet-toned old piano, and as the violin sounds rose, swelled, fainted, he drew towards him the top of a cigar-box and a large brown chalk pencil lying on the writing-table, and rapidly outlined her head, throat, and bust.

It was marvellously like, each delicate turn of lid and lip, the small oval ear, the line of the hair, the poise and droop of the head on the throat.

The colour deepened to vivid carmine on his thin face, his hand quivered and burnt; and ever the picture grew as the violin music swelled, awoke, burst into volume, melody, and grandeur.

As it died down into a wailing miserere, the sketch was completed—a picture evolved from music with minor closing. Gabriel held it out; a look of joy came on his brow, lighting his face like a lamp.

"It's worth it," he murmured, and placing it so that the soft, full light from the window struck and glorified it, he walked quietly away.

He strolled across the lawn till he was opposite the bay window of the cedar parlour, where he became an amused spectator of the following scene.

The "person of the house" stood in fluffy dignity, looking much discomposed on the window-seat; Josline was employed in smoothing her coat, and, it is to be hoped, her ruffled cat-mind likewise, though at present she was growling in an irate manner.

Miss Barbara, with her lustring dress carefully tucked round her, a very high colour on her thin

cheekbones, her dainty mittens thrown aside, and
every fold of her small apron denoting storm, was
kneeling on the floor with a small pair of bright brass
tongs, busily employed in carefully picking up some
silvery hairs from a large piece of brocade stretched
in front of the fire.

It was indeed a Sysiphus-like task ; no sooner did
the snapping tips of the tongs gather a hair than it
fell before it could be safely lifted on to a large sheet
of paper. Miss Barbara was kneeling on a green
square to-day, which of course was not large enough
to support her two knees properly, and every time she
bent forwards to seize a hair, she tipped up and nearly
fell on her face. All the time she kept on a voluble
stream of words, which came out in jets and jerks like
liquor out of a bottle partially unstoppered.

" Just to think of the cat lying on this piece of
brocade, my great-grandmother's best sacque ! so impertinent ! She is getting beyond bearance ; you spoil
her so, Josline," shaking the tongs at the " person,"
who fluffed and jumped, having been awoke from a
dreamless sleep by hearing them snapped within an
inch of her round, soft face.

Josline was in a state of suppressed mirth, but
gravely said, " Fie, pussy ! " with an admonitory tap
soft as silk on pussy's head.

" It's all of a piece nowadays," went on Miss
Barbara, " cats and girls go together. I bring down "
—tip up and nearly into the fire—" my precious

brocade just because Dux insists on my showing it to that artist, who won't care to see it, I know, and then —how these hairs do stick! there! two together!— and then, what? well, and then I find the cat asleep in the very heart of the lotos flower, all amongst those delicate petals. Ah!" Tip up number two. Miss Barbara's pointed nose meets, with severe roughness, the gold centre of the lotos; she raises her head with flaming nostrils, and weeping eye. "And there you stand, Josline, not caring a bit, and stroking that ridiculous mouser. Now just see! six long draggling hairs all on one leaf! disgusting!" Snip, snap of the tongs, snip, snap, and up they came. "I had just gone up to get my little italian, and iron it out properly, and then these small tongs to. place coal on without any dust, and then——" Tip up number three, but this time, quite overbalancing herself, Miss Barbara's small curls lay delicately reposing on the buds and blossoms, her tongs dug into the rug and snapped upon air, and she lay prostrate.

The "person of the house" fluffed straight out of the window, and Josline flew to lift her aunt, nearly suffocated with laughter, and efforts to suppress it. Miss Barbara tilted herself up, like a two-wheeled cart, and not knowing the amount of damage she had done, either to the brocade or herself, sat staring in bewilderment for a second or so. Her first exclamation, as Josline threw out her arms to raise her, was—

"There, child, still on the red square, when I told you to-day was green!"

"Do let me help you up, aunt Barbara," urged Josline, anxiously.

"Ah! I'm on the blue myself!" she said, with a little shriek. "Help me, Josline! Hump!" She was erect and staring at the brocade, which, alas! was sorely creased by the fall.

"Never mind, dear aunt, and oh! look, you have hurt yourself with those horrid tongs."

"Nothing to matter," answered Miss Fairfax, ruefully; "but the brocade!"

"Turgoose will put it all right," began her niece. "I'll run and fetch you some water to wash your hand."

"Child, girl! the *green* squares, I say!" called Miss Barbara after her, as Josline sped with light leaps out of the room.

When, later on, Gabriel was shown the brocade neatly smoothed out, and looking lustrous and infinitely rich and beautiful, and thought with quick retro-active amusement of Miss Barbara's downfall, he could not refrain from smiling at Josline, and whispering, "'Great was the fall thereof,' Miss Fairfax."

It was after breakfast. They were all assembled in the den, looking at and admiring the wonderfully drawn head of Josline. She and Gabriel stood near the window, deeply engrossed in a tray of gems, intaglios, and cameos; the painter was explaining to her the meaning of some of them, and showing her how cleverly and with what exquisite skill the engravers had seized on the veining of the gems to give force to a certain expression or attitude.

" How I should like to travel and see all these beautiful things in their own lands ! " she said. " I always think that seeing the actual places, living in the same atmosphere, surrounded by the same colouring, breathing the same air, would enable one to enter so much more fully into the spirit of the worker."

" Yes, there is much in that," he answered, thoughtfully. " I have read a poem once, and found no clue to its meaning—I mean the meaning it held in the mind that wrote it, which, is after all, hardly ever the signification the reader seizes at first sight ; and then perhaps, after weeks, months, I have read it again not trying for its secret, and suddenly, like a light in a dark chamber, the whole mystery has penetrated my mind in a flash ; then you feel that your mind has met, has actually touched, the spirit that wrote." He paused. " It is most wonderful," he went on slowly. " I suppose it is the divine brotherhood in us, the real equality of our Father's spirit breathed in us at our creation, that thus overflows at times the outward boundaries of our different humanities, and echoes soul to soul. I think this is how we shall know each other in heaven, even as we are known."

" Our souls are like crystals that ring, it would seem to me you think," said Josline.

" Crystals under slime," he answered, with a faint smile. "God's finger touches us, and we vibrate; each time that our spirit rings responsive and true to another, without effort and without simulation, I believe God has touched us."

Josline was silent; her eyes were fixed on Robert, who, standing back from the picture, with folded arms, was intently regarding it. A slight shudder passed over her frame.

"Do you think, then, that such minds would naturally further and further incline towards each other?"

"That depends. If they met much, I think it would be so, and yet not invariably, for further knowledge might show that they only met on mutual ground in one form."

They were both silent; Gabriel thinking of his wife—Josline of Robert Watt.

There was no question with herself; she liked him. From the first day she had been drawn towards him by a force she had not tried to gauge or resist. What it was in him that so particularly attracted her, she had never attempted to define; he was not in the least the sort of person she had ever pictured to herself as an ideal, even in her vague, girlish feelings; but she knew when he was in the room, even if he were not speaking. She felt an undefined restlessness when he was not in sight, she avoided his eye whenever it might possibly be fixed on her, she found herself harkening to his tread, she heard his voice through other voices ; and she knew, without words, that it was the same with him.

The last few days he had been particularly in her mind. He had never shown to such advantage as now, in being careful to help Gabriel Vannier in many small ways, in lifting or supporting heavy books or portfolios, in bringing him without word or question his warm muffler, in closing doors if he thought the artist stood in a draught. Each and all of these small things had been so delicately and simply done, that the painter himself had, she thought, hardly been aware of them, at any rate had not resisted them, and that was the main gain.

There was something very wistful in her face when she again spoke to Gabriel, and a little paleness in her cheek and blueness about her eyes that made her look almost as though she had wept inwardly.

" Do you think both minds feel it at the same time ? " she asked, with a slight quiver in her voice.

" I was speaking of a book," he said, smiling. " If you mean two minds recognizing each other in the same instantaneous manner as the spirit of a book will flash on one's intellect, I think they do."

" Is it a happy thing, do you think ? " Her eyes looked up into his, and he looked gravely down on her, and said—

" Not always; but it implies a great gift for a great purpose."

Her colour faded yet more, and she murmured to herself, "A gift already given."

"All gifts can be redeemed," he said, "excepting God's."

"Yes," she answered.

Here Mr. Fairfax called him to come and look at a most exquisite Zuccarelli—a little smiling landscape in Northern Italy; on the right, a bank with tall trees, two horsemen riding down a glade, and a far-away vista of hills going back into snow.

Gabriel's face glowed with delight and recollection of the landscape, and he began explaining to Mr. Fairfax the scene of the picture. Josline stood for a little quite alone; Robert was listening to the artist, and Miss Barbara was cossetting the "person of the house," who, now quite forgiven, was rubbing gently against the black mittens.

The girl was lost in reverie; her eyes, though fixed on the group near her, yet rested in reality on none of their figures.

"How earnest you look, Miss Fairfax!" said Robert's voice suddenly, close to her. "Were you ever there?"

"No, never. I should so like to go abroad. I have always longed to go," she answered, looking up at him with a good deal of the earnest expression she had been unconsciously infusing into her eyes.

"How I should like to take you!" he answered, as earnestly in tone.

"Ah! that will never be," she said, absently. "One never does what one most longs to do. Oh, how I should like to go abroad! When I look at all these beautiful pictures and gems, I wonder how any one loving art can ever live long severed from the country which produces them."

"Yes, I too used to think that, but it is a great disappointment in reality; these are dead things, not living art, and everything you see produced there now is so infinitely below them in feeling and execution."

"Do you think so? Still I should like to go. How can you stay here, if you can travel, Mr. Watt?"

He looked earnestly at her, so earnestly that again the colour faded in her sensitive face.

"Certainly, there would be the joy of coming back, if my father would let me go," he said, slowly.

She moved a little; her lips trembled.

"Would you like me to—would you wish me to go, Miss—Josline?"

"I—if I were a man, I should go," she said.

"Do you think it would be well for me to go—really—truly?" His voice fell and trembled like hers had done.

"There would always be the coming back you spoke of," she said, faintly.

"Oh! Then I might come back here to see—Miss Barbara, your uncle?"

"Yes, they are not likely to travel."

" And—and you ? "

" This is my only home, I am not likely to wander."

" But you would like to do so, you long to do so. Do you like seeing new people, as well as new places ? "

" I have never seen new places, and I hardly ever see new people."

" Do you get strongly attached to places and people ? "

" I grow accustomed to them, and then—no, I do not like anything very new."

" But do you think you might grow to like even indifferent people, if you got accustomed to them ? "

" I don't know ; yes, I suppose you always grow to endure those you must live with, or else you die."

" But you would like to have the power of choosing your—I mean those with whom you were to live ? "

" I am different to everybody you ever knew," she said, with sudden tears floating in her eyes. " It is quite impossible for you to judge, or generalize from me, Mr Watt."

A passion of anxiety, he could never afterwards define why, shook Robert to the soul. " Why ? " he said, drawing closer, and laying a cold, trembling hand as near her as he dared, which, after all, was only to clasp and grasp with painful force the edge of the heavy writing-table.

" Oh, because—— " said Josline, and stopped with an effort, that made her shake like a leaf.

"*Do* tell me," he leaned lower, till she felt his agitated breathing lifting her hair.

She looked up at him with a wistful, grave, solemn earnestness, that was like a benediction or a miserere.

"I dare not tell you," she said, and her lips trembled, till he thought she would have wept.

"I won't ask you," he said, suddenly; "but, oh! Miss Fairfax—— "

Neither her voice nor his filled the pause.

CHAPTER XIV.

"I know you could do it fast enough if you tried."

It was Robert speaking. He was hanging with feverish eagerness over Gabriel Vannier, who held in both hands the picture of Josline on the rough box lid.

"I don't know. I am not sure—I think not," answered the artist, slowly, "This came to me suddenly. What a heavenly face it is!" he ended, holding the picture further and further from him. "You might make anything of her, Madonna, angel, or—— "
He stopped.

"What?" said Robert, half angrily, striding up and down the room biting a pen, and now and then coming back, seemingly by a stronger volition than his own, to gaze at the picture.

"A woman who would love you to the very death."

"Ha! ha!"

Gabriel sighed, put the picture on the table, sat down in front of it, and settling his chin on one hand,

and shading his eyes with the other, looked long and silently at it.

" What is the good of your staring at it so ? " said Robert at last, coming behind him, and laying his hand tightly over his eyes. " How I wish you would copy it for me."

" I *couldn't*," answered the artist, earnestly.

" Do you think you could paint her again ? " said his friend, after a pause.

" I'll try ; but she will never have that look."

Both of them remained looking at the picture.

" Do you really think her so capable ? Bah ! how can you know ? " broke off Robert, suddenly.

" Of loving, you mean ? " ended Gabriel, quietly. " Yes, but I don't think she would ever let herself do it."

" Why ? "

" It would kill her."

" Nonsense ! "

Gabriel drew a sheet of paper towards him, sketched rapidly the blue vase and the silver lilies, then shadowed in her head like the heart of one of the large flowers, throwing the shadow of a petal across her mouth, giving the wistful, earnest look Robert knew so well.

He stood breathless ; the picture grew. From down in the garden they heard a distant voice, that grew and grew likewise.

" Es ist bestimmt in Gottes Rath, das man vom

liebsten was man hat, muss Scheiden." A turn in the walk caused the voice to fade away, then grow. "Auf wiedersehen! auf wiedersehen!"

Dead silence in the room; the painter sighed heavily, Robert drew a gasping breath.

"Still I like the first one best," said the latter, at last.

"We will take them both to Mr. Fairfax, and let him choose, would you like that?" proposed Gabriel.

"Of course he will choose the one I want, but I don't see any better way."

"I shan't say they are either for you."

Mr. Fairfax truly preferred the Eurydice portrait, as Gabriel was well aware he would; as any one knowing and loving Josline would have done; but he was too kindly and anxious to gratify the artist to press for the choice when he noticed a slight reluctance on Gabriel's part to yield it, although nominally he was given his preference.

"They are both very beautifully done," he said, at last. "And perhaps—well, I know well how she looks by her lilies, and, if I may, I will keep that, and thank you many times for so valuable and beautiful a gift."

Yet all the time he was holding and looking at the Eurydice portrait, and Robert trembled for his resolution.

Finally he banked up the lilies' heart with some

heavy folios, and said, "I shall put it into that old Florentine ebony and tortoise-shell frame."

"That will be perfect," answered Gabriel.

So Robert got his picture, and, when it was fairly his, could do little else than sit and gaze at it.

Josline was quite startled to see another portrait of herself, and admired infinitely the delicate drawing of the lilies, although she did not think the likeness very striking.

"Dux, I wish to speak to you," began Miss Barbara, with much solemnity, coming in and sitting down with palm pressed to palm. "Do you know what is going on here?"

"Going on?" he said, rather vaguely, with his head buried in old music, hunting for the score of one of Haydn's canzonets. "No; anything serious?"

"Robert Watt has fallen in love with Josline."

"Well, why not?" he said, absently. "Where is that canzonet? Everything is so torn and pulled about! I think, dear, the cat must get in here sometimes."

"I wish she did," observed Miss Barbara, grimly. "You think of four-legged cats, and I of two-legged ones."

"Barbara! when you know how sorry I was about that kitten, now, and I told them to kill it quickly, and—— "

"Nonsense, Dux! Don't think of those nasty things!" broke in Miss Fairfax. "How puss could

ever have had it, I don't know" (pathetically and
parenthetically). "What I mean is about Robert
Watt; has he any money?"

"Money? Money would not pay for all this
mischief."

"No, I'm well aware it won't. I don't suppose
Josline will have much. You with your ideas; but I
tell you fairly, Dux, I *will* leave her my mother's
topazes,"—this with some heat—"they will be very
unbecoming to her, but—— "

"Barbara, I really cannot permit this—— "

"They are my own jewels, Dux," said Miss
Barbara, with superb dignity, "and she is your own
niece, though I know—— "

"Barbara, will you listen to reason. These—Good
gracious!"

There was a rustle, down fell a mass of music;
there was a faint squeaking, and, lo, a whole nest of
young mice in the very heart of the canzonets!

The tears actually rushed to Mr. Fairfax's eyes,
and he, ordinarily so calm and patient, stamped his
foot and waved his bow as though about to exter-
minate the whole brood at one fell swoop.

"There!" said Miss Barbara, peering down over
his raised arm. "Now perhaps you will let puss
come in here again; disgusting creatures! Puss,
puss, puss!"

"What! before my eyes? No, I can't see it," and
he fled.

But his sister was not to be put off from her news, she came upon him in the hazel walk.

" What was I telling you this morning, Dux ? "

" Telling me ? Oh ! about—no, I forget."

"What do you know about Robert Watt, brother?"

" He is a pleasant young fellow."

" So is Gabriel Vannier, the artist."

" Yes, indeed," he said, warmly. " I have rarely met any man with a truer, keener love of art."

" But you would not like him to marry Josline ? "

" Barbara ! " stopping short in his strolling walk and flushing to his temples; then he laughed a little low laugh, and said, " Nonsense ! but you startled me."

" Well, I did not mean that, certainly. But how about Robert Watt ? "

"Oh ! as to that—— " a long pause; then he said slowly, " Why not ? "

" I don't know, I'm sure ; it will be certainly—— Why, yes."

" Well, Barbara, she must marry some day, I suppose, dear child—they will always marry sooner or later, somehow," he ended dreamily.

"You and I never did," said Miss Barbara, jealously. " I don't see why she must."

" Oh, us ! But then she is so beautiful, Barbara ; and after all—— " He stopped again.

" Well, after all ? "

" Well, after all, I would have, if I could ; and you might have, if you would."

"But I would not, and why should she would?" said Miss Barbara, in such sudden angry confusion as to forget both sense and grammar. "I don't see why we old people are to have all the anxiety and care and plague of taking thought for them, and then, just when they are beginning to know our ways and be pleasant to us and companionable, and—and of use, then they must just go away with some young fellow, who is nobody knows who, and how he gets hold over them I don't know." She stopped, out of breath, red and quaking.

"Now, Barbara," began her brother, quietly, "you are jumping to conclusions very hastily, and you are wrong in your premises. We do know who Robert Watt is——"

"But has he any money?"

"That, of course, we must discover, not that it is of much consequence, as I have no children and Josline will be my daughter."

"Oh, Dux!"

"Why not, Barbara? after you, of course. Young things must wait; but she is the pearl and joy of my old, withered life, and why should she not eventually be happy? I know she will always love all my old things—my pictures, my gems, my violins, Dumps" (his cob), "this dear, old place, and the walnut trees —yes, she loves them better than you even, Barbara ; she would never dream of cutting down one stick or twig."

" It was only to give you more light, Dux," murmured Miss Barbara, ruthfully, looking at the fine tree she had once nearly sacrificed.

" And then you say, because we have been good to them whilst they were young, the young should live with us when we are old? but then when would they enjoy their own freshness and powers? I think the old will always—as they have done always—live for the young, and the young will live for themselves and in themselves."

" Josline has been quite happy till now," said Miss Barbara.

" She is quite happy still, I think," he answered. " And we do not know, because he cares for her, that she cares for him. Ah, Barbara! she has had a very shadowed childhood; will you blight her girlhood too, from a vain idea of keeping her always all your own? But you could not do it."

His sister flushed darkly.

" I think women are the most generous and unselfish creatures to men, and the most grasping and jealous to each other."

" I am sure she does just as she likes always," said Miss Barbara, hastily. " She has her birds, and flowers, and singing, and—and—— "

" Her *counterpart* ? "

" I declare, Dux, it is not necessary for women to marry."

" And yet 'it is not good for man to be alone.'

Ah, Barbara ! you are on the edge of a great mystery."

They wandered on slowly in silence.

> The little birds sang east,
> And the little birds sang west.

" Then you really mean to make Josline your heiress ? " she asked, at length.

" If Robert Watt wants her to wife, means shall not fail," he said, gravely.

" But, Dux, supposing she were to—I mean—supposing she followed—fell back into—became like her mother ? " she ended in a low, awful whisper.

" Ah, that old pain ! " he said, then paused, bent his head low on his breast, looked up quietly, moved a few steps, and his eyes rested on the old dial. He said slowly and in a deep, grave tone—" ' There is one body, and one Spirit, even as ye are called in one hope of your calling ; one Lord, one faith, one baptism, one God and Father of all, who is above all, and through all, and in you all.' "

CHAPTER XV.

"LADY CLINTON and Miss St. John, please, ma'am."
Upon this announcement the alarmed Phœbe re-
tired, and Miss Barbara rose from the straight-backed
chair, with the lion-headed arms, to receive her guests.
She stood up straight and tall, grim as cast-iron, and
with a most forbidding frown from sheer nervousness
and shyness.

Hermione sat down with her back to the light,
looking at the old pictures let into the panel, more
particularly did her eye fall on sweet Mistress
Margaret.

Lady Clinton soon set the conversation afloat in
spite of Miss Fairfax's monosyllabic answers. After a
few commonplaces she turned a little more towards
Hermione, as though to gather courage from her
extreme quietude, and said, with a kind of spasmodic
quickness of intonation—

"Sir Philip, Gladys, and I hope, so much, that
you will let your niece come to our tableaux later on.

Mr. Crosbie thought, perhaps, if I came and asked, as a great favour, you would allow it ? "

With quick synthetic power Miss Barbara's mind seized and surveyed the position. They had not dared to come direct to herself; they had gone to the god-father; they had, perhaps, gone to the uncle; they had laid a plan; they had a plot; they were gradually going to take away the girl who was the one bright thing in her life. No, it should not be! She would show that she still had power to refuse—to keep back what no one living had so clear a right to—the fresh-ness of this young life, its first impressions, its first gladness. This loving, narrow-hearted woman would cling and grasp, with claw-like force, to the last vestige of her right, forgetting that what she thought of did not exist; for love has no rights, only longings, which may or may not be satisfied; but which can never be compelled into life or power.

Hermione saw instantly that Dorothy had made a wrong move; but it was too late to alter words or expressions now.

Grasping the lion heads, whose sharp angles bit into her hands and added thus to her irritation, Miss Barbara said, shortly—

"Very kind, I am sure; but Josline is delicate and easily tired; I never wish her to go into any ex-citement. Girls are too fond of gadding about now."

" Oh, Miss Fairfax, I will take such care of her; it will be so pretty. Do let her come ! "

" Very pretty, indeed, I've no doubt; but her head is full of nonsense already, and more than enough; since we have had that young artist here, there has been nothing but music and sentiment and goings on," ended Miss Barbara, rather vaguely, and actually against her own convictions, for she had begun to take a real interest in Gabriel, and by no means disliked either the music, the sentiment, or the goings on.

" Oh! is he here still ? " asked Hermione, seeing it would be wise to urge no further at present about Josline.

" No; he left this morning," answered Miss Barbara, turning sharply on her other visitor, and scanning her gravely from head to foot, and then from feet to head.

Now, if Miss Barbara had a weakness, it was for very tall, very fair people; and something in Hermione's voice pleased and soothed her, as a quiet sky will calm a troubled mood.

" Do you know him ? " she added.

" No ; but I have heard a good deal about him. I should so like to see some of his pictures," answered Hermione, feeling that Miss Barbara was suddenly mollified, though she did not define why.

" I can show you one, if you don't mind taking the trouble to come into my brother's den."

They went across the hall in the semi-transparent darkness, and, going into the den, found it empty.

The lilies' heart stood in its frame of ancient work-
manship, leaning against the melodies of the old
masters. So exquisitely was the head shadowed on
the glory of the flowers, that it gave the impression
of being painted on pearl.

"How lovely!" said Lady Clinton; "and how
exquisitely painted! He must, indeed, be all Robert
Watt said of him as a painter. Wouldn't you like
to see the picture he is painting for Bob, Hermione?"

"Yes. I hope to know your niece some day, Miss
Fairfax, if I may," said Hermione; "I hear she sings
so beautifully; and somehow this picture looks as
though she might have been taken after singing."

"That is curious," said Miss Barbara. "It was
not; but one that the young man did at first, and
that was far more beautiful, was done after she sang
some Italian song."

"Is that here?" said Dorothy, looking round
eagerly.

"No. My brother had his choice, and why, I can't
think, with a man's whim he chose this. The other
was far more like."

"What wonderful eyes! They seem to follow
one everywhere. I should like to know her!" said
Hermione.

"I am sure she would be very pleased," said Miss
Barbara, unconsciously becoming more and more
fascinated. "I am afraid she is gone out now;
she was going down to Nan Partridge, the black-

smith's wife, and was to meet her uncle afterwards. He is gone botanizing in Crumb's Bottom."

"Ah! that's where the bogbean grows, Hermione. You'll have to stay on here into next summer, and go and look for it," said Lady Clinton. "Gladys and Robert know all the paths about there."

"Do you care about herbs?" said Miss Barbara. "I have a fine collection. I thought no one cared in these days; no young people, I mean."

"Yes; I am very fond of plants and *weeds*," said Hermione; "but I know very little about them. I find it so difficult to get books about them."

"Dux has several—Giles, I mean. I am sure he would tell you; and I could show you some very strange dried ones, if you like,"

"I should be most grateful," said Hermione, thinking Miss Barbara looked quite pleasant when she smoothed out that knife-like frown.

As they were going away, Lady Clinton said—

"You will let me know, then, whether you could allow Miss Josline Fairfax to come or not?"

"I think I may at once decline," said Miss Barbara, stiffening where she stood, clasping her hands tightly behind her back, and balancing inelegantly backwards and forwards from her heels to her toes, and *vice versâ*.

"I would take such care she didn't catch cold," said Hermione, with her clear, grave eyes fixed on the aunt's face. "I really understand delicate people."

"Of course her uncle must decide; but I am quite against it, quite!"

The horses were just starting; there was no time for more; when suddenly Miss Barbara picked a large spray of sweet-briar, and putting it into Hermione's hand, said—

"We are famous for our sweet-briar; and you said you liked weeds!"

"Oh! thank you!" and they were off.

"Cantankerous old person!" whispered Dorothy. "That poor girl must have a very sad life of it. Now just think of the difference between her and Lady Dunstable."

"Yes," said Hermione, thoughtfully; "but there is something very sincere about her, I should think, inflexibly rigid and just; but there is something kindly, too, in her tone now and then."

"There you go again with your favourite virtue, Justice! I believe you could forgive anything to any one you thought even meant to be just."

"But then, how many need I forgive anything to?" said Hermione. "I am quite sure it is the supreme and rarest virtue."

"I don't know. I think men are generally just."

"To each other, perhaps!"

"*You* are just, Hermione, even to—no, not to yourself, I think."

"The less one thinks about oneself, the better," said Hermione, quickly. "Though, I suppose, trying to act rightly would help one to think rightly."

"Why, that is rather putting the blade before the haft, surely?"

"Oh! there they all are!" said Hermione.

Standing under the walnut trees by the smithy, were Mr. Fairfax, Josline, Mr. Crosbie, and Robert Watt. An old woman, looking like a gipsy in a scarlet cloak, was vehemently declaiming, apparently against Nan, who was standing clinging to her husband's arm.

"Keeping the loaf from your neighbours that fashion, will never fill your bodies or , minds 'wi' good!" she said.

"Why, it's Polly from the gate lodge," said Lady Clinton. "What can she be so cross about? I am sure she can't want anything."

As they came nearer the old body hobbled off, muttering furiously; and they saw that the others were all laughing.

"What *is* the matter?" said Dorothy, leaning out.

"It's only Polly in a rage, because she knew nothing of the goings on by which Charteriss is going to astonish the world," said Mr. Crosbie. "They call that, namely, not repeating news or gossip, keeping the loaf from your neighbours."

"Poor old thing! I'll go down and have a talk to her. Mr. Fairfax, I don't think you know Miss St. John. Miss Josline Fairfax."

"We have been to see Miss Barbara, Mr. Fairfax, and trying to induce her to allow your niece to come next week."

The tall old gentleman bowed, with a side smile at
Josline, who stood quiet and silent by his side, in her
long grey dress and beaver hat.

"Oh, that's all settled," said Mr. Crosbie. "Fairfax knows all about it. I told him I was going to
take her. Bless the child, I forgot she does not know.
Josline, shall you like to go?"

Josline coloured faintly, and looked in a rather
alarmed way at her uncle.

Robert had gradually slid round to her side.
He was looking at her with entreaty; her eye caught
his, and she murmured something so low that Mr.
Fairfax bent towards her, and said—

"Shall we talk it over at home, Anima mia?"
Then added aloud, "It is very kind of you, Lady
Clinton. May I write to you?"

"Oh, certainly. Do come," she said, bending
from the carriage. "We want you to see it all, it
will be very pretty."

"Say yes; do," said Robert, in a whisper which
made her colour deepen.

"It is very kind, thank you," said Josline, in a
tone that might mean anything. But under all those
eyes, and Robert's passionate presence, she could
hardly speak at all, and only leant nearer her uncle,
and felt her heart beat violently.

Then they all parted, Mr. Fairfax and Josline
going towards home, Robert Watt and Mr. Crosbie
sauntering up to the ridge, and Dorothy and Hermione driving to Charteriss.

"Well, what do you think of her?" said Lady Clinton.

"What an exquisite face! But how delicate-looking! She is far more lovely than that picture. What a sweet face!"

"I knew you would think that," said Dorothy, delighted. "Don't you think even Colonel Myddleton might be taken by that face?"

"Indeed I do. It's perfect; such an oval; and what a strange, wistful, far-away look in her eyes! and then that clearness of the skin—it's quite marvellous, it's like the petal of a wood anemone! But surely, she must be exceedingly delicate; she looks as though very little would throw her into decline."

"I don't think she's delicate, at least I never heard of her being so. But really, she lives with those two old people, and one knows nothing of her, except that I have often heard of her wonderful singing."

"Didn't her mother die of decline?"

"Well, yes; but then her husband broke her heart."

They drove on silently; at last, Hermione said, "I wish you could have her more with Gladys; she looks as though she wanted lifting out of herself."

"Ah! they would never allow it. Why, she sees no one but Mr. Crosbie."

"And young Mr. Watt," said Hermione, gravely.

"Why, Hermione! Why, how odd! it never struck me! Of course. Why, how stupid! Why, it's the very thing; how delightful!"

Hermione looked strangely and curiously at her friend. "Would you really wish it?" she said. "I thought you thought he liked Gladys?"

"Oh, that's all nonsense, my dear, they are like brother and sister."

Hermione was silent, and Lady Clinton ran on all the way home about the charming couple Robert and Josline would make.

As they got out, Miss St. John laid her hand tightly on Dorothy's arm. "Dorothy," she said, very low and gravely, "don't mention what I said about Mr. Watt, I *beg* you, don't."

"Very well, Hermione. But, how odd of you!"

Hermione went to look for Gladys with a curious sensation of sympathy in her heart, feeling more drawn to her than she had ever done, although she could hardly have reasoned why, only she kept on thinking of the wet evening when she had found Gladys standing on the ghost staircase with that miserable look in her young face; and in the quivering light on Robert's face to-day she had read, or thought she had read, why.

CHAPTER XVI.

ROBERT and Mr. Crosbie sauntered on up the ridge. Robert was tired, he carried his gun over his shoulder silently. They had had a bad day's hard shooting; he said to himself that was the reason of his depression; but in his heart he was pondering over Josline's manner, and he was weighing every turn of her head, every inflection of voice, as to whether they were in favour of her going to Charteriss or not. How could he care so much whether she were to be there or not? It was all folly; even if she were, she would not be allowed to dance afterwards, he felt sure, and during the tableaux he should see very little of her. Still to know she was there! His every pulse throbbed; to look across the room and see her dear head shining out of the darkness in the pale radiance of her white brow.

"There! I knew you'd do it, if I left you alone," said Mr. Crosbie, with a shout of laughter, giving him a severe pull just as he was walking headlong into the ditch. "What game are you after?"

"Quite as much as I found to-day, I should think," answered Robert, with such savage energy that Mr. Crosbie quite started. Then, recollecting himself, the young fellow pulled himself together, and said, "I beg your pardon. I am so tired, I believe I was half asleep."

"Aye, and dreaming, too," said Mr. Crosbie, dryly.

"It isn't much good dreaming, anyhow," said Robert, "one ought to work."

"Well, I hope you are all hard at it up at Charteriss, for I can tell you that the whole country-side expects you to do your duty."

"Oh, it's sure to be a dead failure, those things always are," said Robert, digging his heavy boot into the mud, and sparing a little starry flower that started by a stone, and somehow made him think of Josline.

"Well, come, now, I hope not, for I do want Josline to see something nice for once; how she will enjoy it! She'll believe it's all real," and the kind old godfather rubbed his hands.

"Oh, she won't come," said Robert, gloomily.

"Won't she, though?"

"No."

Now in his heart Robert thought she would, and was already meditating on the extra fit of his leather jerkin, and trembling lest his boots should be too baggy. And yet, in his mind and brain, he felt convinced she could not, and would not, because she did not wish to meet him. Did not wish? Yes, did wish, but was

afraid. Why did he think all this? How he had
suddenly plunged into these subtle distinctions as to
Josline's thoughts, feelings, impulses—he didn't know.
He spoke because he wanted to be talked out of them;
but Mr. Crosbie was so surprised at his negation, that
he was silent, wondering whether Robert really knew
whether she would or not. At last, he said—

"Did Miss Barbara refuse, then?"

"I don't know, how should I?" said Robert, perplexed in turn.

"Then, why did you say she wouldn't go?"

"Why, she never goes anywhere."

"Pish! is that all? Why, she has never had a
chance, poor child. She'll be as merry as the rest of
them, if you give her her head."

"Do you think so?" said Robert, feeling as if tons
had been lifted from his heart, and noticing for the
first time what a lovely soft evening it was—how
the mists were rolling away off the spurs of the ridge,
and the moon coming up like a silver cup over the
woods.

"Of course I do. Why, she leads such an un-
healthy dead-alive existence, it's a perfect marvel how
she can be what she is. The sweetest bud on God's
earth would grow hollow and pale, and droop and
pine, growing near such a marsh as Miss Barbara's
mind."

Robert brought his gun up cheerily, and lifted his
feet less draggingly; and in a sudden burst of con-

fidence he blurted out, " I say, you know, I was told—
I mean Lady Dunstable implied to me, that Miss
Josline was a Roman Catholic——" He got no further,
for—

" Roman Catholic ! " shouted Mr. Crosbie, making
the welkin ring. " I'll tell you what, I should like to
shake you, Bob, Watt. My Josline a Roman Catholic !
I should just like to know what on earth put that in
her ladyship's head ! Roman Catholic, indeed !
Why, she is my godchild ; I baptized her."

" Oh ! I know that now, I know she isn't now,"
answered Robert, hastily bringing his gun down on the
stock with a vehement bang.

" And pray how ? " asked Mr. Crosbie, suspiciously.
" You don't mean to say you asked her ? though
really I believe you young fellows would do anything."

" I don't see why I should not have asked her,"
retorted Robert, hotly ; " but I didn't, because—— "
He paused.

" Well ? " said Mr. Crosbie, sharply.

" Because Lady Dunstable said there'd been a
row, or something about it, in the family."

" Ha ! well, I should just think there was, and
never been healed over either ; but we aren't going to
let those old worries stand in the way of our Josline."

Robert was silent, and they went on again. Suddenly Mr. Crosbie stopped short, wheeled sharp round
in front of him, and said abruptly—

" What should it matter to you whether she is a Roman Catholic or not—eh ? "

The young man coloured scarlet, and said slowly, " What would it matter to me ? "

" Ah ! "

There was a short silence. A waft of damp odours from the woods below, of crushed moss from beneath their feet, filled the air they were breathing ; a keen small wind came whistling up, swaying over the tall grasses and rank herbage and dock-leaves.

" Nothing," said Robert, slowly and bitterly. " Nothing. I don't know why I wanted to know."

Mr. Crosbie looked sharply at him in the waning light, and then gave a short, quick laugh, turning and going on in silence. They were on the downward slope now. Robert had to turn towards the Red House.

" Good night," he said, taking his gun in his left hand and extending his right.

" Good night," said Mr. Crosbie. Then, hitting him a hard blow on his shoulder he said, " Look here ! Work ! "

They separated. Long into the night Robert sat up with his temples hard held by his two hands, apparently reading a ponderous tome on Italy and art. But ever and ever the sense and words spun away from him ; his thoughts circled round an impalpable form, gracious and grave, that was filling every crevice of his brain and heart—his ideal, his darling, his first

love, his only love.   Staring hard at the page, he
thought he was reading ; at last he dashed the book
together and rose.

"It's no good," he said, "I can't do anything,
I can't think of anything.   How am I to work ?   My
father won't let me go ; he has spoilt my whole life
for me.   I know I am an ass, a half-educated clod-
hopping do-nothing.   What can she think of me in
contrast to her uncle, even though he is an old man,
dear old fellow ?   And then that Gabriel, how stun-
ningly he paints, and how well he can talk !   Even an
artist fellow like that knows a thousand and one
things I never even heard of.   Oh, my darling ! you
say, ' Go, travel ! ' and Crosbie says, ' Work ! ' and
what *can* I do ?   It's a perfect curse, this useless life of
mine.   Why, look at Myddleton, he's been through
ever so much ; and that old Sir Vere, even.   There
are no end of fellows.   Confound it all !   If I had a
chance I'd be at it, too.   I will, I must.   I'll get hold
of Philip and make him talk to my father.   I'll—— "
He stopped, drew a gigantic sigh, and said, "Well,
yes ! I'll go away.   It's no good staying here.   I don't
believe she cares twopence about me.   She'll come up
to the tableaux and see Myddleton, and then she'll
fall in love with him."

He strode across to the cabinet by the fireplace,
tore open the door, and drew out the Eurydice portrait.   Slowly the tossed passion of his face calmed,
his lips closed, his eyes softened, a smile came on his

mouth, and he said very softly, not knowing he was speaking aloud, " My darling, I know you are too good for me ; but if you only would—— " He stood looking and looking till his eyes seemed to have brought life into those wistful, wonderful, pictured eyes. He put his hand quickly over them. " Sometimes," he thought, " I think—I think you will die, and never care for any one."

A distant door banged, and with a sigh he laid the picture back by his mother's miniature, and opening his window leant out to smoke and think far on into the cold autumn night ; and concoct many and divers plans for making his fortune and becoming famous.

CHAPTER XVII.

JOSLINE was very tired. She leaned more and more
against her uncle as they walked slowly towards home,
and her eyes followed with wistful longing, the easy
swinging flight of the starlings and fieldfares that
swept in twittering array from one field, over the
dewy hedges, into the next, at their approach. The
sheep were being folded for the night, and the shep-
herd and his dog went striding away over the ridge,
tall and weird-looking, like a phantom and a fiend
hound. The sharp bark died out; the birds were settling down with quiet little sounds and beat of wings;
the dew fell coldly on the tasselled birches and gemmed
the ruddy spikes of the spindle bushes. Each blade
of grass pierced a diamond or impaled a pearl, according as the moonlight struck the drops or slanted
over them. There was the far-away sound of a
branch cracking here and there in the woods, as the
children went hurrying along the "church path" to
the village, and now and then a merry call or whistle.

Once a woodcock rose from a thicket and darted past.

Mr. Fairfax went on without speaking, his head slightly bent towards the left as though for ever harkening to the divine melody of his beloved violin, his slender hands clasped behind him. Josline had linked hers through one of his arms. Her hat, as usual, had swung back. She looked very tired, and when a sudden sound roused her uncle, he said—

"Josline, how your feet beat! a rapid and most unconnected measure! You are tired."

"A little," she said. "We shall soon be home now, though. I love these quiet, dewy evenings."

He looked round at her. "Ah!" he said, "I hear the fatigue in your feet and in your voice, too." He unlinked his hands and hers, passed one arm round her waist, and almost lifted her along. "Do you know, my dear, when I was a boy I used sometimes to help your mother so. Ay, and in after years, too, I remember," he ended in a murmur.

"Did you, Dux? Did you know her always?"

"Well, it seems to me always; I suppose it wasn't. I was nineteen, I think, and she was fourteen when I first knew her. Do you remember her at all?"

"Oh, yes!" said Josline quickly and low. "I always think of her. You know, one could not forget her."

"No, no; I know. She was very beautiful, and she had a will and a strength and a pride. My dear, she had a pride!"

Josline hung her head. Some pride she had too. Large tears began slowly falling down her face.

" Look here, my dear! I want to say something to you, my child, my little Josline—girl. Look here!" He broke off; his arm tightened round her slender, swaying waist. His head rose; his eyes fixed themselves on the radiant evening star, rising like a passion-flower, purely, serenely against the sky. "I want to say, Anima mia,"—he brought round his other hand and clasped it over hers, folded in front of her—"I wanted to say—you know you are like my own most beloved child, are you not, Anima? you love me?" His voice sank. They were going down into the valley, the great ridge shadow was taking them; our voices always fall in the twilight.

She raised her face. He saw the eyes swimming in tears.

"I know you love me!" he said. "When you sing, I know it, my child, and most when I play for you. I want to say, you are my child, and—and—everything a father has belongs to his child; so—so, my Josline. Hush! don't tremble so! don't sob so!" He had both arms closely round her. "So—so you will be rich, darling; rich—you may do what you like, my little child, my heart's darling. And—and means shall not fail." He stopped, choked; she was lying on his breast, sobbing bitterly. He tried to bend back her head to kiss her eyes and hair; she would not.

She clung with a passionate force and frenzy

almost, that made him fear to hurt her; her slight frame quivered like a chord strung too tightly and heavily strained. And then he became aware that she was trying to speak, to say something; but the words would not come. He bent his head over her, folding her closer and closer.

"You need not speak," he said. "I know you will be like my child to me, and let me be happy in my own way. I understand all, Anima mia."

She bent back suddenly and looked up at him. He never forgot the look on her face; it was her whole generous, noble, pure, upright soul revolting and tearing her heart up by the roots, by every clinging tendril and fibre that had pierced and knotted round her life. "Oh! let me speak," she gasped; Oh! let me speak." Her voice choked, a spasm flew over her face; she suddenly fell heavily forwards and fainted away.

When she recovered consciousness, she was lying on the damp, short stubble of a barley field, and Mr. Fairfax hung over her in an agony of silent dread. The first coming back of life in the lifeless face of one we love is a very awful thing; the flutter of life coming, going, waning, growing, then settling on a face, is full of mystery and silence.

"Hush! don't speak; you are too tired. I ought never to have taken you all round this long way. Lie still a moment. See, here's my coat," tearing it off. "I'll put it round you. Don't speak, it is so damp."

He smoothed her hair and held her face for a second, like a woman might have done.

Josline did not move; she had never fainted in her life, and didn't quite understand what had happened. She only saw her uncle's anxious, pale face; she knew that to be like this, hatless and coatless, was most dangerous for him in this autumn damp, and that something terrible had come to her which—oh, yes, she knew it all now. What had she said before fainting? it was imperative she should know; she sat up.

"What did I say?" she said slowly and solemnly.

"Nothing—nothing whatever, my dear, you only said 'Let me speak.'"

"And I can't, I can't speak," she said more slowly than before; then rising by clinging to his arm, and with a wrung intensity of expression that cut him to the heart, she said, "I remember quite well what you said, Dux, I shall never forget it; but—but——" She paused; then slinging her slender arms tightly round his neck she said, "Yes, you may know I love you, dearly, dearly. I will always tell you so, you may believe *that*; but—in everything else you may disbelieve me utterly, and I will hold you scathless. Oh! Dux, Dux, it breaks my heart, it breaks my heart." She was sobbing this against his mouth, as though she would not let him answer; and he was so entirely startled and shaken that he absolutely said nothing. "I shall never, never want any money; I am unlike any one, but if you will let me I will never leave you till you die."

He still said nothing; he was quite bewildered.

"Come home; you will catch cold," she said, slipping on his coat again. "I will always sing to you, always love you. I will never, never, never be proud to you, Dux, if you will only not believe in me."

They went out of the barley field. The moon was quite up, shining coldly down on the perplexed, grieved, startled face of Mr. Fairfax and on the exquisite marble face of Josline, printing on hers a look it never lost from that night, of a clasped secret. Down the hill, past the great pond with the willows and the broods of young ducks; up the sandy lane, in at the forest path, where the children had gone; along by the deep rut; over the stile on the small bridge, where the stream was murmuring to the alders, hazels, and elders; up the stony road, past the farm, under great elms, and home.

In the shadow of the deep old porch Josline leant once more on his breast, and whispered, "I shall not forget; but we will never talk of it again, dear Dux; you will not need." And then they went in.

In the cedar parlour Miss Barbara was waiting grim and hard.

"Cold as ice, I suppose, both of you; just like the tea! What have you found?"

"A herb or two; nothing much," said Mr. Fairfax, watching Josline going through the room to take off her things, and thinking how terribly, yes, terribly like her mother she had looked whilst insensible.

"Nothing much! so I thought. You look as though you had gathered nothing but wool," with cutting emphasis, "and lost—why, lost your wits."

"I am very tired," said he, sitting down ; then suddenly getting up again. "I think, Barbara, I'll go and play ; I quite forgot to practise that prelude to-day."

"Now, something has happened," said Miss Barbara, levelling a fork, two-pronged and green-hafted, at him, as though he were a potato which she intended conveying to her plate. "What is it? Oh! you needn't say 'nothing much.' Josline looks like my petticoat when Phœbe washes it and irons it the wrong side, and you look like—— "

"We are both very tired. Now, Barbara, do not tease the child, she actually fainted."

Miss Barbara's eyes nearly started out of her head. Then she said, "Nonsense! I suppose you told her she couldn't go to this ridiculous party at Charteriss, and she was pettish ; really what girls are coming to!"

Mr. Fairfax shook his head. "On the contrary, I told her she might go."

"Then I won't have it, Dux; there! she'll faint at me next," said Miss Barbara, quaking with anxiety to get at the rights of the story, and determined not to show her feeling.

"Very well ; of course you will say what you like, Barbara. I don't think she will mind, my dear."

There being no one to contradict, Miss Barbara sat, lost and silent, with a frenzied feeling of being ill-used, and held of no account. Presently Josline came back again, her hair smooth, her hands as white as though there had been no faintings in stubbled fields, but if you had looked closely, you would have seen a slight scratch here and there, and a scarlet prick on the palms. She was deathly pale, and her aunt, watching her keenly, observed that she ate nothing. Miss Barbara had a truly appalling facility for bringing forward dangerous topics, and she at times could not resist saying things that she knew would hurt and stab to the quick, or at least that she thought would do so.

"I hear that young Robert Watt is likely to get into trouble again soon." She didn't know that he had ever been in any, but young men were always going into it, if they were not in it when spoken of.

"Indeed ? how ?" said Mr. Fairfax, nervously.

"It isn't ' how,' Giles, it's ' why.' Why, he has been obliged to sell his hunter, and just at the beginning of the hunting season ; it's very odd to say the least, I dare say some disgraceful debt. They are as poor as church-mice, and old General Watt has always spoilt him so."

There are occasions when people undergo extreme torture heroically. This was one. Miss Barbara

and Mr. Fairfax were both looking at Josline, who
sat quite quietly, trying to spread an infinitesimal
piece of butter on a large square of toast; the slender
trembling fingers nerved like steel, the small teeth set
hard as death behind those closed lips.   The only sign
was a curious quick throbbing on the temples; but who
should see that ?

"Well! no one says anything," went on the
implacable Miss Barbara.   "I dare say you know all
about it, Dux ? "

"I never heard anything about it at all, Barbara.
Well, I must go and play now."   He got up, hoping to
break through the kind of weird spell of his sister's ill
temper, but that was not possible without a storm.
He passed Josline's chair.   Still those small fingers
were spreading the butter neatly up to the edge and
not a hair's breadth beyond; he laid a gentle touch
on her head—in some people a touch is always a
caress.   "Will you come after tea and sing to me,
Anima ? " he said, softly.

"Yes," she answered, not looking up.

Then Miss Barbara burst out—"Oh ! go ! go now,
pray ! you are never content if you are not stringing
and thrumming on that absurd wind-box.   You think
of nobody, care for nobody, but just you two together,
and then I have all the trouble ; and they come to
you and lay a plot, and I know that young Watt is at
the bottom of it, to get Josline away, and set her up,
and make her too fine to do anything.   They came

here to-day. She was quite content till her picture was painted. It's not what her mother would have wished, that she should be gadding about lanes and places, and talking to blacksmiths and rough-riding idle fellows, and sitting to strange artists, and going to see acting. But I hold myself irresponsible, only you shan't go to Charteriss; I wash my hands of you, but you shan't go there. Lady Clinton, with her fine airs, trying to get round me! No, you shan't go; go now, cry or faint, or anything you like. You'll just turn round some day, I know." At last, panting, furious, out of breath, Miss Barbara who had risen, a cup in one hand, an egg spoon in the other, sat down suddenly, and crushed the "person of the house" nearly flat, who flew across the room, with a discordant miau of terror and anger.

Josline had not moved; her head bent lower and lower, like a flower in a terrible storm, but Mr. Fairfax suddenly brought down both hands closely, lightly, and firmly on her shoulders, and spoke—

"Barbara! you don't know what you are saying. Some folly has got into your head; you are tired, and so are we. I don't know what Lady Clinton may have said to you; we met her, and she most kindly asked Josline to go up to Charteriss. I think we keep the child too much shut up here. For our sakes and her own I think it would be better if she went about more, and saw more people. I am her uncle, and give her permission to do just as she likes in the matter. Speak, my child, if you like to go, I can take you."

Miss Barbara choked. " You, Dux, go out again after all these years ! "

" I will take you if you like, Josline, my child. Speak, shall I ? "

Josline stood up, she rocked slightly; but he was still holding her shoulders, that steadied her. Her mouth quivered painfully. " I will do just as you both like," she said, with difficulty. I am very tired ; good night, dear Dux," she stooped her head and kissed his hand ; she crossed the room and kissed the petrified Miss Barbara, and then went out, and slowly upstairs to her room.

And then Mr. Fairfax spoke, and spoke as his sister had never heard him speak before to her. He wound up by saying, " Very well, Barbara, go on as you are doing, but you will kill her, and then who— who will there be left for us to love in the whole world ? "

Miss Barbara made no answer. She sat with egg spoon in hand, wondering whether Dux and Josline had wandered into some fairy ring that afternoon, and came home to glamour her. The facts remained, that Josline had fainted and that Dux had offered to go out at night !

" No, no, no ! " said she, tearing off the precious lace mittens. " It must not be, that little chit winds us all round her finger ! It will be the mother over again."

It was very late. The moon was behind flying clouds, the rain was beginning to drift, the wind was wailing with a whistle, that sounded like water through a rift in rocks, when Miss Barbara suddenly opened Josline's door, and stood, in her huge nightcap, staring in. Josline was kneeling by her bed, her arms were flung wide across it, her nightgown clung round her naked feet, her hair nearly swept the floor; a point of colour caught the candle with a flash, it was the ruby ring; between her lips and the pillow lay the crucifix. She did not move when her aunt came in, and Miss Barbara said in an awe-struck voice—

"Josline!"

She got up at once, and stood there, white, spirit-like, unearthly. For a second there was silence. The rain was pouring now, the ivy went restlessly tossing and bending against the window.

"Josline!" said Miss Barbara, again. "Why are you not in bed?"

"I was saying my prayers."

"It's very late; I am sure you are tired. I came to say——" Here a fierce gust shook the casement with a grim rattle, and Miss Barbara said with a shiver, as her large nightcap frills danced and nodded, "I came to say, I didn't mean to be unkind to-night; you may go to Charteriss if you like."

"I should like to do just as you like," said Josline, in a faint, dreamy voice.

"Don't you care?" said Miss Barbara, uneasily. "It's only that I don't want you to get into the way of expecting gaiety and goings on, when we can return nothing. We were always too proud to do that."

"I see. I do not want to go; it will be better not, I dare say."

"Really, don't you mind?" said the aunt, with a leap of joy, to think she should keep her still all to herself; and a look of almost feline pleasure came in the cold grey eyes. "You know I have always wished to make you happy, Josline. You can go, if you like," said she, magnanimously, now the danger was passing.

"I do not mind; I will stay at home," said Josline, still dreamily.

Miss Barbara thought her manner odd, and came up to kiss her. Suddenly she saw on what Josline's eyes were resting—the crucifix. A passion of anger flew over her face.

"Josline!" she said, and put out her hand to seize it.

"My mother's," said Josline, lifting and holding it against her warm, violently beating heart.

They stood facing each other, girl and woman. Here was a love Miss Barbara could not counteract or quench. The candle-light streamed full on Josline—on her exquisite form, her marble face; her great, burning, sad eyes; her set lips, her braced head; as, staglike, she held it back, gazing with intense, awful earnestness, at her aunt.

~ The wind rose in a shriek, and then wailed away, like a dying soul.

CHAPTER XVIII.

THREE days before the tableaux were to come off the beautiful autumn weather broke up. It began to rain the night that Mr. Fairfax and Josline were so late home, and it never ceased from that hour, except at very short intervals.

"What are we to do with everybody?" said Sir Philip, disconsolately. "The waters will be out soon, and then they won't be able to ride; and as to shooting, the covers are fetlock deep in mud."

Sir Vere, who was shivering over the library fire under an incipient attack of gout, growled out, "Turn them all into the conservatory and let them study botany."

"Not half a bad idea," answered Colonel Myddleton. "I say, Clinton, do you know you have a most deadly poison growing there?"

"Let them find it out and they will plague us no more," muttered Sir Vere, as a twinge seized him.

"I've got something to propose," began Mr. Freeman. "Suppose we light the conservatory and go in there after the tableaux; it will make a break whilst they are getting the things straight again. None of those vulgar coloured lamps, but a small chain of white light running round the cornice the whole way. It's always warm and it would be something quite out of the way of most of the people who are coming."

"And have oranges bobbing up and down under glasses in the fountains, like they did in the first exhibition," said Sir Vere, sardonically.

"Yes; I always thought that the prettiest thing there—how they got in and why they should jump up and down," said Sir Philip, innocently.

"Will you speak to Lady Clinton, sir?" from a footman, closed the roar of laughter with which their host's speech had been received.

"What an absurd girl that Miss Thorold is?" said Quarl, as Sir Philip went out. "She is the most jealous little wretch I ever knew; because I said Miss St. John was to have a tableau nearly to herself, she must, too. Well, she is very pretty, I suppose. I know Myddleton admires her excessively."

Colonel Myddleton raised his head quickly, and then let it fall again with a quiet smile. "Quite my style," he said.

"Yes, money and all," pursued Quarl. "I can see Lady Dunstable has given up Bob Watt and is coming round to somebody else."

Sir Vere's eyes glared angrily. "You always go

P

on so, Freeman," he said. "I don't see that it's particularly good taste to discuss people like that." He took up a newspaper, with a shaking hand, and turned it over sharply.

Colonel Myddleton was still smiling; his eye caught Quarl's, who raised his eyebrows and walked silently to the window, evidently rebuffed.

"The rain is coming down. I shall go out and look at the 'head.' You've never seen it up there, have you, Myddleton? It will be a sight soon."

"I went up there one day with Lady Clinton. She said she had seen it once when the water was within an inch of the top bar of the bridge."

"Ah, yes! I remember Clinton writing about it. Well, they'll have it this time and no mistake."

Gladys was trying to calm her excited nerves by playing the organ. The whole house was in supreme confusion—maids and men running every way at once. Sir Philip was superintending the arrangement of the daïs, and caught Mr. Freeman just as he was crossing the hall. Colonel Myddleton stood in the doorway of the drawing-room and looked in on Gladys. Lady Clinton and Miss Thorold were undoing the jewels which had just come down from London. Hermione and Lady Dunstable were talking by the fire.

"What do you think of Robert Watt?" said the old lady.

"I think he seems a nice, bright, young fellow,"

said Hermione, looking round a little nervously, Lady Dunstable fancied, at Mina; but Hermione was thinking of some one far different. However, the organ tones reassured her.

"I do wish, though, he could get something to do. I think it is so very bad for him loitering about, wasting his life, doing nothing, poor boy."

"He seems quite content and happy."

"Then he shouldn't be," said the old lady, a little sharply. "Life isn't meant to dawdle through like that. He should go away; but that foolish, old father will never allow it, I suppose."

"I certainly think he would do better to settle to something; but I don't quite see what he could do if his father won't allow it."

"Why, he could marry," said Lady Dunstable.

"I suppose he could," said Hermione, thoughtfully. "Only he has no money."

"Money is not everything, my dear," said the old lady, laying one mittened hand gently on Hermione's, "and I know you don't think so."

"But most men do," said Hermione. "They won't marry without it, and they are afraid of women who have it."

"It depends entirely on one thing," said Lady Dunstable, smiling. "And that one thing is the rarest thing on earth now—rarer even than money with younger sons."

"What?" said Hermione, lifting her clear eyes.

"Love, my dear. Ah, yes! You blush; but why? If a man really loved a woman he couldn't help telling her he loved her, were she never so rich, and he never so poor. Ah! I have no patience with people nowadays."

"I don't think I quite agree, though," broke in Hermione. "I can imagine a case in which a man would never speak."

"Then you are wrong, my dear. It means, simply, he does not care enough. Somehow we have wandered from our point, though. I was talking of Robert Watt. It seems he has been up here, talking to Sir Philip about getting something to do. Shall I tell you what that means with him? He is in love."

Hermione again glanced uneasily round.

"Never mind; no one hears. And also that he thinks she will have money. Now, I should like to help him. His mother was very dear to me. Could *you* help him?"

Hermione drew her brows together. Somehow she did not want to help him. "I do not know," she said slowly, but she knew quite well she could; she had had a letter from her agent that very morning, saying he must give up in a year from ill health, and begging her to send him some young man to put in the way of going on with the management of the property. There was one thing in favour of giving this to Robert; it would take him away; but perhaps he would speak all the more quickly; and yet, after all, why did she

wish to prevent his doing so? Supposing that Josline Fairfax cared for him, what then? Could she be
the one to have it in her power to help two people to
be happy and yet hold her hand? Yes, but there was
one other who was very dear to her, whose misery it
would make; and yet, would anything prevent that?

The organ swelled higher and higher. Gladys was
really playing beautifully to-day. Hermione moved
uneasily, trying to beat out her thought through the
rolling chords.

"I will think it over," she said at last. "If Sir
Philip can find nothing, I might perhaps think of
something."

Mina here appealed to her great-aunt, and Lady
Dunstable moved away thinking. "How cold and
calm she is! Even a love story does not touch her.
She never asked who."

Hermione was excessively startled to hear Colonel
Myddleton's voice say suddenly, close to her, "How
perplexed you look! Can I do anything for you?"

"Oh, no!" she said, hurriedly, feeling infinitely
vexed on finding her colour rising in a tide. "I
mean, thank you very much for offering, but it is
impossible."

"I beg your pardon," he said, a little haughtily.
"I thought it might be something you wanted about
the tableaux," and he moved away.

"Indeed, it was nothing any one could help, it's
only something to decide," she said, earnestly and in

an agony, lest she should have hurt him by appearing
to refuse his aid; and yet feeling as though of all
people she could not tell him.

He turned back again and there was a short
silence.

"I do wish these tableaux were over," he said.

"Well, they will be soon; by to-morrow night you
will be free. Why do you wish they were over,
though?"

"Shan't you?"

"No, I think not at least; I like the excitement,
you know," looking up and smiling; "and we shall
all look so odd in our dresses. I do wish, though,
I knew what my dress was for."

"Do you mean to say you don't know yet?"

"No; do you?"

"Well, that's really wonderful. I thought all
women were so curious."

"Well, I should like to know."

"Shall I tell you?"

"Do you know? Yes—no; I mean it wouldn't
be quite fair to Mr. Freeman."

"I thought you would say that. Well, I don't
know either; I did it to see what you would say."

Hermione turned a little pale. "I don't think you
had any right to do that," she said.

"I knew I was right, I knew I was safe," he said,
very low. "Do not be angry, I did not mean to
vex you."

"I am not vexed, only a little surprised," she answered, coldly; but her heart beat violently. Why did he want to know how she would answer?

"Well, Miss St. John, are you consulting Colonel Myddleton? I know he will say a kind word for Robert," said Lady Dunstable, suddenly returning.

"I have not thought any more about it at present," answered Hermione, with so much hauteur, that the old lady immediately said to herself—

"She is angry with *him* about something. I shall go away."

Hermione did not choose to move, though she longed to go away, too.

"What is it about Robert Watt?" said Colonel Myddleton, wishing to change the conversation, and little knowing that he had hit on the most difficult subject he could have chosen; some wilful spirit had changed Hermoine's mood though, now.

"Lady Dunstable wants me to find something for him to do. She thinks he is in love, and wants to become rich," and she looked him full in the face, and laughed lightly.

"It would not be difficult for you to help him," said Colonel Myddleton, in a sombre tone.

"Perhaps not, if I chose," she answered, stung by something in the ring of his voice. She lifted her foot and tapped Jerks's nose, who sat up directly.

"Why should you not choose? Of course, though, because you have the power."

Hermione looked up at him swiftly. "No," she said, slowly and gravely, "you misjudge me; that is not the reason."

"Why then?" He came a little nearer, looking at her straight, his head a little thrown back.

"Because I wish to be just," she said, quietly, "though I know very well that most men do not believe in the justice of women."

He looked thrown completely out in his calculations. "Perhaps I do not judge you as I should judge most women," he said, gravely. "I have always thought you very just. But what has justice to do with this? Has anything been said to young Watt? and do you find yourself bound in any way?"

"No, not at all. I know nothing of his capabilities as an agent, that is all; and that would be the only thing I could offer him. Of course I wish to act justly to my own people, and one is bound not to allow an estate to deteriorate."

He was silent. "I dare say you think I shall make a great many mistakes about everything," she said, nervously, "but I want not to do so. I was just thinking that Robert Watt seems to me very young for such a responsibility."

She was evidently asking his opinion in a regular womanly way.

"It is a great responsibility," he said, not looking at her. "I wonder at any man liking to undertake it."

"Well, it has not been offered yet," she said, quickly; "but there is a very pretty house belonging to it, and the General would be very comfortable, and they could have the shooting."

"And everything else they wanted," he said, suddenly, with a look so penetrating and hard, that Hermione drew back two steps.

"I don't know about everything else," she said, rather puzzled. "I dare say he could." Then suddenly recollecting herself she coloured crimson to the roots of her hair, for of course Colonel Myddleton knew nothing of Josline Fairfax, and it seemed a kind of vague betrayal.

He said nothing, but kept that penetrating gaze fixed on her face as though he would read her very soul. "Some men get everything," he said, in an intense voice that shook her, she knew not why, with a great longing to say, "I will do just as you like." But she made no answer. "Some men get everything because they never try, and others——" He broke off, took up Jerks, and holding the dog as though he were teaching it to beg, an operation Jerks resisted, knowing quite well how to do so, he said suddenly, "Do not give that to young Watt!" His voice shook painfully.

"Why?" said Hermione.

"Why?" He looked up. "I ask you as a great favour."

She was silent, trying to make up her mind. She

longed to say, "Very well, I won't." But something
independent and proud in her nature rose and said,
"No, I can't give in, I will do just what I like."
Before she had made up her mind, he dropped Jerks,
rose to his full height, and said in his natural
voice—

"Of course you will do just as you think best,
though I believe he is a most thoroughly upright
straight-forward young fellow, and will make a most
capital man of business." He turned round and
walked up to the group at the table who were looking
over the jewels. He heard her say rapidly and
low, "I shall decide nothing at present." But he
pretended not to hear, and Hermione went upstairs.

"I have thought of such a lovely plan!" said
Lady Clinton to Sir Philip that evening after dinner.
"What do you think?"

"Something about the tableaux, of course. I
begin to feel quite ill with anxiety," he said, laughing.

"I want you to ask down Robert's friend, the
artist, and get him to take sketches of all the tableaux,
and of all the principal characters afterwards."

"But, my dear! there is not time now. What a
pity! it would have been pretty, certainly."

"Oh, yes, there is time, I am sure. I've set my
heart on it. Don't you think there is time, Mr. Freeman?"

"But it's such short notice, and perhaps he won't
come."

" Yes, he will come, I know. Don't you think so,. Mr. Freeman ? "

" Most people will come anywhere for money," answered Quarl. " And I suppose Gabriel Vannier is like the rest of the world; and besides, if Lady Clinton has set her heart on it, it must be managed somehow. Is the post gone ? "

" Two good hours."

" But we could catch the post at N—— if we sent a groom off quick," said Lady Clinton. " *Do* go, Philip, and see about it; I'll write the letter."

" My dear, I couldn't really do anything in that hurry, you know," said Sir Philip, immovably, crossing his legs and generally settling himself.

" Phil ! " said Dorothy, imploringly.

" I know ! " said Gladys, with a little jump. " Write a note to Robert to-night, and ask him to go up to town to-morrow, and bring Mr. Vannier back with him ! "

" Why, to-morrow is the best meet of the season ! " said Sir Philip; " it's downright cruel to expect a man to go off to London instead."

" It's the only thing to be done, if we are really to get him, though," said Quarl, going over to the piano and opening it. " And to show you what young Watt will give up, I'll sing you 'John Peel.'" He sang it splendidly.

Hermione was listening with her heart hot and heavy, and great tears in her eyes; she never heard

that song without thinking of poor Mark, when
Colonel Myddleton came up and said, addressing her
for the first time that evening—

"Now, should you call this a great or small occa-
sion for unselfish acting? Do you think he will go?"

"I was not thinking about it," she said, in a low,
soft voice, created by her thought of her dead cousin;
but which tortured Colonel Myddleton from giving
him quite another idea.

"You said once that you thought men were very
unselfish in great things; do you call this a great
thing?" he persisted.

"I don't know, I suppose men, hunting men,
would."

"Well, do you think he will go?"

She had been leaning back, now she sat up
straight and looked at him fully and openly. "Yes,
I think he will."

He started. "Why?" he said slowly through his
teeth; "how can you tell? why should you think so
well of him?"

"I don't know that it would be thinking well of
him, exactly," she said, still looking at him; "but
I think he is a kind-hearted, unselfish fellow, and
I think he will go."

"You have thought a good deal about him," he
said, bitterly. "You know how he will act."

"I know how I should expect any one to act
towards a friend," she said, a little excitedly. "Mr.

Watt has always spoken of this artist as his friend, and I think he will act accordingly."

"You have faith in friendship, then?" he said.

"Yes, thorough; haven't you?" It was an unlucky question, she knew it by a kind of instinct the moment she had spoken.

"None," he answered, briefly.

There was a pause. Mina Thorold was singing "The Brook." Hermione felt greatly shaken, restless, and excited.

"I do wish you would sit down," she said, suddenly, with a nervous laugh. "You are so tall, I always expect you to knock that chandelier."

He sat down, lifting the dagger paper-knife and balancing it on his fingers. She felt she must speak, the silence got on her nerves.

"I—I—what you said to-day about Mr. Watt; do you think him too young?"

"Oh, it doesn't matter, you will judge, of course, for yourself, or rather, you have many cleverer advisers than I am."

"But it does matter, very much," she said, beginning to lose self-control under his hard, merciless manner. "I wish for your advice; surely one may be guided by one's friends?" She stopped.

"Certainly, do I not say so?" he said. "You have many friends, I know; they will advise you."

She became very pale. "You wish to imply that you are not amongst them; you will not be a friend to me, and yet——" She stopped; her voice would tremble, and she was afraid he would notice it.

"What can it signify whether I am your friend or not?" he said, slowly, and with a stern emphasis in his voice, that, however, ended with a kind of pathetic thrill. "You have known me some years, I have always spoken the truth, and now, you see, there are many others only too thankful to give advice to you, which also you are ready and willing—*willing* to accept."

Hermione felt as though she were choking; she half leaned forwards, grasping the arms of the chair as though about to rise. "Do you mean to say that you think I have changed, and that that is why you don't believe in—in friendship?" she said, brokenly, for her white lips were so hot and dry she could hardly form the words. "You have misjudged me once before, Colonel Myddleton; I *never* change."

"Nor I—would to God I could!" he said, with such force and passion, such hard-held intensity, that Hermione shivered. "I will speak now once for all, and tell you my whole story, and you shall see."

"Hush!" she said, suddenly regaining self-control in the imminence of peril, for the singing had ceased. She saw he had snapped the gold dagger like a reed, and she knew not what might be said.

"Hermione, come and sign the round-robin to Robert, to get him to go up for Mr. Vannier to-morrow," called Lady Clinton's laughing voice from the other end of the room.

"Yes, and come, too, Myddleton," called Sir Philip. They went. "I don't think I can sign," said Colonel Myddleton, holding out his right hand, shaking like a leaf. "That horrible ague has come on again with all this damp. What am I to do to-morrow for the tableaux? I shall never be able to keep quiet."

"What an awful bore!" said Sir Philip.

"Oh, don't alarm yourself," said Mr. Freeman, coolly. "I shall give him chloroform for the chief scene."

"Very well, I'll take it," said he, grimly.

Hermione signed last, very steadily. Her firm, close handwriting contrasted oddly with Lady Dunstable's flowing letters and Mina Thorold's "cramped impossibilities," as Mr. Freeman called them.

"What an odd hand!" said the little, fair Mina. "It's so clear, like a little child."

Hermione laughed, and Mr. Freeman said—

"It looks like a hand that had carried a gun a good deal."

"I always walk with a stick, if that will help you," she said.

CHAPTER XIX.

Pouring wet met and nearly blinded Robert on his drive to the station the next morning early, to catch the first up-train. He stood up in the dog-cart to look at the mere as he passed the gates at Charteriss.

"It'll be over the banks soon," he said. "My goodness! what a thing that would be! I wish I had run up yesterday to look at the 'head;' it must be coming down there gloriously."

Then he settled back into his seat and covered himself up again. Through the ford the horse was nearly swimming; the station had water running through it; the whole country looked half-drowned. "A nice look-out for folks coming from far!" he thought. "It's lucky the tableaux are to-night, and not any further on in the week. I wish I knew whether the Fairfaxes are coming or not."

The train was just starting, when a groom ran hurriedly along the carriages. He recognized the Clinton livery, and looked out.

"For you, sir!" breathlessly.

They were off. Robert snatched the note and tore it open; it was from Gladys. Three words: "They are coming!"

Of course it was the Fairfaxes. "She is a darling!" he said, reading and re-reading the three words, and seeing a whole evening of joy and gladness spread out before him. "How awfully good of her to write! it's just like her."

Then he threw himself back in his seat and thought over all the possible and impossible things and scenes and conversations that might occur or be done or said by himself and Josline. Then he pulled out the bit of paper and read it again. Finally, he folded it up tightly and put it in his watch-case.

"They are coming!" was written all along the hedges, in every distant copse, on the low-lying down ridges, in the clouds in the sky. He had not believed it. He felt now that it was not Josline's doing; he did not think she would have come if she had been left unbiased. He had seen her the day before. He had gone to Old Court with a message from his father; she was sitting in the cedar parlour looking earnestly at Miss Barbara, who, with her back to the fire, and balancing backwards and forwards from toe to heel, from heel to toe, was evidently holding forth in no measured way. Josline knew he passed the window, but never turned her head; Miss

Barbara had given him a little nick of a nod. He had spun out his time to the utmost, but neither had come into the den, and Mr. Fairfax had said nothing about his going into the parlour. He had admired the lily heart in its frame, and Mr. Fairfax had said, quietly—

"Yes; but the other was the beautiful head; it had Josline's own look in the eyes. I can't think what Vannier did with it."

Robert had turned scarlet and felt like a robber; he stammered something unintelligible.

"I think he must have wanted it to idealize," said the uncle, thoughtfully.

In thinking over this scene now, a sudden idea came into the young man's head. Why should not Gabriel take Josline for his model of the Virgin? He would certainly propose it; and then think of the joy of possessing such a picture! Yes, indeed, then he would be more than repaid for having parted with Redskin.

He found the artist hard at work. In this short time Gabriel had painted till his life, his soul, the essence of his purity, will, love, and reverence had entered into the canvas.

There are times in an artist's life when the power of creation and the knowledge that such power is on him becomes too great for bodily control. Genius rises triumphant, and body is subdued by the subtler and more ethereal essence of spirit. Then, as it were, a sublime possession seizes the thread of his life, holds the throbs of pulse and brain in one steady, burning thrill, and the purity and strength of his soul pass from him unawares and impress themselves with God-like force on some earthly form or substance. It is at such times that a death-light falls on his creation; the intense penetrating struggle between life and expression. The highest of all meanings can only be conveyed by the effort that slays in the utterance. The spirit too highly strung must needs shiver with the force of its own conviction. Perfect power of expression is perfect Divinity.

It was thus, now, with Gabriel Vannier; he stood transfigured, for the time being, in his love, his reverence for his art. His struggling longings to express his soul in his work were being fulfilled before his eyes, and, as yet, he did not realize this; he hardly knew what he was painting. He felt he was working gloriously, but to what it might tend, he could not divine—his spirit within him seemed working in the gloom of semi-day. He would not be able to realize till exhaustion brought reflection; and, being no longer able to act, he could think. He had struck the gold chord of his life, and it was ringing in such perfect harmony with his highest aspirations, that it sounded to him simply as the breath of his breathing, the living of his life.

Robert was startled by the beauty of the design, even in its crude state; he was startled, also, and

greatly shocked by Gabriel's appearance. He was
deadly pale, his face was hollow as a mask; he
looked like an old ivory carving of our Saviour on
the cross. His great eyes were luminous and shone
like stars; his hair was damp, his hands nervous
and restless. He held out his left hand to Robert,
but went on painting with his right, and said, in a
voice that was low from exhaustion—

"I had a sort of idea you might be coming up to
town soon."

"Yes; and well for you I have," said his friend,
sitting down on a tall-backed chair, across which was
swung some blue drapery arranged in exquisite folds.
"If you don't leave that picture of your own free will,
Vannier, you will be carried from it, I see."

"I can't leave it now; it's on me, I must work,"
said Gabriel, with a hollow cough. "I see it's coming
all right somehow; the light is growing in it from day
to day. But, I will tell you something rather odd.
I can't *see* the Virgin's face," he bent his head backwards, and laid his hand over his eyes; "that is to
say, I see only one face it could be. It would be most
perfect, but—— "

"I know," said Robert, eagerly. "You mean
Josline Fairfax. Well now, look here, they want you to
to come back with me, to stay at Charteriss; you would
have every opportunity of studying her head there.
I know she wouldn't mind. Don't you think that
would do ? "

Gabriel turned impetuously towards him. "Oh!" he said, as a wonderful thrilling light came on his emaciated face. "That would be perfect! She is the only person I ever saw who came up to my idea of the Madonna, don't you see? Look!" He seized a bit of charcoal and sketched rapidly a kind of shadowy likeness to Josline, but he had not quite caught the expression. "It is just that which escapes me," he said, with a fierce catch at his lower lip, and a tremulous quiver in his eyelids. "I must see her once more to get it; but don't you know what I said to you about her? It is a face so full of angelic, no, divine purity; so lofty in expression, so tender, so loving, so gentle. Now the Virgin's face ought to have all that. After all, she was a woman like any mother of any of us, and must have humanity in her face. That is where they fail, I think, the Old Masters——" He stopped, then went on rapidly, "Yes, I will come back with you gladly."

"Well, I am glad," said Robert, "for you look awfully bad, and I do hope the rest and country air will set you up again."

"Quite long enough. I only want to finish this," he said, dreamily. "It would be an awful thing to end one's days with nothing to show for it. It's not so much that one does things badly after all, as that one doesn't do them at all. And I always meant to do something."

He was talking in a strange far-away voice, as

though to some one not there, and Robert was rather
held by the tone than by the thought expressed.

"Do you really work for the pure pleasure of
doing something, anything, a thing?"

The painter turned and looked at him with a
grave dignity. "All work brings its own blessing,"
he said. "And how few of us have any one to whom
we can show it, for the mere joy of hearing it appre-
ciated or judged at its fair value!"

"I dare say not," said Robert. "I never thought
of that before. In fact, I've never done anything
worth showing to any one."

"You've done a good work by me," said Gabriel,
fervently, stretching a wasted hand to. grasp the
strong, brown palm of his friend. "You heartened
me up when I wanted a few kind words, more than I
can say." Then as he wandered round the room
putting a few things together, he said, "It's like
a silent love, a few kind words coming at the right
time. It reminds me of what my mother used to say
about God's love for us, that when everything seemed
to end and draw into a tight knot of misery, then
God cut it with joy or—death."

Robert was silent, a little awed, a little puzzled;
the mystic look on Gabriel's face reminded him
strangely of Josline. An uneasy sense of being with
some one whose whole tone of thought and comprehension lies above us is often more silencing than
convincing. At last he said, "Do you think there
is any good in a silent love then, Vannier?"

"God loves us silently," said the artist, plucking his cap from his brow and throwing it on a chair near him.

"Yes, of course. But that's different, you know; He makes us feel it all the same," answered Robert, rather surprised at his own power of continuing this conversation. "But don't you see with a person, they can't know if you don't speak, and how can they tell you do?" He looked up earnestly.

"I don't know—but, well I know not whether you do others good by silently loving them, yet I think unconsciously you do. It's a great thing for them to hold, even unacknowledged, the belief in a silent, deep affection, that waits ready for any lonely time. They hardly realize how much lovingness there is for them till life is beginning to be very empty. But, when all that is in them worth having, in their own eyes, seems burnt out, then to find that there are still those who will gladly take the remainder and value it to the uttermost, is a salvation to their souls. They strive to return it, and thus in wishing to render others happy, they regain the power of happiness themselves." He stopped, sat down heavily and coughed in long gasps that brought the dew leaping on his brow, and shook every limb in its socket. "My God!" he said, as soon as he could speak again, looking up at Robert, who had risen in horror and alarm. "Why do we not accept our lives, not only bear them? for in accepting anything we *use* it in the

best way ; we carry it along, not only support it—— "
He stopped again, putting his hand to his mouth, and
brought it away wet with blood.

"For Heaven's sake, Vannier, don't move!" said
Robert, helpless and desperate. "Let me get you
some water, or what? Don't speak, point, show me."

The painter motioned one hand towards a shelf
on which stood a small bottle. Robert gave it to him,
he drank a mouthful, and gradually the ashy hue died
out of his face.

"Now, do sit still; I'll put your things together."

Gabriel leant back with a faint smile, one hand
holding open his painter's frock.

Steps came suddenly up the old wooden stairs, the
door was pushed open, and a slight, tall, and very
beautiful woman staggered in and reeled towards the
painter.

"Ah, you fool!" she laughed, pointing at him;
"ha! ha! Ah! you fool! ha! ha! ha! . . ."

The mocking jeer rang back mournfully from
the lonely roof and startled her. She stopped, turned
round, saw Robert standing staring in surprise and
confusion, and said, "What was it? Who is it?
. . . ah!" With a sudden cry she rushed across the
intervening space, seized Gabriel's arm, reeled back
against the easel and precipitated the still wet picture
on to the floor.

Echoing her cry, the painter shook himself free
from her grasp, and pushing her fiercely into his

vacant chair, lifted the picture, smeared from top to bottom. He stood trembling, not wholly with rage, but in a kind of dumb despair. "Look!" he cried, at last, with passionate utterance, holding it towards her. "Look!"

"Yes, I see. Very pretty! very pretty!" she answered, shaking her head gravely, and smiling the while.

He quivered from head to foot. Then suddenly dropping the picture on the easel, he sank on to the remaining chair in the room and hiding his face in his hands, he said, "It's of no use; you always drag me down, always, always."

She stared stolidly at him, making no reply. Robert stood silently between them.

Going down in the dusk of the evening, through the sodden land, Robert's heart smote him that he was taking this delicate artist into all this damp and fog, and yet, too, he felt that it was actually better for Gabriel than staying in town with that haunting misery, from which he could never be free. Gabriel had led Viola from the room, and no words had passed between the two men about the scene; but before leaving, the painter had turned the canvas with its face to the wall with a sigh, and Robert felt inclined actually to cry.

They went straight to Charteriss, the close carriage meeting them at the station—a kind thought of Lady Clinton's for Gabriel's sake. In the hall,

Sir Philip came out to meet them, with a most cordial and delighted welcome. But Gabriel was so exhausted, that he had to go at once to his room and lie down.

"I say, Bob; how awful he looks!" said Sir Philip, who, after seeing that he had everything he wanted, had persuaded Robert to come into the morning-room to tea.

"And how good of him to come!" from Lady Clinton.

"How good of you to go!" from Gladys.

"How delightful to be painted!" from Mina Thorold.

"Another sick animal!" from Quarl, ended the chorus. "I tell you what, Colonel Myddleton has got a most ugly touch of this fever again, I don't know what we are to do with him to-night, really." He looked so concerned that everybody became uneasy. "I wonder whether I dare give him chloroform, really?" he said. "What do you think, Sir Vere?"

"Try it," said the old gentleman, laconically. "I think if you do, you will have very little trouble with him afterwards."

"What does everybody say?" said Quarl. "Don't all speak at once," as silent dismay was his only response. "He is quite willing, but——" He got up, went and stood with his back to the fireplace, and held his chin meditatively.

"Phil, what do you think?" said Dorothy, looking anxiously at her husband.

"It's an awful bore!" uttered the oracle. "I don't like to say. Suppose, Freeman, you give up the scene with him in it."

"No, that I won't," said Quarl, shortly. "What do you say, Lady Dunstable?"

"Give it up," said the old lady, gravely. "It can't matter, and I think it will be a great risk his appearing at all.

"What a fuss about that stern, hard man!" said Miss Thorold to Hermione, who, with a face, the tension of which was painful, sat clasping Jerks against her knee.

"It would be a pity, though, to injure him just for our amusement," she answered.

Mr. Freeman turned to her suddenly. "It's all his own fault, he won't give up that scene."

"Can't you talk him out of it?" she said, shortly.

"No."

Her brows contracted painfully; she appeared about to speak, then closed her lips again.

"Suppose you ask him, Miss St. John," said Mina, looking only half up from under her large lids.

"What nonsense!" said Hermione, with the same pale severity in her look that had once before awed that young person. "Colonel Myddleton is the last person to be persuaded by any one unless he chose."

" But he might choose in this case, you know,"
persisted Miss Thorold.

" If Mr. Freeman has failed, I should not attempt
it" (very coldly and proudly); and she rose and walked
quietly into the hall.

" I believe they are all afraid of him," murmured
Mina. " *I'll* try."

" We all know that angels rush in where fools fear
to tread," said Quarl, dryly.

" Yes, yes; we all know Mr. Freeman is very
cross," she retorted, nodding her head gently at him,
" so we forgive him."

Hermione stood in the hall, watching the gardeners bringing in rare exotics and palms. A bush
of evergreens on fire, falling close to her, made her
start; she helped to re-arrange them in their place
after the fire was put out, and all that she touched
seemed to stand up and fall together again gracefully.

" Will you let me help you ? " said a voice at her
elbow, and turning with confusion, she saw Colonel
Myddleton. It was the first time he had left his room
that day, and he certainly did look very pale and ill.
She spoke before she had time to think.

" Oh ! I wish you would not act to-night."

" Why?" he said, holding up the trailing creepers,
and twisting wire round the balustrade of the gallery.

" Because Mr. Freeman seems to think you ought
not."

Their hands met in fastening the wire, and his

voice sank very low in answering. "I *cannot* give it up; it's only this one night; you don't know what it will be to me, it may alter my whole life." His voice shook so that Hermione hardly heard the words, though by some strange instinct she caught their meaning.

"It will make you ill," she said, very low.

"What does it matter—afterwards? nothing will matter much then. I thought, I meant——" He broke off, grasping the balustrade; then he went on with energy. "Do you know? no, of course, you do not know; but I mean, it's an awful thing to see— to see all you want within your very grasp, and you cannot, dare not put out your hand and take it." He was looking at her a little wildly; his face looked fierce and thin. He put out one hand, it was cold as ice, and laid it on hers; she did not withdraw it. "You said once, about justice," he went on, brokenly, "'You must put *self* out of court.' I have tried, I am trying—but there are things, feelings in one's nature; they must have play. Even a jury gives a recommendation to mercy." His mouth, ordinarily so stern and sharply cut, was quivering now. Her eyes were full of tears. "I only ask for to-night," he said; "only this one night to act with you, to be with you, near you. Do not ask me to give it up, for I cannot refuse you if you do; give it me, will you?"

"Yes," she said simply.

"God bless you! I knew you would."

Hermione was in such an intense state of excitement that she felt quite blind and giddy; she could not have said another word if her life had depended on it.

The gardeners were all busy at the other end of the hall, wreathing the pillars and the front of the daïs; presently they appealed to Colonel Myddleton for advice, and he called Mr. Freeman out of the morning-room. Hermione stood still by the gallery, trying to think. What could it be? what could it mean? It could not be only because she was so rich. Lady Dunstable had said if any man cared enough they would speak. To think that he did not care now would be sheer folly; it was evident that he was shaken to the very heart. But, what could she do? absolutely nothing, nothing; tied by every sense from helping the one person most dear to her in all the world. She could have taken her heart out and wrung it, as she did her slender fingers, till the diamond ring cut into the palm, and brought the blood springing. Oh! for one hour of manhood to speak and bid him speak! for one hour of dire, horrible peril that should shake or tear his secret from him, and free her! She almost prayed for it. How glad, how thankful she was afterwards that she had not! She felt that she must be alone, must have air, must think without walls round her. The front door opened with a rush of icy, wet wind. She must go out.

She turned and walked slowly to the door ; they were all busy raising a "wing" covered with splendid creepers and orchids ; they did not notice her, she thought. She went out, turned to the left, and beat along under the terrace to the conservatory. Ah! there it was all quiet, warm, passionately scented, and quite dark; they had not begun to light up. She walked up and down, up and down, her hands clasped behind her, thinking.

Hermione's was a grand, calm nature, quite capable of waiting any time for a given action, but it was this dead blank of uncertainty and powerlessness which fretted her now ; it was like being bound with spider's webs, and who knew but that by waiting she might not be allowing them to tighten and strengthen, or that by moving she might not bring the whole edifice crumbling around her ? If he had not seemed to feel it all so greatly she could have borne to go on any length of time, she thought, but it was the light of misery in his eyes that had shaken her so to-night; the sort of look of a baffled hunted creature at bay. It was altogether so unexpected from him, he who was always so calm and so self-contained, that it worked on her with tremendous power. Through all her anxiety pierced the joy of feeling that she was very much to him, must be far more than she had ever dreamed; and yet with counter force came the conviction how dread, how all-powerful, must be the barrier that kept him back. No mere question of wealth could stay him thus. She knew by the very pride and nobility of her own nature that his love would rise above that now; it would become a low and vulgar bar, that he could not allow to remain between them. Then what could it be? Something that had occurred in India? Something that in some way bound him, or that he fancied did so? It must be. The only question was—was it irrevocable? could not even her wealth free him? Doubtless, only there —now she seemed to see why he did not speak. How could he owe his freedom to her? " Why not ? " she thought, as the blood came leaping and tingling like flame to her cheeks and brow. " Oh ! my dear, my dear, what is all my wealth worth in comparison with your happiness ? "

She walked more slowly ; her heart beat so loudly that she hardly heard the rain coming down in sheets and torrents on the glass roof. Now and then a great drop fell with startling reverberation on the marble floor, or shook a flower on its stem, like a passionate kiss. How hard it was to know what would be best to do for him ! If, indeed, his happiness, his highest happiness, namely, his belief in her, and his respect for himself, consisted in not speaking, then would she be of all most miserable if she urged him into utterance. Whereas, on the other hand, if by speaking, by the truth being faced, " things " might be brought straight—then, why, by some conventional inanity, keep him back from it ? Hermione's lofty, noble

nature had a widespread belief in the strength, the
all-healing power, of truth and light; she had always
faced things herself, and from having done so strongly
and acted accordingly, forgot that often no one had
been aware of the fact save herself.

They were coming in now to light up, and Allan,
the head gardener, came up to her and asked her
whether she had looked out and seen the mere. No,
she had not. She went to the centre door and saw it
through the belt of trees; it was white and swirling,
and looked like a sword drawn hastily and in anger.

" It's coming down at the 'head' most awful," he
said. "And do you see that thin white line, away
westward, miss ? That's the river breaking its banks."
The drift and swish of the rain was deafening now
on the glass, overhead. "If so be you've never seen
the 'head' in flood-time, miss, I advise ye go down there
to-morrow, first thing."

" I will, indeed," she said. " It's the very thing
I most want to see."

CHAPTER XX.

"There's Josline!" said Gladys, clutching Hermione tight, and peering through the curtain hung in front of the daïs. "How sweet she looks; and, oh! there is that dear old Mr. Fairfax. He is just like Lord Strafford, that horrid Charles's Lord Strafford."

"Don't say 'horrid Charles,'" said Hermione, laughing; "though, certainly, that was horrid!"

There was a great buzz of excitement; the band was playing softly, "Could ye come back to me, Douglas?" up in the gallery. People were still arriving, and every fresh person seemed more and more imbued with the idea that they were the very last who would be able to cross the ford, and that all succeeding visitors would have to remain on the further side, which, as the speakers were safely in the house and in the midst of warmth and pleasure, added fresh zest to their enjoyment of the whole scene.

Sir Vere Temple received the guests, in the absence of Sir Philip, called twenty ways at once; which caused a little confusion.

Presently, there was heard a loud command: "Take your places.!" There was a bustle and settling in, the hall darkened, the music died down. People began whispering; everybody got near those they wished to speak to, and Josline found herself sitting next to Gabriel Vannier, much to her astonishment and pleasure. He was in a kind of loose frock of brown velvet, and, with his fine peaked beard, oval face, large eyes, and tossed hair, looked like a Vandyke stepped out of its frame. Josline was entirely in white, without a single ornament of any description. There seemed to be a little hitch in the arrangement; people began talking, when suddenly, a trumpet sounded twice, and the curtain went up. It was the scene of " Catherine Douglas barring the door."

The queen and her ladies were huddled at the end of the daïs; Gladys was clasping Disko in her arms, an afterthought of Quarl's, which had been received with acclamation. Old Lady Dunstable, looking her part most perfectly of all, perhaps, stood a little in front of Mina, with her ebony stick extended in feeble protest.

Lady Clinton was kneeling, fastening down the trap-door on the king, whose hand only was seen. The door was in the act of falling. "Catherine's" arm was broken; she was leaning back against the shivered timbers; her hair, partially undone, had slid across her face; her other hand was convulsively grasping the iron of a partizan, which had pierced the wood close to her side; her lips were unclosing in the act of fainting; her long dark riding-dress swung on one side, showing her small feet, firmly planted in a kind of despairing energy. Through the fissures you saw the faces of the pikemen—Sir Philip, Robert, and Colonel Myddleton.

The grouping was perfect, the energy of all the figures was wonderful; but Quarl's training had not been in vain. His last words, "Now *do* try," had braced them with a strange wish to please him, after all his trouble; they knew he really cared.

Robert began to shake a little, even before the curtain fell swiftly; for he saw Josline and Gabriel, side by side; they had both risen to see better, and those two beautiful heads in close juxtaposition would have been remarkable anywhere, and by any one. They had not recognized him behind his planks and in his morion, but yet he felt as though his eyes had met and held Josline's for one brief second of intense feeling. She was a little stirred by something, at any rate, for she turned involuntarily and touched her uncle's hand, whose long fingers closed over hers instantly, with that quick sympathy of intuition so often noticeable in those who are highly gifted.

"Did you like it?" he whispered, through the ringing plaudits.

"Yes, very much, but she looked as though her arm was really broken," she answered, with a little shudder.

"She *was* Catherine Douglas for the time being," said Gabriel; "every muscle in her arm was actually braced. It's one of the finest pieces of still acting I ever saw in my life; and did you see the tightening of the nerves under the eyes? Marvellous!"

The band was playing that sweet old song of Paêr's: "Hélas! c'est près de vous, O ma tant douce amie, que mon âme a trouvé nouvelle vie."

Mr. Fairfax turned round with joy in his fine face. "I do love that air," he said. "It's so simple and so touching. Remind me Josline, when we go home, to hunt it up."

A grave discussion was going on as to whether the monkey were real or not; and many criticisms were being uttered about the whole scene, but admiration predominated.

Again came the command to be seated, again the trumpet sounded, and then there was a scene from Dumas's novel, of the "Reine Margot," where Du Mouy had taken refuge in the queen's bed-chamber, on the St. Bartholomew Night, and she was standing in front of him, whilst all the guards were pouring in. And now Josline saw Robert. Half-dying, he had drawn the magnificent dress of Marguérite round him, and was lying half-insensible between her and the bed. He did it fairly well, though, considering that his eyes should have been shut, and that, instead, he was gazing fixedly at Josline, his acting could not be said to be perfect; however, it was only for a moment, and, as his gaze never wavered, why, it did not so much matter. Miss Thorold really surpassed herself; her tiny figure was drawn to its full height; her gorgeous dress added dignity to her manner. She was supposed to be saying, "This is the bed-chamber of the Queen of Navarre. Stop!" and she looked as though she could say it, too.

The furniture, the hangings, the whole arrangement was marvellously in keeping. The jewels were superb, and I do not think that that little fair person who wore them so bravely had ever been so happy or so elate in her life. Her French blood told wonderfully in the carrying out of the character, and she looked all that Marguérite de Navarre might have looked, with her small, childish face, beautiful, fair hair, *mignonne* figure, and exquisite hands and feet.

The audience was generally enchanted, and there was no criticism whatever. Robert did not pay her half compliments enough; but she was so pleased with herself that she forgave him. He was dying to go amongst the audience, leather jerkin and all, though really the fit of it was not quite what might have been wished, as he said to himself, as he tore at the waist-belt and tried in vain to screw the strap tighter. "Confound that ass! But she won't mind, I know; perhaps she won't even see. I believe she doesn't see things that other stupid girls think of."

"I know you're dying to be off," said Quarl, suddenly coming on him. "Go then! You look uncommonly odd in that get up."

Robert jumped. "What do you mean?" he said,
with suppressed anguish.

"Never mind! Go along! I want everybody out
of the way now."

The band was now playing Beethoven's Symphony
in C minor. And one or two people said, loudly,
"What a horrible noise!" But it was only at the
beginning. When it came to the part where the
great chords go slowly rolling, and the violins worked
up and held them and silence came down on the
audience, Josline drew closer to her uncle, whose
face was turned towards the orchestra.

"He has picked his men carefully," he murmured,
now quite at home and perfectly happy. "What a
pleasure to hear it played like that!"

The hall grew darker; a strange, red, lurid light
shone below the curtain, and a kind of low, hissing
sound made every one start and hold their breath.
No need now to bid them take their seats, the music
had kept them still.

The curtain rose just as Robert entered the door
and he stood transfixed; even Josline was forgotten for
that moment. It was the scene of "the forsaken
sentinel in Herculæneum." The glare of flame came
down a narrow gallery on the right, and struck on
Colonel Myddleton's face. He was standing with his
arms folded round his spear, very quiet, very calm;
he had evidently made up his mind to die and was
waiting for it to come. It was the strange waiting

without expectancy that struck every spectator with
such crushing force and made them feel as though
they were looking on at an actual sacrifice.

"And all for a word!" said Gabriel, breathless.
"It's awful! he must have felt that! gone through
it actually! What a face!" He was leaning, saying
this in Josline's ear, who could hardly keep from a
sob of excitement and anxiety.

She was pressing up against her uncle, who was
too much moved himself to be aware how fast her
heart was beating. The mournful, grave, intense look
on Colonel Myddleton's face became graved in two
hearts that night. It was a longer time before the
curtain fell than any before and then the applause
was deafening.

"Out of the way, everybody!" said Mr. Freeman.
"Come here, Myddleton! Now for the scene of the
evening. Everybody not wanted go into the hall;
everybody!" He hustled them all out, only Colonel
Myddleton remained.

"Surely I am not going on again alone?" he
said, rather wearily, looking round to see if Hermione
were there, and feeling his heart sink with a sick feeling of disappointment. "I thought you said——"

"Wait!" said Quarl, looking eager and very
anxious. "I'll tell you what, Myddleton, I'm in a
most horrid fright. I've never told Miss St. John
what it is she is to act, and now, supposing at the
last she should refuse, my dear fellow, I should be so
horribly vexed."

"Well; but is she even dressed?"

"Oh, yes, sometime ago, I went to see." Quarl was striding up and down the room, snatching at his chin violently, very red and nervous. "She looks so awfully beautiful I didn't know what to do not to tell her. Look here, do you think there is any human being who could persuade her not to mind?"

"But why doesn't she come?" said Colonel Myddleton, in a short, sharp voice.

"I told her not till the last minute. Oh, I wish I weren't such a fool!"

"But she said she would do just as you told her, you know."

"Yes, yes, that's all very fine; but there are some things I should never dare to urge her to do."

There was a little silence. Suddenly Colonel Myddleton said slowly—

"Look here, Freeman! I think she will do it, if you don't put it into her head that you dream of her refusing."

"Very well," said Quarl, desperately. "I'll call her, then."

The band was playing the swan song in "Lohengrin;" the sweet, sharp, reedy notes were beating through the hall, with that piercing cry only known to violins. Not a soul present knew what it was excepting Mr. Freeman, who had heard it in Germany, and had insisted on the band learning it for this scene. They were playing it wonderfully; from

far, far away the exquisite lament seemed to come ; so
still was every one, that you could hear the rush and
beat of the rain outside, the wind rising and whistling
like a demon chorus.

Colonel Myddleton leant back against the side
wing, waiting. His heart beat thickly ; a great sadness flooded his whole soul, under that mournful, be-
seeching wail.

Suddenly Quarl's voice said, in a rather shaky
tone, " Look ! "

He did look. There stood Hermione ; but what a
Hermione !

Clothed entirely in a white stole, which fell straight
from her throat to her feet ; her magnificent hair undone and falling in one wide, golden sheet to her
knee. She was looking at him with a strange, wistful
inquiry. She was so exceedingly beautiful and looked
altogether so unearthly, that the man who loved her
and the man who did not, were equally speechless.
They were all a little unnerved—Hermione by not
knowing what she was going to do ; they by trying to
tell her.

" Oh ! " said Colonel Myddleton, suddenly advancing and holding out both his hands. " Do not refuse !
It would be such a pity."

" I promised to act with you to-night," she said
quietly, looking straight at him. " And I never
change my mind or go from my word."

" Hush ! " he said, in a voice dense and dull with

a fierce anguish and passion that startled both his hearers. "You know no word holds good to me; I died just now! I hold no one to their word!"

Mr. Freeman thought he was playing on the part he had just acted; but Hermione had seen the look in his eyes when he first saw her—the look of a creature shot through the heart; they had seemed to break, and that was one reason why she looked so pale.

"How long they are!" "Something has gone wrong!" "What is it?" people were beginning to murmur, when the band suddenly ceased; there was a profound hush and the curtain rose on a representation of Noel Paton's picture of "Mors janua Vitæ." On the left was a towering wall of creepers, exotics, orchids, palms—drooping, lovely, faintly scented; down from above them, glittering through them, bursting triumphantly through crevice, tendril, leaf, and bud, struck light, white, intense, pure, wonderful; shedding its rays into the furthest recesses of the hall, piercing and searching like an organ's tone or the trumpet-call of an angel. On the right was darkness, dying leaves, broken branches, stagnant water, crawling things.

Immediately in front, knelt Colonel Myddleton, in full armour; bruised, pierced, broken; the straps giving way, rust on everything; a crushed helmet had rolled against a gigantic thistle, and was full of down from the seeding plant; his broken sword was slipping from his grasp; his face, full of a terrible heart-broken anguish, was turned towards the streaming light, every line came out as though carved in iron; he was dying, and of a broken heart, a wasted life, a trust betrayed. Close to him, with one hand lifting his, stood Hermione. The light fell over her, completely transfiguring her as she stood looking almost transparent; there had been no need to powder her face, it was pale as a sculptured angel. Behind her, actually touching her (though she never knew it even afterwards), was a gigantic representation of Death. Her hair swept over the knight's figure, he felt it lying on his neck, he let his hand lie in hers, not colder than her own; for those brief seconds she was his good angel, and they gave him strength to bear, to be true.

The curtain fell; it was the last scene. There was no applause, somehow the tableau had been too real, every person present had more or less been overcome by those two figures; even the arrangement of the scene was more perfect than any of the others. It was still in everybody's mind, when the hall was quickly relit, the band began to play a lively air, and each spectator said—"Well!" or "The Last!" or "Wonderful!"

Gabriel was lost in thought, Josline was shivering from head to foot.

CHAPTER XXI.

In the warm, dimly lighted conservatory, every one was walking up and down, talking over the scenes and dresses, whilst the hall was being cleared for dancing. Colonel Myddleton had been talking over the scene to Mr. Freeman, who was perfectly satisfied, radiant, and exultant.

"Didn't I ask you to name the most noble-looking woman you ever saw?" he said, hugging Disko with effusion, and stuffing him with sugar. "*Did* you ever see any one look so grand as she did? She is a grand creature. God bless her! I am grateful to her for having made no fuss, but just taking her place at once, and looking it to perfection. If that lath of a painter isn't madly in love with her, he ought to be. I never saw such a figure; the sweep of her arm was superb. And then that hair! Heavens! it would have tingled to my finger-tips if it had fallen over my shoulder, as it did over yours. She *looked* the good angel. Yes, for such a woman, one might even be content to die."

" Or to live," muttered Colonel Myddleton, stooping to pick up his helmet, and trying to steady his voice.

" I thought it was all up with her once, though ; just when the curtain was coming down, her whole face was as white as her dress, did you see ? "

Colonel Myddleton nodded.

" And then how oddly it altered her ! her hair all being down, eh ?   Her face looked so small and sweet and soft ; one only knew her by her great eyes. What hair ! " and he laughed.   " I can't get over it ; now do you honestly think that's all her own ?   It's just like her, somehow, too," he added, musingly ; " so massive, so fine, so soft ; for, do you know, I felt it.   I couldn't resist ; I took up a strand of it, it was just like spun gold, and she never seemed to think about it at all.   My goodness ! what would the little Reine Margot give for that hair ?   She acted well, too. Well, I must go and look after my children, and if you take my advice, Myddleton, you'll go off to your bed, and not show till to-morrow ; you look uncommonly beat."

" Ah ! well, yes ; I'll go, anyhow, and get rid of all this toggery," he said, with a grave, tired smile ; and he walked away, with his head down over his gorget, looking like one who has indeed fought a losing battle.

" Why the deuce he doesn't speak, I can't think. Is it his health that stops him, I wonder ? " muttered Quarl.   " I thought I would prod him up by talking so about her, but the pride is gone out of the man. Well! 'How are the mighty fallen!' He doesn't look much like a hero now. Not that she would care; she loves the ground he treads on, I believe. Why, their eyes literally *met* when he said she must act, and she said she had promised him and she would stand by it. Well, Disko, my child, I'm mighty pleased, and in a good temper for once. I'll see if nothing can help them. I suppose there's nothing ugly in the background, no entanglement or anything. No, he doesn't look like the man for that; it's that confounded money, or else he knows more about his health than he will allow."

Colonel Myddleton went slowly across the great hall, through the dining-room, through the long stone corridor, along the cloisters from which he saw the lighted conservatory, and heard the band playing faintly, and into the beautiful oriel chamber. He had been walking almost mechanically, thinking over the scene, and now, finding himself suddenly at the foot of the great staircase, he recollected the ghost story, and thought of Hermione. His foot was on the first step before he looked up, and then a thrill of superstitious dread shook him from head to foot.

Standing on the haunted landing, all in white, her hair still floating round her, was a tall woman's figure. She was looking down. There was hardly any light, he could not see her face, but he knew it was Hermione. For two breathless seconds they neither

moved nor spoke; it might have actually been Sir
Sydney and the hapless lady of the legend. They
both knew the story; the strange significance struck
them both. She had left the hall immediately after
the last tableau, and had been crossing this quiet way
to her room.

"Do not move," he said, at last; " I am coming
to you."

He began slowly mounting the stairs, very slowly,
for he wanted to *see* what he was going to say. At
last he trod on the top step. He stood quite still,
looking at her; her face was very pale and grave.

"You see," he began, in a strange, hoarse voice,
"they maligned Sir Sydney; it was a lie, he never
broke his word to her, his word of honour. They
killed him, but he came."

"And she waited," said Hermione.

Doors opened and banged; a train of servants
came through the room below them, carrying lights,
fruit, and wine; they were in darkness, no one saw
them. The doors closed again on distant laughter,
merry voices, stamping feet.

He stretched out one mailed arm towards her, and
spoke again, very low, but she heard every syllable, as
though it had been a voice of doom.

"God bless you for keeping your word to me, to-
night! It has helped me at my utmost need. I am
going away to-morrow. I may never see you again
in this world; I will say good-bye now; but believe,

believe—oh! God grant that you may believe—that if I live a long life, or a short few years, no woman on the whole earth will ever be to me what you are, what you have always been to me." He stopped, trying hard to master his emotion, which half strangled him, and with one hand he struggled to undo his gorget.

Hermione did not move. She stood as though turned to stone; she felt as though dying.

He came a little nearer, he knelt down suddenly, gathered her hair in his two hands, held it like golden water to his lips, and then looking up with his eyes dim with unshed tears, he said, " I have believed in you, Hermione, all my life, will you believe in me ? "

She tried to speak. Oh! what would she not have given for power to utter, if only a few short words ? She could not move her lips ; her heart beat so loudly, he heard it.

" Perhaps in a year, in a few short years, you will have reason to think I have wilfully deceived you," he went on; " but it will not be so. I shall still hold to my thought of you as the one woman in the whole of God's world whom I love—to the death." His straining, eager look held her like an arm of steel, otherwise she must have fallen. " I am going now," he said. " Will you speak once—say my name once—say you forgive me—say you will believe in me ? that I may carry that thought with me till I die, and can tell you the truth." She did not

move, or utter, or alter her look, rigid and cold as
stone. " Oh, my God! my God! you cannot, then!"
he said, breaking down suddenly, letting his head
fall on the hair in his clasped hands, and sobbing
frightful, tearless sobs.

She made a sound, her lips parted, she struggled
to speak, she lifted her hands vaguely, blindly towards
him; an awful look of untold love, faith, misery
came into her beautiful, tearless eyes. She thought
she had spoken, she thought she had said, " Tell
me, tell me why!" but there was no sound.

" God bless you," he said, not looking at her, but
rising to his feet. " You are true even in not speaking ;
you said there were some things better never known,
but I thought you ought to know that—that I—I
mean what I think of you. Good-bye. God bless
you!" He lifted her hair again, kissed it passionately, then turned and walked slowly along the gallery
and through the great door at the end.

It was too late.

The instant he was actually gone Hermione recovered herself a little. She staggered to the window-
seat, still staring at the place where he had stood,
and she said, alas! now out loud, " she had loved
him all her life!" as though speaking of some one
else. " She believed him! she — believed — him!"
She lifted her hair and looked at it, and then clasped
it tightly to her. Then on her came a passion of

anxiety to be dressed, to go down, to meet him again ; for of course he would be amongst the others. She got up and went to her room in a fever of excitement. She was deadly pale, her eyes glittered, she looked fearfully ill. But what did she care? what did anything matter? who would look at her, or she at them? She hurried her maid frantically; she caught up the first jewels and flowers that came to hand; she twisted up her hair in long golden coils, fastened her dress with trembling fingers, heard Gladys's voice calling her, and went hurriedly to the door. Somehow she couldn't find the handle ; everything rocked. She tried to call, but failed, and sank into a chair as Gladys ran in.

" It's nothing ! " she said, as soon as she could speak. " I often feel faint; I think nothing of it, I assure you. Don't look so ghastly, Gladys, you foolish child ! Give me some cold water." She was shivering, and deadly cold; her teeth chattered in her head. " Now let me get up ; here, give me your hand, Gladys; so ! I am all right. Now don't say anything about it. Come along; Marton, give me that flask ; it's horrible, but I must have something, I suppose," as her voice failed her and she drooped her head on Gladys' shoulder. " Pour it out, Marton, a teaspoon, two." She was shivering, so that the chair against which she leant rattled. She drank it and the colour ebbed back to her cheeks, though her lips looked thin and white, and her nostrils kept quivering in. "Now, let us go," she said, with a faint smile, "I am all right, really. I am tired, yes, very tired, but that's all."

Gladys didn't dare say anything; they went down to the hall.

CHAPTER XXII.

Mr. FAIRFAX and Josline were in the drawing-room looking at the statue of Night. Robert was with them, longing to ask her to dance, but not daring to do so. She seemed so strange and silent; she clung to her uncle with presistency, refusing to move a step without him, and looking confused and startled at every word addressed to her. Gabriel Vannier was sitting in a low chair watching her every movement, noting every turn of her head, every expression of her mobile face. She was quite unaware and unconscious of this, though; she felt no fear of him whatever, and if he had talked to her, or watched her all night, would probably never have remarked it.

"What would aunt Barbara say to us?" said Dux, smiling as they sat down under the grouped shrubs. "She would be startled beyond all words."

"It must be nearly time to be returning," said Josline, with flushing cheeks, as she caught the passionate entreaty of Robert's look.

" Oh ! Miss Fairfax, you really must wait for supper—won't you even walk to the doorway and see the dancing ? "

She shrank a little and Mr. Fairfax said directly—

" Ah ! Josline, yes, do go and see how they all get on."

Reluctantly she rose, and side by side they went to the doorway. She made no attempt to take his arm, and he was so abashed by her manner that he dared not offer it to her.

They stood quietly looking on, when Lady Dunstable came up on Sir Philip's arm and said—

" Robert ! is that Miss Josline Fairfax ? " There was surprised pleasure in her voice and a little tremor too.

" Yes, madam," he said, bowing.

"Ah ! how like ! Will you let me kiss you, mon enfant ? " she said, with stately kindness, and breaking into her native language, " Your mother was Lucille's only friend. Grand Dieu, how it all comes back to me ! I see her, tall, young, beautiful."

She stretched her two hands, drew the young girl's head towards her, and kissed her gravely on the brow. " Your hair grows with the same sweep," she said, with tears in her voice ; " so smooth, so heavy ; I loved her very much ! Alas ! poor child." She remained looking gravely at Josline, who was looking equally grave at her, with trembling earnestness and curiosity.

Sir Philip and Robert were talking together, the latter hearing every word with keen double hearing. The dancers whirled past, the music went on with lively beat, the wind roared, and the waters came down.

"I say, Freeman, where are you going with that ridiculous monkey? Its looks bewray it; it's terrified to death and horribly sleepy."

"I am going to take it to bed," said Quarl. "It's done its duty like every one else. When are you going to have the supper room opened?"

"Soon. Where's Myddleton?"

"I sent him where Disko is going, long ago," returned Quarl. "He's dead beat."

"I wish I were there, too," said Sir Philip, stifling a prodigious yawn. "Do listen to the rain! I begin to be horribly afraid half the people will have to stay here."

"Then Disko had better go at once, or they'll have to steal his bed."

"Robert! where is Gladys?" said Lady Clinton.

"Gone to fetch Miss St. John; I suppose they got talking," he answered, rather shortly, for he saw Josline being carried off by Lady Dunstable.

"Here I am, if you want me," said Hermione's low voice at their elbow. "Gladys is dancing."

"My dear, how tired you look!" "Do let me get you a chair," from Lady Clinton and Robert, simultaneously.

"No, thank you, I'm all right," she said, with a smile that looked cut on her face.

"Ah! there's Gladys. I've caught her eye, she must go and speak to old Mrs. Crompton." Lady Clinton left them.

"I don't see Colonel Myddleton, is he dancing?" said Hermione, with extreme quietude.

"No: he's gone to bed," said Robert. "I heard Quarl tell Philip so just now. Do you want anything? Do let me do it for you."

"Oh! it's nothing, thank you; I only wanted to answer a question he asked me, that's all."

There was silence. The supper-room had opened, and people were drifting towards it. Robert felt he ought to ask her to go in, but he didn't want to let Josline out of his sight. Gladys came past them; she too looked tired.

"Bob," she said, smiling, "why don't you ask Josline to go into supper? she knows no one. I'll follow soon, if you go towards the left. Hermione, will you let me introduce Lord Edward Morton to you?"

There was no help for it. Hermione went into supper. What she talked about she never knew. What Lord Edward was like she never knew—tall or short, or fair or dark. He said afterwards that the great heiress was the most beautiful and the most silly woman he had ever met, for she laughed at everything, and said yes to everything, and talked so fast he couldn't hear himself speak. There was a slight discrepancy in this statement.

Hermione was only conscious of one miserable fact : he evidently would not see her again ; he was going away, and she should never, never speak to him more. She watched the people coming in now in shoals; every one looked happy, excited, flushed, satisfied. Was there then, indeed, only her own one miserable heart? She was vaguely glad to hope so, to think so; but yet, oh ! if she could only see him once more, see his tall, strong figure come in at that opposite doorway, for example, come up to her, touch her, speak her name! before all these people, yes, before them all, she would have to speak ! So strong was the yearning on her that she began to be afraid she was saying something. She thought Lord Edward looked strangely at her, so she smiled and said by a great effort—

"We are all rather tired and stupid to-night, I think."

"It must have been awfully hard work. Oh! I say! who is that lovely girl ? "

" That is Miss Fairfax. Would you like to know her ? "

" Oh, I say ! yes, you know I should."

Hermione had no scruples, for she saw Gladys talking to a man she knew she could not bear, and determined to release her. The dancing went on again after supper with renewed zest. It was not every day that the county had an opportunity of dancing on such a floor and to such a band, and they certainly made the best of it.

Quarl was disconsolately leaning against the doorway when Hermione slid past him.

"Good night," she said. "Don't betray me, I must go to bed, I am so tired."

He started forwards. "Don't go," he said. "I am going to get Miss Fairfax to sing."

"What now? to-night?"

"Yes; I mean, I know she will if you ask her uncle. That young Watt has bothered her enough for one night."

"Oh! I don't think it would be kind, she is too excited and tired; don't ask her."

"Do you think so, really? Well, look here, will you take one turn with me in the conservatory?"

"If you wish, yes. I am rather tired."

"I won't keep you two minutes. Come along," he said, rather unceremoniously.

They went in. One or two people were walking about, the Fairfaxes amongst others.

"Do sit down," he said kindly.

"I would rather stand, I think," she said.

"Well, now, Miss St. John, I'm a very odd person, you know. I am going to say something odd, shall you mind?"

"How can I possibly tell till I know?" She drew back rather coldly.

"Oh! you needn't go off like that. It's only that

some one we know gets horribly hipped, and thinks he's going to die or something, and he isn't a bit. That's all; don't you mind."

Hermione laughed. "He never told me so, why do you think he does?"

"Well, he will tell you. Don't you mind."

"I should mind very much if he did," she said. "I have known him a long time, and should be very sorry; but I think you are mistaken. Was that all? Well, I am sure you meant very kindly. Good night, now. By-the-by, he is going away to-morrow, isn't he?"

"Yes; he says so. I don't think he will."

"He generally does what he says," she answered. "Good night."

It was the last piece of heroism she was capable of. She reached her own room safely, and then broke down, and sobbed such passionate, bitter tears as she had never wept before. "Oh! why, why did he say that? Oh! why, why did he not give me time to answer? Oh!——" with a long, low wail, stretching her arms out across the darkness of the room to the shadows cast on the wall like living things. "Oh, my darling! my darling! come back to me! give me time! do not leave me! do not leave me! I am so alone in all the world—alone, alone!" Then she hid her head in her arms, and wrung her hands in impotent misery and despair. "I never could, I never could say anything in a hurry. He might have known; he might have waited. I meant to speak; he knew I would speak;" and she sobbed and cried, like a broken-hearted, beaten child.

Robert and Gladys were putting Josline and Mr. Fairfax into the lumbering old clarence that was to take them home.

"Are you quite sure the ford is passable? shall I not come with you? I wish you would let me," he was imploring; and Josline was saying—

"Quite sure. No, thank you," in a hushed whisper, like some one speaking in their sleep.

"You will come soon, then? and I will play as you wish," Mr. Fairfax was saying to Gladys, with whom he had made great friends. "But don't, please, stand out here in the damp. I beg your pardon, but I always look after Josline, and get an idea no one ought to do anything."

They drove off, leaving Gabriel looking after them, and Mr. Freeman saying, as he tapped the artist on the shoulder—

"'A chiel's amang ye, taking notes.'" Then he strolled off through the rapidly emptying rooms, thinking over Hermione's manner. "I begin to think she doesn't care, after all. And perhaps he knows it, poor wretch! Well, she's a mighty cool hand; but when she does care—my eye!" with which adjuration he bethought him that he had two, both of which were heavy with sleep, and so betook him to his rest.

Sir Philip had just begun to wake up, and he and

Robert walked the conservatory for ever so long, smoking and talking over everything.

"Well, it all went off very well, I think, don't you, old fellow?" This from Sir Philip.

"Yes, very," from Robert, who was utterly miserable, and had probably never passed so wretched an evening in his life.

"Everybody looked very nice, I think?" tentatively.

"Oh, very; they all danced." Horrible falsehood, for Robert had not taken one turn.

"You're half asleep, and no wonder. I say, you did look so odd in that jerkin, ha! ha!"

"Ha! ha! did I?" in feeble misery.

"Well, never mind, I heard that sweet, gentle Fairfax girl tell Gabriel Vannier you looked just what she fancied a pikeman would look."

"I wonder what that would be?" meditated Robert, flying up to Paradise again.

And so the evening ended. It left most of them wondering what something would be, excepting little Gladys, who lay down to sleep, quite certain how something was gone from her for ever.

CHAPTER XXIII.

THE old clarence lumbered along the heavy rutted lanes. Mr. Fairfax was humming softly to himself "Hélas! c'est près de vous." Josline was wondering whether "going out" always meant this extraordinary mixture of excitement, disappointment, scraps of conversation, rushes of music, beat of feet, snatches of laughter, and above all, and over all, two eyes that followed you everywhere. If so, she thought she would never care to go anywhere again. She was tired out. They splashed through the ford, just not too high, and at last they stopped by the wicket gate, and saw Mrs. Turgoose standing in the porch with a lantern. How strange she looked, thought Josline, in a scarlet flannel petticoat tied round her neck, and both her arms stuck awkwardly out of the placket-hole! It was raining heavily. Josline, holding up her delicate muslin dress, tripped lightly in, and Mr. Fairfax followed, and was received with the cold muzzle of a gun planted in his chest, and the words "Come no further!"

"Nonsense! Why, Barbara!"

"Dux, is that really you?"

"Of course. What is the matter?"

"I thought the driver might come in and want some beer, they always do on a wet night."

"How can you be so foolish? We are dead tired. Josline had better have something hot and go to bed out of the damp and wet."

"Ah! starved? They always starve you at a rout; that comes of going out." Here Miss Barbara brought the gun down with a bang and a click of the lock, that made Mrs. Turgoose scream slightly. "Turgoose!" said her mistress, angrily, "how often have I told you to-night that a gun not loaded can't possibly go off? I assure you, Giles—I dare say you thought the hall smelt horrible, this foolish woman thought fit to go into hysterics when I brought out the gun, and I was obliged to burn feathers to bring her round."

"I don't wonder," said Mr. Fairfax; "that gun looks deadly, and I believe it *is* loaded, for not long ago, I was going round the wilderness with young Watt, and I know I loaded it then, and——" Here he walked up to Miss Barbara, who, holding the gun up by the stock, shook it well, as a dog would a rat. "Take care!" he shouted, loudly. Mrs. Turgoose had sunk on the floor, dropping the lantern with a bang, and drawn her scarlet drapery over her head with shrieks of terror. Josline turned a little pale;

but Mr. Fairfax rescued the weapon, and said, after an examination, " No, fairly discharged. Now, do go to bed. Just come to my room for a moment, Josline, you know where that air of Paêr's is ? "

" She must not sit up," said Miss Barbara. " I shall come and see she does not." She stalked on in front, looking a very spectre, her tall night-cap making night hideous. Miss Barbara had no respect whatever for people's "feelings," and said that "You were always yourself, no matter how you were dressed,"—a curious assertion, when thought over.

" What are you going to do with that gun, Dux ? " said she, when the piece had been found, and the uncle was saying good night to Josline.

" Keep it here," he answered, smiling. " I don't want my lungs blown out, or rather in."

" It's a very heavy gun," said Miss Barbara, meditatively. " I think it must be loaded."

" No, no, happily it's not; now good night." He was tuning his violin already.

Miss Barbara was so accustomed to hear the sounds penetrating faintly and dreamily all hours of the night, that she didn't think of objecting to his nocturnal harmonies.

" I shall come in whilst you are undressing," she said to Josline, and accordingly she sat on the small white bed.

" How did they all look, child ? You don't speak," she said at last, sharply, for she was really dying to know. " What did you think of it all ? "

Josline was holding her slender arms high over her head, and said in a tired, faint voice, "There was a great deal of light, and some nice music, and they danced; it was rather like the Watteau in the den."

"I don't think you will care to go out again, much," said Miss Barbara, curiously.

"I will do just what you and Dux like, always," said Josline.

"Well, you are a good child; but Josline, you know, the other night——" She stopped.

Josline turned slowly round and faced her, not speaking, but with a curiously blended expression of intense terror, and yet intense determination.

Miss Barbara frowned. "You should not look like that, child," she said, sternly. "I should never have looked like that at my mother."

Josline began to tremble nervously, then she suddenly clasped her hands together, and held them out to her aunt, trying to speak. At last she said—

"Oh, please, please aunt Barbara—*please* don't say anything, I am so tired, and I do mean to do what you would like, I do mean to try; but, but—*please* aunt Barbara, I can't bear to hear anything about—about mamma."

"Child! I loved your mother," said Miss Barbara, rather moved, in spite of her standing no "feelings," for if she had any leniency in her nature, it was for this fragile creature, whom she had seen reared under their roof. "There, there, I will say no more to-night; you are tired, as you say. But don't get up to feed those doves so early in these cold mornings, my dear, and do try and not wander about the lanes so long by yourself. And if you would help Turgoose to darn the damask table napkins, I think you would do it more neatly than Phœbe, and I would lend you a ball to do it over, so that you need not prick those small, thin fingers. Now, good night, and if you are afraid of—of anything, why, come to my room; or perhaps you would like to have the white puss to sleep here. No? Well, I will go now. There, kiss me, like a good child; you know your old aunt is really fond of you, in spite of your going about with other people."

A little bewildered, Josline gave the required kiss, and Miss Barbara left her in peace. As she stalked along to her room, she muttered to herself, "What a delicate look anxiety gives that child! Ha! hum! I don't think she had better go out any more. Anyhow, she will have more time to mend those napkins; the pattern of Pharoah's head is really quite going out."

CHAPTER XXIV.

ALL night long the rain came down in blinding torrents; the wind roared and drove the waters before it;
both rivers had burst their banks; the "head" came
thundering; birds and beasts cowered, with fur and
feathers rough and drenched. Twice before the dawn,
Sir Philip rose to watch from his window the conservatory, which absolutely rocked, a circumstance which
probably saved it. It was a wild and fearful night,
but at eight o'clock in the morning wind and rain
ceased suddenly, so suddenly that the pause was
almost more alarming than the storm and whirl had
been.

By nine o'clock Hermione was dressed and out.
Everything was drenched and dripping. There was an
undefined restlessness and excitement in the movement
of the boughs; tiny streams of water still raced and
tore along the gravel walks on the terraces. Great
drops fell on her head, she could hardly have told from
where; the clouds were rending above her, leaving

huge fissures between them, through which shone soft gleams of a pale, stormy, sea-green; adventurous birds were blown widely out of their course; no one was in sight as she stood for a few seconds undecided, on the steps of the portico, looking right and left. Behind her was a faint smell of burnt wax, singed leaves, crushed flowers, old damask; before her a wild, breezy fragrance of all things washed pure of any scent, save that of their own nature. The air tossed her fair hair in wild tendrils round her pale, grave face, and tinged with delicate rose the soft oval of her cheek. She had a way of carrying her soft beaver hat in her hand when her head throbbed, as it did now, and she went down the steps and along the drive to the left, with her hat in one hand and her stick in the other.

The exultant beating of the wet pure air was like strong wings urging her on, down under the pines to the mere, which was tossing and foaming and fretting its banks away like an impetuous, ill-trained heart. She went quickly along, meaning to cross the "head" and come home again by the hollow way. The swans were on the bank, pluming themselves and hissing softly. Broken branches, massed leaves, mud, weeds torn up by the roots, strewed the path. A squirrel darted across her path; the little moor-hens swam out with a rustle. On she went; the air allured her like a presence—soothing and loving and silent; it pressed against her, it wound her heavy dress round her, it bore her along.

She reached the "head" at last, and stood on the bank, close to the bridge, looking at the water. It certainly was what Allan had said, "coming down most awful;" one wide, blinding sheet of foam and fury. The roar was tremendous. She stood looking on, and back in a flash came the memory of the day she had stood there by Colonel Myddleton and he had said, "I should think you liked everything with a dash of conquering and danger in it." And her answer, "Not for the mere reason of conquering, I think; but when everything is smooth in one's life, one does sometimes wonder whether one would have strength if it were necessary."

She lent over now, watching the frightful turbulence and unrest of the water, then looked on and saw how smooth it was further in the pool, where it only fled away with a great rush, sweep, and depth in unconscious and tremendous strength. "It really is like life," she thought. "After all the struggle comes the deeper knowledge of how to endure. He looks as though he had been through fire and come out knowing how to bear it, whilst I——" She looked up, to sweep the spray from her face, and saw him coming down the hollow way. Her heart gave a tremendous bound and then seemed to stand perfectly still. Then her resolution was taken, the next instant she was on the bridge. At this moment he saw her. She saw him throw up his arms and heard him, even in that unearthly din, call something to her. She smiled and

held out one hand, and—the next minute the bridge
gave way, with a cracking sound, and she disappeared
in the whelming and triumphant water !

He didn't utter a sound after one shriek of piercing
agony ; but he tore his coat and waistcoat off as he
rushed madly down the bank. He knew she would,
she must come into the pool ; to have jumped in
where the bridge fell was only immediate death for
them both. In his heart was such terrible anguish
as only the strong can know. In those few seconds
his whole life rose before him. He was entirely
speechless, almost pulseless, all his energies braced,
as they had been several times in his life, to *wait* and
gather for the coming struggle. There was an awful
silence in his heart, wrung through and through as it
was, in which echoed only the cry of " God ! " So profound and penetrating was the tension, outward utterance would have slain him. He shivered like one in
extreme and mortal fear.

At last, yes, there came her head, pale, with the hair
sweeping over it. In he plunged. A fierce struggle
to reach her ; yes—no—yes, he held her, he had
her ; and then for the bank. He had to drift ; fiercely
he spat out the foam and surge, the slime, the foul wash
of weeds and mud. He was praying now, and, God
knows, he wanted help. Her heavy dress was heavier
with wet, it clung round him ; her hair undone, coiled
round his throat—her beautiful, heavy, silken hair—
and nearly strangled him ; her head lay heavy on his

shoulder and kept down his breathing; but they were
not far from the bank, the very rush of the water
helped them. He was a magnificent swimmer. Once
he raised his voice in a vain attempt to "Coo-ee!" but
his voice died; he was too exhausted. Something
struck his arm down and both heads went under, but
they came up again; he was nearly blind. Then—
was it shouts or was the water coming in his ears?
One desperate effort! What happened? He was no
longer swimming, he was floating. He heard, surely
he heard, a voice saying, softly, "Let go!" Then
darkness, dense darkness—death——

No, not death. Death is not so lightly come by.

   *   *   *   *   *

They all walked up to the house, except Hermione,
who was carried, hurriedly, by four men—insensible?
dead? Who knew? Not Colonel Myddleton, who,
though he walked straight on, leaving a track of slime
and foam behind him, was led by Sir Philip, held by
the arm, staring straight before him like one walking
in his sleep; he had received a blow from the boat-
hook on being dragged out, and had been slightly
stunned. He was still praying in a dead kind of
hollow whisper, and as the words fell from his blue,
cold lips they sounded almost horrible. No one else
spoke; you only heard the panting of the gardeners,
as they went as fast as they could go, at a kind of
double, up the hollow way. As they turned the corner they were met by two grooms, on horseback,

laying their horses to the ground, in search of a doctor, having been warned by a runner. The hall door stood wide open; in the hall a group of terrified servants.

"This way," said Lady Dunstable. "Lady Clinton is in Miss St. John's room."

Tramp, tramp across the marble floor. Sir Philip paused; Colonel Myddleton nearly dragged his arm out of the socket, still going mechanically forwards. The butler and two footmen caught him, and pushed a chair towards him, on a sign from their master.

"Let me go—on—on," he said, struggling.

"Stop a moment, Duke, for God's sake," said Sir Philip, nearly exhausted himself. "Sit down for a second, my dear fellow. Oh, it's awful! Brandy!"

"Here," said Gladys's voice, and she held out a glassful, with her small hand shaking. "He *is* so wet! after the fever!" she ventured to add.

"Yes, yes. There, drink this! We must get him to bed. Order the big bath to be got ready."

"It is, Phil; it's waiting; Robert has everything ready in his room."

"Come then; now, Duke. Here, take my arm."

Colonel Myddleton still stood in the middle of the hall, staring straight in front of him, with that vague, awful intensity of a corpse.

"Come, my dear fellow, do come," said Sir Philip. "Oh, Freeman, here you are! Make him move, for God's sake, make him move; I feel quite sick at his going on so."

"Come, Myddleton, come along," said Quarl, quietly but firmly. "I want to know all about it; come to your room."

Suddenly Colonel Myddleton turned round and covering his face with his hands, he burst into tears.

"Go away, everybody!" said Quarl, with an angry stamp of his foot.

The servants went. Gladys ran into the library and shut the door. Sir Philip shook from head to foot.

"All right now, Clinton," said Quarl. "Come along!"

      *   *   *   *   *

"Well, what do the doctors say?"

Sir Vere, Quarl, Robert, and Gladys stood in the library.

Sir Philip, who had just come in, walked to the window. "She has just come round. They know nothing, but——" He stopped; he was choking.

"Philip!" Gladys was clinging round his neck, sobbing, she couldn't help it, poor child.

He struggled for composure. "They think the shock—I don't understand—the heart is somehow affected. They fear—paralysis——" He stopped; there was a dead horrified silence. "I can't—I can't —I *can't* tell Myddleton; he's nearly out of his mind now; they say he must be kept quite quiet, I——"

"I heard," said Colonel Myddleton's voice in the doorway. "Then there's nothing for it but to wait."

He stood still in his shirt sleeves, wringing wet, with a ghastly grey pallor on his face. "I have waited before," he said, with a strange quivering smile, looking round in each hushed awe-struck face. "I had better have waited a little longer, and let her die at once."

"Duke!" Sir Philip was holding his arm, choking back his tears.

"I think," he said, slowly, "my arm is broken. I will go to my room now, if you will bring the surgeon."

*   *   *   *   *

It was in the evening. The house had settled down again, the London doctor had left, the country doctor was to sleep in the house. Lady Clinton and Gladys were still hard at work writing to put off the fancy ball for the following evening. Lady Dunstable was sitting in a large chair by the fire, looking sorrowfully into it. Mina Thorold, grave, for perhaps the first time in her life, sat at her knee with her hands linked. At last Lady Clinton gave a great sigh, and pushing the writing materials together, she said—

"I think that's the last, Gladys; do come and rest."

They both got up and came to the fire, very silent, and Gladys trembling a good deal. Lady Clinton put her arm round her.

"I wish you would tell me, Lady Clinton, how was

it all done ? " said Lady Dunstable, sliding into idioms
as she did when deeply thoughtful.

"I really hardly know, Phil is so confused, and
can't speak about it, scarcely ; but he said Allan came
to him and said he didn't think the bridge safe, and
supposing any one crossed and fell in ?   So Philip
thought they had better go down and see, and if it
were dangerous they would fasten boards across so
that no one could go over ; and he and Allan, and five
of the men went down, and when they were in the
hollow way they thought—they thought they heard a
cry, and—and—they ran, and they saw." Lady
Clinton stopped, crying bitterly, and hid her face
on Gladys's shoulder.

"Ah ! yes, I see my dear, I see.   Well," after a
pause, " and how are they now ? "

"They've set his arm ; it must have been struck
by the timbers of the bridge, they think, and he is
very quiet and calm, and they hope no fever will come
on.   Philip says his head has swollen up frightfully
where they struck him with the boat-hook, but that is
a good thing, I believe, and he doesn't seem to want
to speak, he hasn't asked anything at all.   When Phil
goes in, he just says, ' She's just the same,' and then
he closes his eyes again, but—but—Phil says he looks
as though his heart was broken."

There was a little pause ; no one spoke.   Lady
Clinton cried quietly.   Then Miss Thorold said—

"And how is she ? "

" She is in a kind of stupor, but they think that is the best thing at present. Sir Henry is coming down again the day after to-morrow if we don't send before ; he says the only thing is to wait, time will show, there is nothing to be done. Oh ! it's horrible," she said, breaking into a wail, and giving way entirely. " It's horrible ! I love her so, and there is nothing to be done, poor darling ! "

" Dieu sait ! " said old Lady Dunstable. Then she added, " We are going away to-morrow, my dear ; the house ought to be very quiet, you know, and everybody will have plenty to do. Sir Vere says he will accompany us up to town."

" Oh, no ! " said Lady Clinton, piteously. " It will be so lonely." She looked almost frightened.

" It will be best, my dear, really," said the old lady, kindly and gently holding out her hands. " We will come back to you in the summer, if you will let us."

The truth was that, kindly and gentle as she was, the old French lady had the most intense terror of death, and she firmly believed that one, if not both of the " poor drowned ones " would die.

Just then the gentlemen came in, and Robert Watt came up to say good night ; he was going home. Gladys went with him into the hall to find his coat.

" Robert," she said, " how sadly it has all ended ! "

" Yes, indeed," he answered, with a shiver, " he's awfully bad, you know, Gladys ; you should have seen his arm, ugh!—a horrible compound fracture, sticking through the skin; and he never said a word all the time, for fear they should think of him and not her. The agonies he must have gone through! He fainted twice when they were setting it."

"Robert, you didn't see him cry, though; that was most awful," said Gladys. "I never saw a man cry before."

"Ah! poor fellow, how horribly ashamed he must be!" said Robert, sympathetically. "It was the counter shock, of course. How horribly ashamed I should be! I remember once I got a most tremendous cropper over a post and rail, and how I got home I don't know. Redskin took me, and when I got in and got off my horse, I sobbed and cried like a baby. I *was* ashamed, I could have thrashed everybody," he ended, his cheeks tingling at the recollection. "Don't ever tell anybody, Gladys."

"No, of course not; but I don't think he knew, he was quite odd after that, Quarl said."

"Well, perhaps not. It's altogether a bad look-out for them both. Poor Miss St. John, she was as nearly dead as possible; fancy owing your life to any one, eh, White Cat?"

"I should not mind, I think, if it was any one like Colonel Myddleton," said Gladys. "He is such a grand, kind man."

"Well, he's saved lots of people before now in the Mutiny, and killed lots, too," said Robert, meditating.

"I think I shouldn't mind saving people's lives now and then. Well, I must go, I hear the dog-cart coming round; it's altogether rather sad. I say, Gladys, I am awfully glad it wasn't you! What should I have done? Just think!"

Gladys smiled faintly. For one wicked moment she almost wished it had been herself if he would have cared so much. He was holding her hands and looking down in her face, and he said, very softly—

"I should have been sorry. You look so pale to-night, Gladys, do go to bed soon. I do wish you'd smoke; now don't you think you might try one little pull? it makes one feel so comfortable."

She shook her head, she felt too sad and anxious to carry on the joke; but he wasn't joking entirely.

"It's a great pity Gabriel Vannier went down to Old Court," he said. "I don't believe you'll ever get painted now, Pussy; and I had so set my heart on your being done in the hood, and the scroll out of your mouth."

"Don't Bob," she said, half crying, for his words brought back the merry, dear, happy past, and now everything seemed so sad and dreary. She was thoroughly worn out, too, with the past excitement and bustle; and now the exceeding quiet and gloom of the house weighed her down. They were standing on felt, the whole house was laid down with it. The bells were all blocked—such perfect quiet was considered necessary.

"My dear little Cat," he said, tenderly. "You do look so sad! but you must come down to the village, and do go to Old Court, and Mr. Fairfax will play to you——"

She interrupted him with a startled, nervous look. "Oh! Robert, don't. I feel as though I never wanted to hear music again. I keep on hearing the Lohengrin, over and over and over, and seeing his face; it was like a kind of foreshadowing of it all; he dying, and Hermione being the angel, and Death close to them. Oh! it's horrible!" and she hid her face against his breast, for he still held her hands. "Do you know, he looked just like that this morning when he came in here," she murmured, burying her face lower and lower.

"My darling," said the young man, tenderly. "You are worn out; do go to bed. Good night, poor little thing!" and he softly kissed her hair—so softly, she hardly felt it.

It was the first time he had ever kissed her gravely, in comfort; though often in fun he had kissed her hand. It broke her down quite—she began to sob and cry, and he was in great distress. But the hall door opened to show him the dog-cart was there, and she went quietly away.

"It's an awful ending," he thought, as he tucked himself in. "How upset she is! I do wish girls smoked. What a gentle, loving little thing she is! Well, it is horrible altogether! I am glad Freeman is going to stop; it will be somebody for Philip."

CHAPTER XXV.

IT was a few weeks after the accident. Colonel
Myddleton was up and about again, with his arm
still, of course, in a sling and useless. The enforced
rest had done him good in some ways, though the
great anxiety about Hermione had tended to diminish
his rapid recovery. He was a man who had gone
through desperate things in the way of wounds and
escapes, and thought comparatively little of his
broken arm, though it was a very ugly wound, and
not quick in the healing, and at times he suffered
frightfully; but he never said anything about it, but
just bore the pain as he best might, going away by
himself when no longer able to bear up without its
being apparent that he was suffering.

Hermione had not yet seen any one but Lady
Clinton and Gladys, and they only once ; the slightest
excitement or exertion brought on fainting fits, which
were of all things the most to be avoided. Sir Henry
said it was the shock, and would, he hoped, wear off

in time, but that the action of the heart had been so
lowered by the shock, the long immersion, and the
thorough chill, that it would probably be months, a
year, even more, before she really recovered. She
was worn to a complete shadow, and looked literally
"all eyes." Her hair had not been cut off, though,
and hung round her in all its beauty; making her face
look so sweet and soft and small, as Quarl had said
it did the night of the tableaux. She had never
mentioned any one by name yet. She had, indeed,
a very confused idea of the whole occurrence, and a
kind of nervous dread of trying to aid her memory.

Matters in the village went on much as usual.
Gabriel Vannier had gone back to London with a
most lovely sketch of Josline's head for his picture.
And if all went well, he was to come down in the
early spring to Charteriss, and do a picture of Gladys
and Lady Clinton together.

Although Miss Barbara watched Josline with lynx
eyes, nothing very remarkable occurred to strengthen
her daily-growing conviction, that Josline was taking
her own line, and was gradually drifting from under
her guidance and counsel. Robert came very little
to Old Court, though most of his rides and walks
led somehow past the house. He could not keep
away; stronger and stronger became the longing
that drew and urged him to move in any line which
might, by any possible means, end in seeing Josline.
Yet in these weeks he had only seen her twice, and

each time with others. Was it really the case that
she carefully avoided her old haunts? or was it only
unlucky chance that was against their meeting? On
Sunday mornings he always contrived now to be
within sight of the parsonage gate, when he thought
she would bring the flowers to her godfather; but
these heavy rains had destroyed the few remaining
flowers, and Josline came no more. He was con-
stantly up at Charteriss, and saw a good deal of
Gladys, but Gladys was going up to London to stay
with Lady Dunstable for change, and then even that
indirect means of hearing of Josline would be gone.

He became so restless and easily irritated, or so
moody and silent, that old General Watt could not
divine what had taken the boy, as he still thought of
him and spoke of him; and the father began to
ponder whether really it would not be as well that he
should allow him to try for some further employment
than looking after the few cows and sheep at the
Red House Farm. Mr. Crosbie had several times
lately started the idea, "That all young things, men
and mice, and such small deer, should have *work*, my
dear sir. It makes their eyes bright, their coats
glossy,"—("and a tailor's bill then!" from the
General, testily)—"and their appetites healthy,"—
("and a butcher's bill then!")—"and it's an infal-
lible cure for bad temper, gout, and dyspepsia."

Colonel Myddleton's arm did not heal satisfac-
torily, and the fever and ague still clung to him so

persistently that the doctors insisted on his wintering abroad, and starting at once for the South. Their decision was first made known to him about two months after the accident. In the beginning he would not hear of it, but at length, when they told him that it was his only chance of complete recovery, and that otherwise he might, in all probability would, remain an invalid for life, he decided to go.

He was in London at the time, and after the consultation he went for a long, lonely, cold, and damp stroll in the Park, which of course was not likely to help him towards recovery. Then he went home and wrote a letter to Sir Philip and one to Lady Clinton. Both letters were answered by return of post, begging him to come down to Charteriss at once. He went on the following day but one. Lady Clinton met him at the station, and they drove home almost in silence through the dusky quiet lanes.

"She does not know you are coming, we are only going to tell her to-morrow," said Lady Clinton, "as we fear the least excitement might still give her a sleepless night."

"Is she still so weak?" he said, in a quiet, level tone.

"Yes, but much, much better. Sir Henry had come down by the very mail that brought your letter. We asked him about your seeing her, and he said on the whole he thought it might do her good, if she did not know of it too long beforehand."

"I am glad of that."

"You know she has been talking of you lately, and of the accident, too; she does not know much about it, though; it's quite odd to see how little she knows. She knows you saved her, and that is about all."

"There is not much to know in that," he answered.

"She thinks so," answered Lady Clinton, a little vaguely as to sense and grammar.

Then they were silent again. It was very cold, but the horses went fast; and though Colonel Myddleton was longing to be there, for the night to be over, to have seen her once more for the last time, as he kept on asseverating to himself, still he almost wished the drive to be prolonged, too, for he knew that he should soon be going back over the same ground as fast—from her. He thought over again that first night they had spent together at Charteriss—how he had believed her to be married, then been quickly undeceived, then remembered he was no longer free, dared no longer love her; how he had gone out and walked up and down, and up and down, said he would go away and yet had not gone. On the whole, now, he was glad he had stayed, and he would act fairly and honourably at last and tell her all, if she wished, if even she would see him; perhaps she would not wish to do so when the time came.

But she did wish.

It was Christmas Eve; a bright, beautiful, mild day. She was lying on the sofa, in the morning-room, doing nothing, looking a little vaguely and mournfully out of the window, across at the conservatory, which ran out at right-angles to the house. It was a cheerful room, full of pleasant books and pictures and flowers; and the window near her sofa was open, and you could hear a robin singing close to it, in a weeping holly, with a loud and beautifully rounded whistle. Lady Clinton came in, lifted the shawl that was lying over her feet a little more to the left, and then said, in a voice which slightly trembled, "Hermione, how do you feel to-day?"

"Very well, thank you, dear. You are all so good and kind to me. I was just thinking I ought to be going home again; I am quite strong now!" and she gave a little quiet laugh, as she tried to lift the heavy Indian wrap with her wasted hands, and failed.

"Don't, don't talk of going away!" said Lady Clinton, in an agitated voice. "You are much better, I know, but we can't spare you yet. Some one else is going away—I mean Colonel Myddleton, and he is come down here to ask how you are. Would you like to see him?"

The colour flew up to her very brow, then faded even from her lips, leaving her ashy pale.

"Yes—now—at once—alone," she said, in a voice so faint that Dorothy hardly heard her, but alarmed though she was, Lady Clinton knew quite well what to do. She poured out some drops given her by Sir Henry, and put them to Hermione's lips. And in a few seconds she said, much in her usual tone, "I should like to see him now, please."

The door opened and closed; they were alone.

Neither spoke; he came forward and took the two hands she held out to him; the last time he had touched her they had both been at the very gate of death.

He was the palest now; a burning colour stained her cheeks a vivid and beautiful hue, and her eyes glittered with excitement. She spoke first.

"You have been very ill," she said, slowly, looking at him solemnly and sorrowfully. "And all to save my life; and I have never even thanked you ! "

"You have thanked me," he said, in a low tone, " by living."

She said nothing in answer. Under the heavy shawls he *saw* her heart beating. He thought her face had grown smaller, softer, and sweeter than ever. She lifted one hand and pushed back a heavy mass of hair that had fallen forward on her trying to rise on his entrance, and her lips quivered. He, too, was speechless. How could he go away and leave her like this? He had not counted on seeing her look like this, somehow. She was trying to say something, he saw, and he would not speak. As last she said, in a broken gasp—

" Do you care, then? Are you glad I am here? "

"My God!"

The two words that had been wrung from him the night he had first seen her. He found no others; in his beating throat, on his dry lips, no other sounds would come. He was kneeling by her now. She lifted one hand and laid it on his shoulder.

"Hush!" she said, as though to still the convulsive trembling that shook him, for he had not said any more. "I had wanted to say something to you. I have tried—to live—for' that. *I believe you*. You know you wanted to know." She said it in a whisper, and held him off a little, trying to see his face. "It would have been dreadful to die—unanswered," she ended.

"Hermione," he said, as every muscle in his face contracted, "I am bound by my word of honour to—another!"

Her eyes dilated, then closed; her hand relaxed; he didn't attempt to clasp it; he thought she was dying. The beating of her heart was frightful, then it seemed to stop; but he saw the pulsation go slowly and unevenly through her whole frame. He didn't dare to move; he felt as though the movement of a finger would kill her. The ashen colour spread over her face and over her throat, and she lay quite still for a few seconds. In his heart he said, "I have killed her." But life returned; she opened her eyes again; they looked dim and did not seem to see. Then she said, in a voice like that of a person miles away—

"I believe you.—God bless you!—Go!"

He stood up; he felt he must leave her; she had said it. He dropped her lifeless hand gently; it slid down and hung against the couch. She was looking at him intensely, with an awful look of yearning heart-agony. He went quietly to the door; there he stood. He could not go so. A strangled sob shook him; and yet—for her sake—he turned back. He did not touch her; but he stretched his hands out towards her, and he said—

"I swear to you, before the Almighty God, I believed you were married; and I did it for the best!"

"I believe you!" she said; and then he saw she had fainted.

He sprang to her and raised her head; he thought she was dead.

"Hermione!" he said. "Hermione! my love! my darling! God and my soul only know how I love you!"

He did not attempt to rouse her in any other way. For a few seconds he knelt holding her so, and looking at her. Then a wild terror of—he knew not what, a feeling like murder, came over him. He laid her down, and rushed for help, meeting Lady Clinton in the doorway.

When he heard that she was recovered, and that it had only been one of her bad fainting attacks, he said good-bye to them all, and started just in time to catch the up-train.

CHAPTER XXVI.

OLD COURT was quiet again. The lily's heart hung
in its ebony and tortoise-shell frame in Mr. Fairfax's
den ; and sometimes, when he was playing quietly to
himself, her uncle found his eyes fixed on Josline's
picture.

Mr. Crosbie came as usual on " odd evenings," as
he called them, " to squeak on the fiddle," tease Miss
Barbara, and pet Josline, " the only godchild he had
ever had, the only child God Almighty had ever given
him." Josline would put his favourite chair for him,
prepare his tea, and have always a spray of some
shrub, or flower-bud, for him. There had been no
more trouble with musically inclined mice, and Josline had sewn together the torn canzonets, and blotted
in neatly the partially erased notes.

It was well into spring now. Nan Partridge was
learning the saddest of all lessons—that the dead die
quickly, in the gentlest way ; for the myrtle had
hardly taken root on her baby's grave before there
was a new hope for her.

Gabriel wrote occasionally to Robert, saying that the picture was getting on well, and that he hoped it might be finished by the early summer.

"Robert has been talking to Phil again about going away and getting something to do," said Lady Clinton, one day, coming into the morning-room.

Hermione, who was writing, looked up with a start.

"Now, that is odd!" she said, brightly. "I was just thinking of him, and writing about him. Old Mr. Doon is going to give up work altogether, and I ought to have appointed some one long ago to help him; but being ill, I forgot about it. I heard again to-day, though, and I really must settle. Do you think, Dorothy, that Mr. Watt would accept it?"

"Oh, my dear! how delightful!" said Lady Clinton, excitedly. "That would be nice. Why, it wouldn't be so very far away; and under you, too. Do let me go and tell Philip!"

"Shall I come, too?"

"No. I'll go and fetch him!" and Lady Clinton literally ran out of the room.

Hermione sat still, looking out of the window, which stood wide open. It was soft and warm; the crocuses and snowdrops starred the border, and periwinkles ran in and out in beautiful gleaming lines. The window faced up the lime avenue; a fine tachamahac tree scented all the air with its bursting, gummy buds; and, somehow, the fragrance carried Hermione's thought far, far away, to Southern France. She seemed to see the waving palms, the silver grey of the olives, with their lacy leaves; the tall iris blood-red sceptres, or standing like spears of molten metal of purest white; the geranium hedges, the weird-looking cacti, the soft-coloured young eucalypti trees; the clouded emerald and turquoise of the water deepening into mystic purple, almost black under the rocks; the tall heath, one sheet of silver blossom, under the fragrant pines; and the melancholy cypresses, like shrouded statues, in the sloping gardens. A hand seemed laid on her quickly beating heart; her eyes filled with tears. What was he doing all these weeks and months? There had been no word or sign. Somehow she had thought, had fancied, he would write and explain; and yet, would it have been like him to do so? If she only knew the rights of it. The worst pain was not knowing how his after-life might be affected by it, by the promise that held him, held his honour. She had thought and thought over it all these weeks and months, but could form no sort of idea as to what it could possibly be. Something that did not make him happy; something that gave that grave, absent look to his face, that cut that sharp, grey shadow on his temples, that drew such an intense look round his mouth and eyes. She felt sure that though he would abide by his word to the very death, it was nothing that could make him happy.

She dropped her pen, and folded her hands in

front of her. " What is happiness? " she pondered. " Is anybody happy? I suppose the great thing is to be content; you can be that without being happy, though not happy without being content. I wonder what the most perfect form of earthly happiness would be. I suppose being able to make others so. How well I remember his saying, down by the water that day, that one was never happy long, because one didn't know all. And now, it seems to me, that if I did know all, I should be happy; no, not happy, perhaps, but more content." She lost herself in thought. " Well, I must wait—— "

The door opened, and Lady Clinton and Sir Philip came in together. Hermione rose.

" Now, let us all sit down and be snug," said Dorothy; "Hermione in the big chair, Phil on the sofa, and let us talk."

" I was going to propose asking Mr. Watt if he would like to become my agent," said Hermione, a little nervously, feeling as though she were committing a slight impertinence in proposing anything of the sort to Sir Philip, for his cousin. " You know there is a very pretty house, a small farm, and the income is five hundred a year."

Sir Philip opened his eyes very wide, but made no remark; but Dorothy gave a little shriek, and said—

" Five hundred a year? why, that would be wealth! "

" I thought perhaps he wouldn't mind trying it;

and then, perhaps General Watt would like to look after the shooting. It used to be first-rate in poor Mark's time, and, of course, they won't care for a lady," said Hermione, with a little quiver; "but if General Watt would be kind enough to see that they didn't neglect it too much, it might get up again."

"Ha!" from Sir Philip.

There was a little silence. Dorothy looked at him anxiously, and pinched his arm now and then. Hermione sat motionless, her head resting on her hand.

"If you don't think it enough, shall I say seven hundred a year?" ventured Hermione.

"Certainly not," from Sir Philip, bluntly. "He isn't worth it."

"Philip!" from the indignant wife.

"Now, look here, Miss St. John. Bob Watt is as good a fellow as lives, but whether he won't get the whole of your affairs into inextricable confusion in a few months—well! As to the General, he is a meddling old woman, though he can shoot very well; but, on the whole, it's an awful risk."

"One must risk something in everything. Mr. Watt is just, and I should think not above being taught, is he?"

"No, there he's safe enough; but then he does such idiotic things, only about his own interests, I mean. Well, perhaps, after all, he would be all the more careful about other people's."

"Then you wouldn't mind my offering it to him, anyhow?"

"I should think not, indeed. But I'll speak seriously to him; it may be the making of him. It's very good of you. If he's under Doon for eight months, he'll do, I think."

"And how about asking him? would you mind?" said Hermione, shyly.

"Not at all, if you wish; but why shouldn't you and Dor drive round that way this afternoon, and see the General?"

"Oh!" said Hermione, crimson and pale, by turns; "I am rather afraid."

Sir Philip laughed. "I'll tell you what, Miss St. John. He'll be so polite, you won't know what to do to get away, that's all. He came up here yesterday about Bob, who has been rather moody and short in his temper lately, and his father is finding out at last that my young gentleman is getting a little too much out of discipline, I fancy."

"And no wonder, with that old bore," said Lady Clinton, sympathetically.

"It's funny though that being in love is so trying to the temper!" said Sir Philip. "Was I horribly odious, Dor, when I was in love?"

"Well, not to me! I dare say Gladys found you a trial. Mine has come since," said his wife. "I always think the so-called easy-tempered people are the most difficult to get on with."

"Why?" said Sir Philip, laughing.

"Because, of course, they never *are* out of temper,

and if anything goes wrong, it must be your fault, and that aggravates you, and makes everything worse."

"You goose!" said her husband. "What a good thing it is that you don't live with Quarl!"

"Yes, indeed! Now I never did see him out of temper; he always controls himself, and only says cutting things."

"Quarl in love would be an appalling spectacle!" said Sir Philip, solemnly.

Hermione, who had been sitting silent all this time, said, "I couldn't imagine Mr. Freeman in such a condition."

Sir Philip and Dorothy looked at each other. Sir Philip began to laugh; Lady Clinton pinched his arm vehemently. He began to speak, and then stopped, then began again—

"I say, I heard from Myddleton to-day; he is getting on all right. Now, there is a fellow who will never fall in love to his dying day."

Lady Clinton had never made up her mind as to whether Colonel Myddleton was in love with Hermione or not, though of course he ought to be, as he had saved her life. She looked keenly at Miss St. John now, with all a woman's quiet perception as to change of colour, or intonation of voice; but Hermione's delicate colour never varied; and as she did not speak no change of voice betrayed her. She remained looking stedfastly out of the window, and Sir Philip went on—

"Awfully dangerous his going out to Cannes; everybody marries out there ; nothing else to do."

"Then he won't," said Lady Clinton ; "he never does what other people do."

"Ah ! he'll be caught some day. How do we know what——" Sir Philip stopped short. "The worst is, that talking to you, Dorothy, I never know when to stop," he said, good-humouredly, getting up and walking to the door. "Well ! I suppose you'll go and tell the General this afternoon? I've kept Broom waiting all this time, about the chestnut." He went off, whistling.

Lady Clinton got up, came to the window, near which Hermione was sitting, and leaning against the shutter, she looked out, and said, "I do wonder about Colonel Myddleton, too, don't you, Hermione ? "

"I don't see any good in wondering," was the quiet, matter-of-fact answer, but Hermione's heart was beating quickly. Ah ! how she did wonder ! Yet a curious thrill of subdued satisfaction ran through her, too. She felt convinced that she knew more about him than any one else did ; though how little that was !

"I should like to know, though," persisted Dorothy. "There are not many people one cares to know about—I mean to know the ins and outs of their lives; but there is something about Colonel Myddleton which makes you feel that he must have gone through so much, so quietly ; even when he is talking of quite common things, you feel as though he was enduring something, there is something so unsatisfied in his expression; don't you think so, Ione?"

"Well, I don't know; I dare say he often thinks of all he has gone through."

"He is so quiet. I often think, do you know, Hermione——" Lady Clinton paused, for Miss St. John raised her head, and fixed her beautiful, clear, grave eyes on her friend's face. "Don't look so entirely above everything and everybody, Ione," said she, kneeling down by her quickly, and putting her arms round her. "I don't care, though, how you look, I *will* say it, there! I often think you were made for each other, and how happy you might be." Lady Clinton bent backwards, and looked in Hermione's face, half-defiantly, half-fearfully.

If anything, Miss St. John grew a shade paler, but she said quietly, "What a pity we did not think so too, Dorothy! that would have completed the idea, wouldn't it?"

"You will never care for any one, Ione," said Lady Clinton, sorrowfully. "It is such a pity."

"'The pity of it, Iago; the pity of it!'" quoted Hermione.

"Ah! you needn't mock me, Hermione; you, too, will be sorry, some day."

Miss St. John was silent for a few seconds, stroking Dorothy's hair. At last Lady Clinton spoke again—

"Do you—is it that you find it so difficult to make up your mind?" she said, timidly.

"I don't think it is difficult to make up one's mind about great things, Dorothy."

"Don't you?" said Lady Clinton, surprised.

"No ; they must be right or wrong. I mean, you see it at once. The difficulty is in small things, where it really matters very little, but where, perhaps, you would like to please everybody."

"Well, that is a funny idea. Why not please yourself, then, in little things?"

"Because," said Hermione, gravely, "'every little makes a mickle,' my dear Dorothy; and if you begin like that, why, it makes all great things difficult."

Lady Clinton sighed. "You live such a noble, impossible life, Ione," she said. "I do wish, oh! I *do* wish——"

"You were not so foolish!" finished Hermione. "Come, and let us go after General Watt. If you only knew the fright I am in; I have no moral courage whatever."

"Why, your hands are quite cold!" said Dorothy, laughing.

"Yes; I wish it were over!"

CHAPTER XXVII.

WHEN Hermione was well wrapped up in furs, Sir
Philip came to put her in the carriage. She was still
extremely weak and shaky. It was the first time she
had been out, and the fresh, sweet spring air seemed
to make her quite faint. As they drove along she
watched the first green glamour coming on the hedgerows, with here and there an adventurous spray,
stretching forth delicate pink fingers to test the
warmth of the sun; or brown buds, folding back on
themselves, like small brown hands. Everything was
growing in fragrance and strength and beautiful life
and joy.

The ponies were very cheerful, and Lady Clinton
had quite enough to do at first in guiding their way-
ward wills in some direction approximating to the
centre of the road.

"Hermione, you have such a strange look in your
eyes. What were you thinking of?" she said, suddenly, as they came to a severe rise, and the ponies

thought fit to relax their strenuous efforts to run away.

"How beautiful the spring is !" said Hermione.

Lady Clinton smiled. "I don't think you were only thinking that, you looked ever so far away. That is so odd about you; sometimes you look *out* of you, as it were, as if you were looking through years, through time, not space."

"Sometimes you think of so many things at once, you don't know what you are thinking of, you mean, and then you say 'nothing'—but that isn't true ; and so I said I thought the spring beautiful." There was a pause ; then Hermione said, "Everything seems so complete in nature, somehow. Did you ever notice that, Dorothy ?"

"Well, I don't know. How do you mean ?"

"Why, one thing leads on to another. You never stop at a half thought in nature. I mean, if you see a twig, you know a bud will come, and then a leaf, and then fruit, and then seed. But, somehow, in human nature that sequence is very unlikely. Lives stop sometimes so uncompleted, of course in the Hereafter—— It is like a sudden early frost; and yet the harvest might have been worth the garnering." Hermione was thinking deeply. "I think the best and noblest lives never do end here ; at least, they seed and sow other lives with noble germs, but their own never fill, somehow, with golden grain."

"I do wish, Ione, you would not look so dreadfully

far away," said Lady Clinton, uneasily. "And you are so blue around your eyes, and look so pale. I think we had better go home."

Hermione roused up directly. "I was only thinking hard. I am all right. Oh! don't turn; do let us go round by the river, and then through the long pine wood; that will be delicious, Dorothy; do!"

So they turned to the left and went down into the valley.

Conversation ceased now perforce. They had turned in between some aged gate-posts, leaning against mossy banks of gorse, and had come on to a wild, waste land, better known as Crumb's Bottom, a kind of dried marsh. There was only a faint track; the ground was very rough, springy, and full with sprouting reeds and marshy growths of every sort; the ponies, feeling the rebounding turf, required real handling to restrain their impetuosity, and the light carriage swung and tossed almost like a ball of thistledown. Away on their right lay the ridge, with its hanging woods. In front of them the land swept away to the river. A distant gleam came now and then in view through a broken line of willows, putting on in haste their silver coats of palm. A faint cry came from some wader or water-bird; the little tufted weeds or ruffled reeds sent out now and then a gleamy fly or moth. It was very still, warm, and fragrant. Squish! squish! went the ponies, with tossing manes, and jerking tails; and Hermione leant back in her furs, and thought it was "all very good."

Now they went down a hollow; the growths ceased,
they were on sand, part of the river-bed; then over
the hollow, low, wooden bridge, up the other side,
through groups of wild-looking, small, velvet-coated
cattle, one or two sheep; then on over marsh-land
again; then rising gradually and imperceptibly, the
reeds grew taller and more sparsely, gorse grew in
closer clumps, then heather, then withered fern, and
here and there rough curls of young bracken, then
trees—willows, birch, alders; then up on to the track
again, under the hanging woods, with the river brawl-
ing over its stones on their right; past the old mill
and farm, along the sandy road, and so on to the pine
woods; through the gates, and slowly along the
deeply rutted track, where, as a rule, only timber-
waggons went. It was so still, you heard a wood-
pecker tapping. The faint, gummy odour of the
resinous stems impregnated the air; cones lay thickly
everywhere, with mysterious-looking fungi, scarlet
and pale yellow, black and imperial purple; here
and there wood-sorel stood waving tiny veined cups in
sudden and precipitous little dells, caused by the up-
rooting of some large tree; moss hung on the stems,
with fairy scarlet spikes ready for war; the wood-
pigeons were cooing in a dreamy way; and over all
brooded silence, like the wings of some great Angel of
Peace.

Both Lady Clinton and Hermione were quite
silent; the ponies pulled no more, their small feet

slipped here and there on the needles, or cracked a broken branch. The groom had got down, and was running by their side to ease the springs. You could see far, far away into the pine stems, as they stood in their ranks, brown and slender; and then at last, just as you thought: there, your eye would pierce beyond and gain the sky, one tall stem stood up in its burnished armour of brazen flakes, and stopped all egress, and somehow your eye travelled back along the stems, and you were content it should be so. The wind swayed softly, like a hand stirring the branches; and now and then there came a kind of pressure of branches altogether, which was as though some mighty arm had leaned upon them, and was pressing music in a solemn undertone from out their power so held and subdued.

"It is so peaceful, I should like to be going on for ever," said Hermione, slowly and softly. "I always think that nothing in the world is like violin music but a pine forest."

"My dear! Well, the connection would never have struck me, but now you say it, I seem to see it, too, somehow. Oh! it is a pity, a thousand, thousand pities!" Lady Clinton stopped suddenly,

"What?" said Hermione, in a dreamy voice.

"Why, you know—— Well, I don't care, but I must say it. If only you could have liked Colonel Myddleton; he is just the man who would understand all your ideas and everything. Now, honestly, don't you think so?"

"How can I tell?" said Hermione. "I never tried."

"I know you didn't, but don't you see, I know him very well, and if once you get over that cold, hard, unimpassioned manner, he has such deep feeling, and he is so very like you in many ways; but of course, I know it can't be helped, people can't like each other because they want to."

"My dear Dorothy, why should he want to?"

"Well, he ought to, then; men are so tiresome. I suppose he will just go and see some little miss at Cannes, and get entangled in some ridiculous way, for he is quite mad on the point of honour and all that, and—— "

"But he is not the only person," said Hermione, hurriedly, feeling as though a knife were being slowly turned in her heart. "I suppose I might get entangled with some little master."

"How absurd you are!" said Lady Clinton, laughing, but really vexed. "I had set my heart on it, and of course after saving your life and all."

"Oh! hush, Dorothy!" broke in Miss St. John, turning very pale. "It's nothing whatever in saving my life; why, any man would have done the same. Why, you would not let a dog drown if you could save it, and then on account of that to expect him to— to—— It's quite cruel," she ended, with such a beat of agony in her voice that Lady Clinton was silenced and startled. At last she said—

"You have such a way of putting things, Hermione. I never saw it in that light; of course not *expected*—only for his own sake."

"I don't think we can discuss it, Dorothy," said Hermione, faintly. "One never knows a man's life. He——" She paused, then said very coldly and quietly, "I should think he had cared all his life probably for some one whom, for some reason, he cannot marry."

Lady Clinton sat thinking. "Yes, he looks like that, perhaps. I dare say Philip knows all about it."

"I dare say he does," echoed Hermione. She had said the very bare truth, and yet she knew there was no danger of Lady Clinton ever striking on the actual heart of the matter. They had reached the edge of the wood before Lady Clinton spoke again, then she turned rather flushed to her companion and said—

"If he had Hermione, would you?"

"I never thought of anything so improbable," said Hermione. There was something in her voice that made Lady Clinton wish impotently that she had not spoken; then she said, half aloud, "Well, he said he wondered how you had always contrived to be so cold and unimpassioned."

"Did he?"

"Yes; and I said I supposed it was because everybody liked *you*, so you didn't care."

"When did all this conversation take place,
Dorothy ? "

"The first night he came ; he was so odd. I did
think then he cared for some one, but then afterwards,
I don't know how, the impression died out."

They were out of the wood now, running rapidly
down to the valley again.

At the Red House they were shown into the sitting-
room, and left for a little.

"I am afraid the drive has tired you dreadfully,
Ione," said Lady Clinton, undoing the heavy fur wrap.

"No ; I like the spring air," was the answer. "I
am in such a fright about the General, though."

"How cold and cheerless the room looks ! Well,
poor Robert might be glad to go any where else, I am
sure."

"Yes, it wants a woman to set the things straight,
certainly. Rooms look so dreary when no one cares
to live in them."

At this moment there was a loud cheery whistling,
and in came Robert. "I've found it," he began, then
stopped short on seeing who it was. "Oh ! I thought
it was Mr. Fairfax," he said. "I've got the root he
wanted."

"Where is General Watt ? " said Dorothy.

"Gone off to Old Court. Do you want him ? "

"Yes ; never mind, we'll go after him."

"All right, then I'll come too ; I must take this
root to Mr. Fairfax."

"We'll take it for you, if you like."

"No, thank you," said Robert, getting rather red. "I think a short trudge won't do me any harm."

Hermione pulled Lady Clinton's cloak, who said suddenly, "Here's a good idea. Charles can follow on foot; Robert, you shall go in front and drive Hermione, and I'll sit behind, and then you two can talk."

So it was settled, and by the time they had reached Old Court, Robert knew all about the agency, and was partly in an ecstatic state of bliss at the idea of getting work, and partly in depth of gloom at the thought of leaving Josline.

"I am afraid I am awfully stupid, Miss St. John," he said, scarlet with excitement and gratitude, "but I'll work hard and try and get up everything, and a fellow can always learn if he means to."

"I am sure you will get on all right; I am so glad you will come, it's very good of you," said Hermione, devoutly hoping the old General would be half as easy to talk to as she had found his son.

When they drew up at Old Court they found Miss Barbara going round the windows with a little iron rake; hitching them to and fastening them outside as well as in.

On her head, over her cap, was a gigantic hat-bonnet, rather like a hen coop, of very coarse straw; it threw into fine relief her sharp nose; her small black apron had got twisted on one side, her dress was tucked up very high, and she was standing in a critical position on the verge of the violet bed.

"Ah! it's you, Mr. Robert," she said, sardonically, and quite ignoring her other visitors. "Well, I am just going out, so it's no use your coming in."

"How do you do, Miss Fairfax?" said Lady Clinton, springing lightly down from the back seat, and advancing in apparently profound ignorance of Miss Barbara's speech.

"How do you do, Lady Clinton?" said Miss Barbara, holding the small rake inelegantly at right angles to her body with one hand, and letting a cold and fish-like hand descend frigidly into Lady Clinton's extended right. "I am just going out, and am closing the windows," she added undauntedly. "There are so many tramps about and lazy people."

Here a short waterproof cape which clothed Miss Barbara's gaunt shoulders became unfastened in some mysterious manner and descended, slowly at first, and then with a sudden pounce, on the "person of the house," who fled, carrying round its portly person the black cape. Even Miss Barbara had to laugh, as pussy darted hither and thither, trying to get rid of the cape, and scattering the pigeons in all directions.

By this time Miss Fairfax became aware of Hermione's presence, and with a gentle look she went solemnly forward and held out her hand, saying, "Oh, Miss St. John! I didn't see you; it is the first time since your accident. I am very glad to see you out." Then she put her hands behind her in embarrassed silence, tippeting backwards and forwards from heels to toes.

"I have your sweet-briar still," said Hermione, smiling. "I put it in water at first, and then I kept it in memory of this dear old garden, and of your kindness in giving it to me."

"Did you?" said Miss Barbara, really touched, Then putting out one hand timidly, she said, "Won't you come in? or mayn't you?"

"I should like very much, but aren't you going out? I should not like to stop you."

"Oh! that doesn't matter at all. Do come in and have some tea. Don't move; I'll go, and get something," with which mysterious promise Miss Barbara marched into the house, and presently reappeared, rolling before her, with strong kicks, some matting, which ran to the carriage. "There!" she said. "Young people are so careless, and damp is very bad when you are weak. Here is my arm."

Hermione was privately laughing, but would not have allowed Miss Barbara to know it for the world.

They all went into the cedar parlour, which was quite stifling from being hermetically sealed on account of robbers; but Miss Barbara speedily reopened the windows, then turned to Robert, and said, with great asperity, "Well, young man, and what brought you here?"

" I have found the root Mr. Fairfax wanted."

" Take it to him, then ; he's in his study with your father ; and tell Josline I want her."

Could anything have been more cleverly cruel ?

They sat talking for some little time after Robert's departure ; Miss Barbara not doffing her hat-bonnet, but sitting on a high stool with glittering eye.

Now Robert didn't mean to have all his woe for nothing but the mere message to Josline.

He found Mr. Fairfax pasting carefully in some rare botanical specimens, and his father reading out the names to Josline, who was writing them in delicate characters on small labels. He was joyfully received, and even Josline looked delighted at his " find."

After a short discussion as to its merits, Mr. Fairfax and General Watt went off to the cedar parlour, and Josline was following, when Robert placed himself desperately in her way. He didn't speak, but his whole face was so full of supplication, so quivering with emotion, that Josline stood still and trembled.

" I want to tell you—I want to ask you—shall you mind my going away ? " he said, in a burst.

" Going away ! No, of course not. Why ? " she said, puzzled and doubting.

" Oh, I don't mean the going away we spoke of that you wished, that I said I would try for. This is only work, plodding, dry work, and I am going to be paid for it," he said, a little bitterly. "You know, I mean, I am very poor, I have nothing, I——" He stopped. Josline looked up at him, a slight quiver came on her face; she made a little movement, so slight, like a leaf blown sideways on its stem. "I am not rich, I never can be rich, but I am young and strong, and I will work, and rise; I am not afraid of toil, I will work day and night, I will work for years; only say 'yes; do try.'" He stopped again; he didn't attempt to touch her, but he stretched his hands to her, whilst a great surging longing to gather up that little fragile, gentle creature shook him to the soul. In one hand he was holding some of the dried specimens; they slid and fell rustling to her feet, withered leaves.

She looked at him gravely and silently. Into her great, stag-like eyes came a look of dumb misery, like a creature being struck in the dark.

"Speak to me," he said, softly. "Will you not speak to me, and say 'work?'"

"Work!" she said, softly too, like a child repeating a lesson.

His face lighted; he came a little nearer, stooping his head in the low doorway. "Will you say 'work for me?'" His voice fell to an almost inaudible whisper. The passion in his eyes swept over her heart and found it cold, and left it cold.

She let her eyes fall, leant back a little, and said slowly, "Work is always noble and good; I am glad you are going away."

"Ah! how can you?" he said.

She was silent; in her slight body you could see the vibration of her heart.

"Then you are glad to be rid of me? Oh! I had hoped——" He stopped again. "Oh, Josline!" he burst out, suddenly, "I love you, I love you; don't you feel it, and know it? I have loved you from the very first moment I ever saw you; oh, I love you so, I don't know what to do! Answer me, say you will wait, say you care, say I may work for you; oh, do, do speak!" He was speaking rapidly now, in violent, throbbing, beating rushes of sound; his eyes were full of tears, his whole frame shook. "Oh, do say 'yes,' do say 'yes!'" He would not have 'nay.' He came close to her, he almost took her in his arms.

But quiet and still as a vision in a dream, she made no return of sound or gesture, and something in the supreme stillness, as in the silence of a dream, struck him suddenly motionless and silent, too.

They stood looking at each other; then she made as though she would have passed him. "Ah, dearest!" he said, "won't you answer? then, do you hate me so much?" He paused. She slipped her small hand inside the front of her dress and held something, at least, afterwards, he vaguely and dimly thought so; her lips moved, and he bent forwards to catch what she said, but she did not speak aloud. She looked so strange, so pale, so unearthly, that Robert's heart began to beat thickly.

"Are you faint?" he said. "Have I frightened you? Shall I go away? I am so rough! I did not mean—if you would only say one word, only one word, I will go."

"Go!" she breathed.

He started; he had not meant that. "Oh, Josline!" he said, "do think; it is so hard to bear. I love you so! If you only could know how I love you! I will do anything you wish; only couldn't you say something?"

"You have said enough—quite, quite enough," she said, shivering.

"Are you angry, then, very angry?"

She shook her head gently.

"Not angry? Then—then—oh, Josline!"

He held her two hands, he bent over her slight fragile form, his breath shook on her forehead, he trembled from head to foot, his every nerve and pulse leapt and quivered. A feeling of such intense happiness shook him that he felt quite faint. "Oh——" He couldn't speak, his voice choked.

She let her hands lie in his for one brief moment. For one brief moment Robert was happier than he had ever dreamed he could be, to be for ever after more sorrowful. Then she said—

"I did hope you did not care, would not go on caring. I am very sorry. I can never, never be any good to you!"

He dropped her hands, a scarlet burning tide flew

over his face, dyeing his very eyelids. She remained
deathly white.

"There is something about me you do not know,
no one knows, I cannot tell you. Oh——" For a
second she lost self-control, the sobs rang through her
voice. "I would if I could, I would, indeed." Then
as he lifted his head with a kind of start, she said,
as before, coldly, like a voice in a dream, again pulseless, "But I can't, it can never be ! I shall never
care for any one but my uncle ! "

"But that—that is quite different," he said, passionately, feeling as though he might plead her out
of some strange, horrible glamour and possession.
"I assure you it is different. Oh ! I have frightened
you ! I am so rough ! But, see, look ! I will be so
quiet and gentle, and I won't speak to you again for
a year, years—any time."

"Never ! " she said, quietly ; "never ; it can never
be ! Do not urge me ; it can never be ! "

He stood looking at her ; he saw she was shivering.
A strange idea seized on him. "Josline," he said,
slowly, "are you determined never to care for me ? "

"Yes, I am—determined," she answered, as though
constrained by his look.

"Is it because I am poor ? "

"Oh, no ! " she said, with a sort of cry, coming
forwards two steps, her whole face convulsed with
deep feeling.

She looked so infinitely sweet and lovely, that the

young man's heart rose in despair. " Oh, my dear ! "
he said, taking her head suddenly in his two hands,
and kissing her reverently on her forehead, " I shall
never love any one but you ; *can't* you love me ? "

It did seem a little hard, he loved her so ! Her
touch seemed to create a change in him ; he said,
suddenly, " I believe—Josline, is it possible ? I believe you could love me, and you won't ! "

The wonderful alchemy of love had given him a
power of prophetic insight into her mind and heart.
She made no reply, she hung her head and stood
like a flower in the night, enwrapped in its own
essence, pure and untouched.

" Can you not answer me ? will you not ? dare you
not ? "

Silence. A heavy step came through the hall,
a hand was laid on Robert's shoulder, and Mr. Fairfax's voice said—

" You must come now, Robert."

Josline came forwards. She put both her arms
round her uncle's neck, and said, with a sob, " Yes,
take me and keep me, I have only you."

She was shuddering violently, but tearless. Mr.
Fairfax made Robert a sign, and he went away
through the darkening hall—the darkness took him.

" I shall be ready to start to-morrow, Miss St.
John," he said, as they all parted on the ridge.

" That will be good of you ; you know you can
always be running backwards and forwards till we

do up the house for your father. I am so glad you will come, and it is so good of General Watt to spare you."

"Yes, very," answered Robert, and strode away down the hill, feeling as though a heavy waggon had gone over him and crushed all life, and hope, and youth, and strength out of him.

He was still young, though, for when he got home, he went to the cabinet, took out the picture, the Eurydice portrait, and sobbed bitterly over it; then he fetched some wash-leather and did it up tightly, sewing it carefully together at the edges with huge stitches of white silk, pricking himself horribly the while, in his fierce misery and distraction.

"The worst of it is, I don't know what she is at!" he thought. "What can she mean? and she looks so delicate, and seems so miserable. Oh, dear! oh, dear!" Then he kissed the wash-leather where the face ought to be, and put it away, and vowed a vow he wouldn't look at it again till he was a rich man and didn't care any more. Then he got into bed, and thought over every word and gesture and expression, and more and more he became convinced there was some mystery; only what could it be? He wondered whether Gladys could find out. He would write to her; both together they would try; and then at last some day they would all be happy. Perhaps he had frightened her, but surely he had been very gentle; only she was so fragile and so easily frightened; why, he had seen her jump at a moth, and he was a very big moth, and how his wings did burn with a curious frizzle, like sweetbriar hedges done up in matting, which he knew could never possibly be put into so small a pie-dish as Miss Barbara's hat-bonnet, and— he was fast asleep.

END OF VOL. I.

PRINTED AT THE CAXTON PRESS, BECCLES.

www.ingramcontent.com/pod-product-compliance
Lightning Source LLC
Chambersburg PA
CBHW020945030726
47496CB00005B/1355